WAIVERINGS

A BRAINWAIVER ANTHOLOGY

CHANTAY M JAMES

Midwest Creations Publishing Titles
By Chantay M. James

The Brainwaiver Series
Waivering Minds
Waivering Lies
Waiverings, A Brainwaiver Anthology
Waivering Winds
Waivering Times

Other titles by the Author:
Valley of Decisions
(Xulon Press, 2005)
(Midwest Creations Publishing, 2017)

Anthologies featuring the Author:
A Hawk's Tale
(KDP) Electronic Version (MOBI)
----Author Alias: Chantay Hadley---
(*with P. Lee, D. Outlaw and A. Johnson*)

Waiverings:
A Brainwaiver Anthology
Chantay M. James
Midwest Creations Publishing

Midwest Creations Publishing
St. Louis, MO 63114
Visit our website at midwest-creations-publishing.square.site

This is a work of fiction. Names, characters, places and incidents are a product of the author's imagination or are used fictitiously. Any resemblance to actual persons (living or dead), locales, events or establishments is coincidental. The publisher does not have any control over and does not resume responsibility for the author or any third-party (reviewers, bloggers, booksellers, social network etc.) or their content.

Waiverings: A Brainwaiver Anthology
Waivering Winds Novella 1.5
Waivering Times. Novella 2.5,
The Brainwaiver Series
Copyright pending ©2021 by Chantay M. James.
All rights reserved. No part of this book may be reproduced by any means (including but not limited to

electronically via scanning, mechanically printed or handwritten) nor copied or shared without the express permission in written form from the author or publisher in representation of the author; the exception being a direct quotation of a paragraph or brief passage by a reviewer or blogger.

Cover Illustration copyright ©2021 by Chantay M. James. All rights reserved.

Edited by Midwest Creations Publishing

Designed by Midwest Creations Publishing

Scripture quotations are taken from the Complete Jewish Bible.

Printed in the United States of America

Originally published electronically via KDP by Midwest Creations Publishing

For Eunice...
I love you Mom. I wish I could hear your voice, one last time.
Even your laugh would be good. I'm not picky.

Prologue

September 13, 1994

"De-lie-la the liar, lying like a lion..."
Jacob Redbird didn't see the punch coming. The little blond girl had swung just that fast. Before he knew it, he was spitting out the dirt he'd just licked, hunched over on his side on the ground.

And that was exactly what Delilah had intended to do.

"Delilah Jean! You get your behind over here this instant!"

Little Delilah huffed and crossed her arms in a show of attitude. But that's all it was, just a show. Her great aunt Grayce May Dancing-Wolf didn't play around. When you were disrespectful or acted out, you got your behind tanned, plain and simple. And there wasn't no calling child services out here on the Res either. Something she strongly disagreed with since she got her behind tanned more often than not.

But running always made it worse. Because she wasn't a dummy. At a height considered tiny for a 7-

year-old with short legs to match, she wasn't going to get far before Aunt Graycie caught her. And then she'd wish she were dead. And she knew that from experience. A thought that made her frown more. Regret. That was the word her Dad had used to explain what she was feeling now. She regretted not thinking before she punched that snot rag in his nose. "That's gonna be the death of you Delilah," her dad had said, "you better start thinking before you act girl, or life is gonna wipe the floor with your behind."

With dangling arms and her head bowed, she dragged her feet as she inched her way toward her house three doors down. Wishing her Daddy were here now to say those very words, instead of being overseas, fighting a war that her Aunt said had nothing to do with them. Wishing that she could actually do it, so she wouldn't be getting this spanking. And wishing most of all, that she regretted it enough not to do it again. Because the truth was the truth. She didn't regret hitting Jacob where it hurts, not one bit. And that scared the life out of her.

It was why Delilah knew with all her heart that she was gonna die young just like her mom. Because she didn't need to think about what was right and what was wrong. And she didn't bother worrying about con-see-qweenses like she should. If she saw wrong, she acted on it; without regret. And she wasn't sorry. Not at all.

So, death was gonna come for her; her daddy never lied. And when it did, she promised herself that no matter how much she feared it, she'd punch it in the nose too, just like Jacob Redbird.

Chapter 1 – Run with the Wind

July 17, 2004 – San Luis, AZ

"You wench!"

At least that's what Delilah thought she heard. It was hard to hear annunciation with Jell-O stuck in her ears.

But she'd been through this before and found that sticking her finger in her ear, wiggling it around and coughing helps. Except there really wasn't time for that as her opponent was coming right at her.

Swinging Sue was her opponent's stage name; born and raised Susie Watkins from Arkansas. 5'11" tall, African American and slim, Susie had a long reach and a dangerously high kick. The kicks were no concern, they tended to throw Susie off-balance. Delilah had learned a long time ago (as in just three months ago when she'd been introduced to the Jell-O wrestling circuit) that kicking never worked out very well for the kicker.

Backstage Susie and Delilah or as her stage name goes "demonic Delilah" were the best of buds, but in the ring, it was no holds barred. Something Susie all but proved as she rushed Delilah, diving in for a takedown.

Sliding slightly to the left Delilah stuck out her ankle and like a cartoon character Susie tripped, slid and torpedoed right under the ropes and out of the ring. Cue the standing ovation as Demonic Delilah added another victory notch into her belt. That was code for a $300 bonus for the win on top of the $250 she made per match.

While blinking quickly to dislodge the Jell-O from her lashes, Delilah's right hand was snatched up by the moderator aka Mike the Mullet (it was really Michael Hansford, but the girls called him the Mullet due to his "business in the front and party in the back" mullet haircut.)

The crowd roared again. And Delilah kept blinking away the Jell-O fragments, her fakest and brightest smile frozen on her face as she waved enthusiastically at her so-called fans. Three months ago, it had been exciting; the crowd, the attention... the freedom.

Dismissed by Mike as he announced the next match that would take place in fifteen minutes; Delilah tipped her way out of the ring, pretty much a pro at navigating the raised platform littered with warm ooze, still blinking. She hoped her vision would clear by the time she got to the ropes. As a novice two months ago, she'd tried to wipe away the Jell-O only to realize that her hands, coated with the stuff, just made it worse. Hence all the blinking.

The crowd continued to roar. Mindful of her bosses admonishing to make the boys happy, Delilah waved with both hands and hips one last time before exiting the ring... and ran smack into a wall.

It wasn't a wall, but it might as well have been. It was a chest. A chest she knew. A big, burly, barrel one that caused her heart to lodge in her throat as fear snatched her voice.

"When are you gonna learn, girl? You can't run from me. Wherever you go. Wherever you hide, I'll find you."

Delilah swallowed. She didn't bother to look up. There was no need. First, her lashes were still crusted with Jell-O. And second, she knew what she would see.

The expression in Brody's eyes was always the same. Sad. With a little bit of compassion mixed in. But it never stopped him from dragging her back to Zeke. Back to hell.

Delilah didn't even bother with trying to snatch away from him like she had the first couple of times he'd found her. Brody was well over 6 feet 5 inches and outweighed her by over one hundred and fifty pounds. To say that she was battling outside of her weight class when it came to him would be more than accurate.

So now, instead of blinking away Jell-O like she had been before, she was blinking back tears. Her nose burned with the effort of trying to keep them from falling. But she knew she would win. She always did.

From the day three years ago when Zeke and his band of not so merry men snatched her away from the Res (with the guise of stopping to ask for directions) there was one promise that Delilah had kept to herself – never let them see her cry. She didn't then. And she wouldn't now.

***

K.C.

"I double-dog dare you!"
I laughed.

Rick, my bunkmate and best friend since arriving here at the Marine Corps Air Station, was one funny dude. Not because he was a comedian or nothing, which I firmly believe he could be, but because his responses reminded me of my ten-year-old cousin every time I was about to do something that made him uncomfortable.

Like go into this here bar and see what this Jell-O wrestling thang was we'd heard so much about.

I had to remind myself that Rick was still wet behind the ears at just 18. Since I had about four years on him, I usually tried to go easy when it came to stuff like this.

That is until he had to go and pull out a double-dog dare on me. I grinned and shook my head.

Not bothering to respond, I headed toward the entrance. We would need to return to base soon, and I wanted to get this over with. Because this wasn't just a double-dog dare from Rick, it was a challenge from Bradley Herrington, a ranking LCpl like me, also a guy I pretty much hated.

Just thinking about the guy put a bad taste in my mouth. Almost tasting my disgust of his petty, entitled, trust fund having, snake in the grass acting behind, I almost missed the shadow of a big guy dragging some reluctant girl toward an SUV idling about 20 feet away.

I paused. It could have been some guy just hauling his girlfriend to the car after an argument. It could have been some disgruntled dad dragging his daughter away.

But for some reason, it didn't feel like that. This felt... wrong. My gut told me that it was too important to look past. I never ignored my gut.

During my one-year stint thus far I've seen a few missions and have had a few risky call outs. Every time I did, I knew that I could trust my gut and my God, the primary influence in my life, to keep me out of harm's way. They didn't fail me then, thus the reason I heeded them now.

Changing direction before I could change my mind, my long stride turned into a light jog. It was hard to miss my approach as our military issued boots were not geared out for sneaking up on the enemy. And I knew that this guy was exactly that.

I figure he heard my approach at about the same time as I addressed his back.

"Hold, sir. Ma'am, you okay?"

It was his not turning around to address me, but rather, turning his head to the side to "dismiss" me that raised my hackles.

"She's good." He grunted at the same time she strangled out an, "I'm fine."

But I didn't believe him. And I really didn't believe her.

"Sir, I'm gonna need you to release the lady and step away."

I assessed him closer as I cornered off and widened my stance. This guy was big. He had at least four inches on me and about fifty pounds since he was taller with more lean muscle, while I had a stockier build.

So, even though I was more muscular, I was smaller and probably quicker despite his leaner body type.

The lady's strangled, "No really, I'm okay," didn't move me.

Because I knew she wasn't. And I didn't bother to repeat my command. He'd heard me the first time. And that meant one thing. He was going to let her go, or I was going to make him do it.

I watch as the guy took a deep breath before turning to focus on me.

"LCpl, huh. Expected you to be an MP the way you're talking."

Again, I didn't speak. Because I wasn't military police, nor was I armed.

In fact, technically, I had no legal authority or right to halt a private citizen for any reason. I wasn't law enforcement, not in Yuma, here in San Luis, nor on the base.

I wasn't even an NCO – non-commissioned officer yet. But that didn't matter to me.

This girl was in trouble. Standing by and doing nothing while she was being dragged away just because I didn't have a legal dog in this fight wasn't an option.

"You do realize that I don't have to do what you say?"

I didn't answer that either. Both of us knew he didn't. Both of us knew that it didn't matter either way. Because if he didn't comply, I was going to make him, plain and simple.

"You good K.C.?"

That was Ricky who was now at my back. Still a PFC – private first class, Rick didn't have the right to interfere either. But he had my back. We were Marines. It was how we rolled.

I almost missed the shadow of a smile from the guy as he released his hold on the girl. I didn't miss her edging away from him though. Just like I thought. He'd had her against her will.

"You a former Marine?" That question came from Rick and was directed to the guy who'd crossed his arms at us before widening his own stance.

And just like that, I saw what Rick apparently saw. The tattoos on his left arm, one of which was the badge of a Sergeant-Major. I cursed under my breath, but I didn't back down.

My gut told me not to. That, and the fact that the girl was still edging slowly away from the guy.

"Yep. Retired four years now. Which is why I will do you boys the courtesy of providing this warning only once, you need to go on your way and make sure you wipe our," he says as he jerks his head in the girl's direction, "existence out of your minds. Never to be seen or heard again."

I settled my weight on the balls of my feet before I responded.

"Can't do that."

The guy frowned. "You have no probable cause for detaining us. Nor do you have the right as you aren't local, state or military law enforcement. What am I missing here?"

I shrugged but didn't bother refuting any of that. All of it was true. But it still didn't matter.

"Delilah! Get back here." This the guy said on a growl. My gaze shifted to whom he had to be addressing.

The girl cringed and stopped moving. And just like that, Rick was at my side.

My fingers curled into fists as I bounced once in my

stance. This was going to happen fast.

Ricky read my body language seamlessly, something I knew because he was also now on the balls of his feet, his body positioned slightly more toward the girl. I was going to have to take down the big guy while Rick got her safe.

I could tell that ex-Sergeant Major read us because he went to reach behind his back. He was quick, but I was faster.

Launching myself forward, I didn't bother trying to secure or hold the man, he was huge. Instead, I leveled my punch right into his gun hand's inside wrist with precise force as I grabbed the barrel of the gun and deflected it up.

The fingers immediately released allowing me to take possession of the firearm just in time for me to duck the left hook that came at my head.

I spun with the secured weapon in hand and pulled the magazine back to let the big guy know that it was locked and loaded. Apparently, he didn't keep his safety on since I didn't have to disengage it.

His hands went up, and he took a step back.

I heard Rick asking the girl if she was okay and if there was anyone he needed to call.

She answered no there wasn't and told him that she just had to go in and get her bag, then we could see her safely home. Which was good since we had less than 45 minutes to get back to base.

The big guy kept backing away until he reached the SUV that was still idling on the side of the building. He smirked at me before opening the door from behind him, turned then hopped into the front seat.

The SUV took off in a cloud of dust, and I took a breath for the first time in what seemed like an hour (in reality, it had only been about 5 minutes).

Ten minutes later...

"Dude, we have to get back to base. Why don't you go in to see what's taking her so long?"

I grinned. Rick was always about the drama.

"You want cheese to go with that whine? Man, the girl just had an ordeal. She's most likely trying to compose herself in the bathroom still. Give her a few more minutes, will you?"

I hadn't even finished speaking before the door to the place opened and a tall, beautiful caramel skinned lady stepped out.

Well, she looked like a lady from far away anyway. But, having caught sight of us and now jogging our way, I could see as she approached that she was barely old enough to drive.

I could feel Rick beside me starting to squirm. That, and the sudden rock I felt sinking in my stomach told me this was not going to end well.

I was not wrong.

"Hey." The girl half panted, something that concerned me since her jog hadn't been all out; thus, she should barely be out of breath.

"Hey. Everything okay?" That came from Rick. I didn't bother asking because I knew it wasn't. I just hopped down from the hood of our ATV Jeep, crossed my arms, and waited.

"You the guys that helped Delilah?"

I nodded while Rick affirmed verbally.

Reaching into the pocket of her velour jogging pants, the girl pulled out a wad of bills and held them out to me.

"She said to tell you thanks for the assist, but she found a ride home, so no need for you to wait around."

I just looked at her hand, my eyes narrowed, before focusing again on her face. Her eyebrows went up as she shook the money at me. I still didn't take it. Because she was lying.

"Okay then..."

"Who with?" I asked, cutting Rick off.

The girl froze. I could see her grip tighten on the money as her eyes shifted quickly to the left before refocusing on me.

"Uh. Um. Her ah... her dad. Her dad came to get her."

"When? We've been sitting here for ten minutes. There have been no new arrivals as far as we can see." My eyes narrowed again. I hated lies. And I hated liars. So, I could always smell a lie a mile off.

"I meant that he is coming... coming to get her."

I shook my head. I was about to turn away and wash my hands of the whole thing when the girl surprised me by reaching forward and grabbing my hand, jamming the money into it.

"Anyway, she said to tell you thanks. You're her heroes."

As the girl's chocolate eyes met mine, I saw what I missed before because anger at being lied to had clawed at me. There were tears there, hovering just a blink away from spilling over. That was what gave me pause, what made me wait for it. I didn't have to wait long.

"I didn't know guys like you still existed. But thank you. Thank you for stepping up for my friend. I wish there were more out there like you two."

With that, she blinked, and I watched as if in slow motion, the tears spilled over.

I knew, right then that this was why I enlisted. This was why I put on the uniform every morning. To be a hero. Whether the world recognized me as such or not.

Chapter 2 - Low Winds

April 22, 2008 – Las Vegas, NV

"Stop pulling my shirt!"

Delilah felt her eyes roll back. She tried to stop it; she really did. But as always, when it came to these three; the eye roll overpowered her desire to appear unemotional and detached.

"I didn't pull it. Anyway, it's my shirt. You stole it out of my closet."

"I didn't steal it out of your closet!"

"You did!"

"Maria -," Delilah was cut off as she knew she would be.

"No, I didn't! I stole it out of Delilah's closet."

Ugh. There goes the eye roll again.
"Tandy -,"
"You're nothing but a huge thief!"
Delilah paused in her next attempt to interrupt at the shake of Maddie's head.

Maddie was the youngest of the bunch at 12. As her story goes, she was sold to Zeke by her uncle to pay out a bet. Somber for one so young, Maddie had an appeal – everyone wanted to protect the kid; including Delilah, which is how she found herself in this position in the first place.

The pause gave Maddie time she needed to do her thing. Which, in this case, was orchestrate a fall.

And just like that, at her small chirp when she faked her trip and hit the ground, both girls immediately stopped arguing and rushed to her aid. They helped her up and dusted her off. Maria, the hardcase of the bunch that reminded Delilah of herself even clutched Maddie's face to peer deeply into her eyes as an older Latino mother would do to make sure the kid was okay.

Delilah thought older Latino mother because that's what Maria acted like and was (though young). A mother. One that made wrong choices. At only 15 her story was the darkest of them all.

The details were too gruesome for even Delilah to bear, but the result was Maria showing up at a fake adoption company to hand over her newborn. Only to have herself and the baby snatched and sold, the baby on the black market, and Maria to Zeke.

Then there was Tandy, the 16-year-old, brushing Maddie off like she fell into an invisible pile of leaves instead of in the parking lot of a run-down motel.

Tandy was the oldest and had the strongest protective instincts. She reminded Delilah of the kind of person she would have wanted to be.

Good down to her soul, Tandy had sold herself into the life to provide food and money for her brother and sister to travel cross country to their aunt in Florida.

She and her siblings hadn't had enough to escape their drugged-out mom and her drug dealing boyfriend. The same boyfriend that planned to sell all three of them.

So, Tandy had taken it upon herself to steal his contact, have her brother Randall (a fifteen-year-old that looked like he was 18) make the sale and turn her over. Randall and Michelle were on a bus to Florida that next day. Tandy ended up here, on Zeke's roster.

And then there was Delilah, the reformed escape artist. She'd escaped at least twelve times over the last four years; only to be dragged back all twelve times by Brody. She finally stopped trying just six months ago when the other three were pushed slash dragged into Zeke's shabby headquarters.

The girls had been green. They were so green and so innocent; Delilah was sure that they would be eaten alive.

And the survivor in her didn't care one bit. They weren't her kids. She didn't know them. Since no one had bothered to care about her when she was forced into this life, she had no intention of caring about anyone else.

Until Maddie with her gorgeous red hair pulled up into ponytails flashed her soulful, tear stained gray eyes Delilah's way.

She'd been lost and found at the same time. A purpose had been sparked inside of Delilah at that very moment.

While she had been the cash cow for Zeke over the last few years, the truth is that her allure must be fading. Delilah didn't think it was because of her looks. No, Zeke believed in keeping his property fed, fit and looking good.

That meant, visitors that could care for and style hair, nails and condition skin stopping by on the regular. It also meant consistent visits from physical trainers.

Delilah didn't know how much they banked on her services, but it had to be a lot. They gave her to the high money clients; the fat cats that oozed class.

And in the last year, when she'd turned twenty, she had become highly visible arm candy to many. Some of which required a happy ending, some that just needed a hot date.

Either way, Delilah had been Zeke's go-to when it came to money material. So, she often remained by herself with Brody as her personal guard since she had high dollar value.

That's why it surprised her when "the three," were dragged through and thrown into her space – a suite of heavily secured rooms in the basement of Zeke's "headquarters," aka rental home on a flat of land without any neighbors nearby, not far from the mountains.

The way it went, Zeke and Brody had about forty girls that were divided into groups of four to eight. The groups of eight were low level earners. They were girls usually saved for what they called "quick hits," aka truck stop runs, casino grabs and conference grabs. In other words, the tourist or traveler scenes where a quick lay, quick pay and quick exit were required.

The groups of four tended to be midlevel earners. Most of these girls were targeted toward specific clients, could behave in public and were usually so cowed that they needed no supervision or management. These are the ones that had been so beaten into submission, that even if a way of escape stood up and waved a flag, they'd wave back to say hello and go on about their business.

As one could guess, these types didn't last long. Most of them were managed by drugs and were constantly rocking the blowpipe (heroine), or were depressed and, as a result, suicidal. Neither of these situations guaranteed great health and long life.

And then there were those like Delilah. Those that had spirit and high potential to earn. Sad to say, most clients liked a little fight in their bed. Even sadder to say, most mistook resistance for passion, something that Delilah could never understand.

But it was at the sight of these three that Delilah's world had unraveled and re-stitched itself into something different. Something more than just survival.

Brody's distaste at the change of play had been another consequence of adding the girls to her group. When he'd brought them in, he'd stared Delilah long and hard in the eye, like he was trying to give her some kind of secret message or code. And seeing that they'd spent hours on hours together (which was why she knew how the set up ran in the first place) she was irritated beyond belief that she had no idea what his pointed stare had meant.

But what she did notice is that his hanging around to guard her had all but stopped. They had one bodyguard or two on occasion that guarded the door. The same guy that would retrieve them and usually take them where they needed to go. And that was when she realized how fast her heart was beating in her chest.

Because, even if she'd finally given up on ever being free from the hell on earth that her life had become, there was no rule that stated she had to sit and watch these three become victims too.

And that had been that. On the night before her 21st birthday, Delilah vowed to herself that Tandy, Maria and Maddie were going to escape successfully. And Delilah was going to make that happen if it was the last thing she did. All she needed was a plan and the perfect moment.

December 12, 2009

"Dee, come on. You can't stay here."

Delilah remained mute. Instead of explaining for the fifteenth time to Maria that someone had to stay behind to make sure that the girls made a clean get away, she reached forward, grabbing the now sixteen-year-old, she pulled her into one final hug.

Delilah's eyes squinted shut as Maria clutched her back tightly. Because, while Delilah had never had a mom, she'd had a great aunt whose death still haunted her. And she'd learned enough in those short ten years to last a lifetime from Grayce. One of which was how to love and believe in a kid that everyone else couldn't see the good in.

Delilah saw the good in Maria. And Tandy. And Maddie. Unsurprisingly, they'd bonded to her like chicks to a mama hen. And for over a year now, Delilah had to watch as they were pimped out like she had been. Hurt like she had been. Until the time finally came. The time where her plan would be realized, and the girls would finally be free.

Delilah blamed the dreams. The dreams she had of platinum blonde hair that was far from feminine, covered in a Marine issue military cap and a shadowed face that a flicker of light had revealed possessed silver eyes. The eyes of a hero. And had it been any other woman in the world, he would have been one – a hero, that night.

But not her. Delilah didn't get to have a hero. She didn't get rescued by a handsome stranger and swept off her feet. Her life was about one thing and one thing only: survival. And winning. If she lived to see another day, she won. For every year she lived past her mom's age of death, the ripe old age of 20, Delilah won against death, against life and against every condemning stare.

However, the dreams didn't agree. They haunted her. They poked at her. And, even when she'd zone out to her happy place while her body was being used, her once effective coping strategy now possessed huge silver eyes, accusing ones. Eyes that refused to let her rest until she worked out the plan to help those girls. The original plan had gone from just helping her three to helping all the girls if she could. Barring that, she'd settle for just her girls if she had to.

And so, the planning began. Since Delilah had stopped running away last year, she'd become the bottom girl. The bottom girl was like the headmistress of all of those that worked the strip, circuit and truck stops. There were twelve girls total now; three teams of four that were marched to their assigned locations with one group resting and out of the rotation for some recovery time. Something that she'd argued the girls needed until they got it.

And the girls needed it first and foremost because some men liked it rough. Zeke didn't care so much if they payed to play. But Brody did. His disgust was apparent. In fact, he seemed disgusted all the time lately. It was for that reason that he and Delilah had developed a dependence of sort on each other in the last year. They weren't friends necessarily. Brody relied heavily on Delilah to take care of the girls and their various needs (like tracking their menstrual cycles and such). And Delilah depended on Brody to treat the girls like humans... like the kids they were; even when the lifestyle that they were trapped in called them everything but.

That said, it was more like an uneasy truce. Delilah knew that If she tried to run, Brody'd haul her back in a minute and watch Zeke beat another lesson into her like he did all those other times.

At twenty-two, she was still the oldest among them. There have been a few that have managed to escape over the years. And while she didn't help all of them get away, she didn't provide any help toward them getting caught. Even for the girls Delilah didn't like, she'd crossed her fingers and prayed in her heart that they'd made it. That they got away safe. Some did. Some didn't. And some... some she knew would never come back or be seen anywhere else, ever again.

Blinking back the tears she never allowed to fall, Delilah pulled away, clutching Maria's face between her hands the way she always did when she was telling the girls something important.

"His name is Andrew Talbot. He has a bumper sticker on his truck with the initials TAT on them. There will be three women with him about your height that will arrive in a separate SUV parked on the other side of the truck stop. Repeat what I just said."

Delilah nodded as Maria repeated it.

"Good, you meet in the bathroom and switch clothes, they won't let you go alone so remember to time your approaches. Brody will be watching but Frank is the one that you really don't want to make suspicious. Brody will just bring you back for Zeke to deal with. Frank will beat you up right there in the parking lot. After you switch clothes, then what do you do?"

Delilah listened as Maria rattled off the plan exactly as she'd explained to them two nights ago. It was dangerous. It was definitely not foolproof. But it was the best she had.

It was a plan born out of desperation. Two weeks ago, Delilah stumbled upon a documentary on A&E called Traffick in the U.S. The documentary featured stories about the increase of human trafficking in the states and how advocacy groups were popping up to try to help as the crime itself was so difficult to prosecute. And that's when she saw them. Truckers Against Trafficking, an advocacy group made up of Truckers that had started just last year.

Delilah had been transfixed. She remembered seeing a few trucks with the TAT bumper sticker on them. She remembered the one man, Marty, who'd asked her if she was okay. When she'd climbed into his truck he'd just wanted to talk, unlike so many before him. And, though she hadn't said much, she'd listened to him talk about his family, his two grown daughters, and couldn't help but smile as he paged through pic after pic of his grandkids on his cell.

When the knock on the window came from Frank letting her know it was time to move, she'd been sorry to say goodbye to Marty. It must have shown on her face because he'd grabbed her hand and placed a business card in it. He told her if she ever needed to talk or found herself needing help, she could call that number.

Delilah hadn't paid much attention to his words. There were always johns promising to take her away from the life or to save her from the streets; but that was because they didn't understand. She belonged to Zeke, mind body and soul.

There were even a few that had approached Zeke, offering him loads of cash just to take her away with them. Zeke always said no. And to those that didn't take no for an answer? Zeke said no in a way that they had no choice; with Brody's fist. It didn't take long for those few that were adamant to figure out that she wasn't worth the trouble.

 She could have saved them the trouble of finding out the hard way had they simply asked her. She would have told them that she wasn't worth the money or the beat down.

So, Delilah had pocketed the card in her jacket and had forgotten about it. The card had stayed there for months, untouched, while the dreams turned into nightmares and the accusing silver eyes haunted her.

Thinking about that card hauled Delilah's attention back to the here and now and not a moment too soon.

Maddie now stood in front of her where Maria had been before, clutching her waist and crying silent tears. The silent tears thing had always fascinated Delilah.

"Gonna miss you little bit." Delilah grimaced as the kid's hug tightened into a death grip around her waist.

And Maddie, as was her way when she was gripped by the silent tears, said nothing.

And Delilah, at that moment, decided she was done.

She was the hard case. The cutsie blonde with a smart mouth and bad attitude. She easily made the most bank and was the one that had quickly become the favorite and too tough to mess with.

She didn't cry. She didn't tear up or have a shaky mouth at the sides to contain her wails of agony. Delilah picked herself up, again and again, and kept it going.

And this time was no different. Pulling from Maddie and ignoring the stubborn pointed look that Maria threw her way, she snapped her shoulders back and smiled at her girls one last time.

"What are you heifers waiting for? Let's do this."

Chapter 3 – Red Sky

June 18, 2010 – Hollywood, CA

When Delilah woke up this time, her mouth tasted like it was full of cotton. And everything was fuzzy. It was as if her eyes refused to focus.

And because she'd never felt the vertigo effect when she was lying down before, she felt disoriented and confused.

Was she standing up or laying down? Was she inside or outside? There was a bright light shining right down on her that could possibly be the sun. But everything was too fuzzy to tell.

And there it was again, the nausea. A sickening, lurching feeling that was quickly followed by fear, then anger. She knew that she wasn't dumb enough to get pregnant, nor was she as stupid as so many of the girls were to eat whatever a john set before her. So, either she'd been drugged or beaten up so bad she couldn't function.

Those were usually the thoughts that flickered through her mind at the speed of light before she remembered. Those thoughts despite the change in wording at times and those exact same emotions. Until she heard the shouts, the screams of rage from Frank and the gun shots that followed.

Until her mind, in perfect sync with this torture routine called memory, recalled with perfect clarity the horror of watching Tandy fall forward, two bullet holes appearing like magic in her back as she'd leaped toward Maddie to protect her.

And as before, that yawning void of coldness swallowed her, drowning her in the agony of her failure.
They'd gotten caught. Maria had been beaten, Tandy killed and Maddie? Gone.

No one knew where or how. It had been the one flicker of hope that Delilah felt, remembering that; the hope that Maddie, at this very moment, was somewhere safe. Somewhere living the life of a trucker's daughter; a girl with sisters, a mom and a family to keep her protected. A girl that could grow up normal, right and beautiful; scarred maybe, but not broken.

It was a hope that Delilah desperately wanted to cling to, knowing she would need it for what came next. And since this time was just like all the others, she knew that it would follow on that hope's heels like clockwork. The memory did not disappoint.

Franks fists. His kicks, punches and feet - stomping her middle, her shoulder and her hip. Hitting her everywhere. Then Brody's yelling and pulling him off her.

The gun held to her head as Frank threatened to blow her freaking brains out for what her little stunt would cost him and how the boss would think that it was his fault.

The room growing quiet as Zeke entered, something she'd only known because she could hear him greeting his guys as his presence filled the room causing a hush to fall over it.

And he hadn't been alone. There had been two short old guys, dressed in khaki and older than father time himself, along with a young man of average height, average brown hair and beady eyes.

"Hell son," Old man number one said, "you break it, you bought it. And since I just paid twenty- grand to own it, I don't think you can afford it."

Like a fool I remember thinking that Zeke had somehow tricked the two geezers into believing I could shoot gold out of my nose or something, for them to pay twenty-thousand dollars for just a night.

It wasn't long before I'd learned that I hadn't been sold for a single night, but forever. Along with several other cattle that belonged to Zeke.

"Don't worry Sirs, "Zeke soothed, "this one looks beaten now but she's tough. And cleans up real good. I think she will be the perfect Guinea pig for your experiment. Let me know how the surgery goes, then I'll send over the rest of the girls in groups."

I'd grunted and weakly pushed his nudging toe away from my arm, gathering my strength for one last effort to get the heck out of there. Only to end up with his foot on my back while the two old men chuckled and cackled with the beady eyed guy joining in.

"What you think Lance? Will this one work?" Asked old man number two while beady eyes squatted down beside me and flipped me over onto my back.

Weakly I'd swung and missed as his head dodged back. That was when, for the first time in a very long time I felt the terror that engulfed me when doc pronounced Graycie Mae dead and gone. As those beady brown eyes narrowed on me, a smirk like one I have never seen on any comic book or cartoon villain, stretched across the bottom half of his face, giving him the appearance of those creepy Marionettes. It was the first time I'd ever prayed for death in my entire life. I instinctively knew, in that moment, that surviving would not be winning. Not to sound narcissistic but, it was times like these that I hated to be right. And there's not a day that goes by that I don't wish that I was wrong.

***

K.C.

San Luis, AZ

"Staff Sergeant!"
I grinned before saluting, then took a swing at Rick. Ducking and laughing as he spun away and did his "float like a butterfly and sting like a bee" dance, I shook my head again at how everything around us changed even while it stayed the same.

In the middle of that thought I was almost tackled to the ground before being caught up in a bear hug that near to broke all my bones. Rick had apparently been working out. And Ricky hadn't just gotten ripped, boy had gotten strong!

"Put me down, man! That's an order!"
I tried hard to give that command in my "command" voice, but that's difficult to do when you're laughing and can't breathe at the same time.

I was laughing because Rick was a nut. And because I missed my guys. I'd been 6 months on special ops overseas with six guys and four gals from another unit, two of which were on a farewell mission as they were on their way out of the corps this month. The rest of the crew had traveled back down to San Luiz with me for a layover before we head out to the Twenty-Nine Palms base in San Bernardino County. There we were ordered to hook up with the 3/7

(The Third Battalion 7th Marine Regiment) next week. We were headed back overseas, but to Afghanistan this time. Our destination would be the Sangin District in the Helmand Province. We were the second unit being sent for relief from the 3/7, the first having pushed out in May of this year. While we were supposed to be a relief for British forces and work cooperatively with them, I had a bad feeling about all of it. Which was why I'd petitioned my superior for more men.

And this time I got to choose my own crew, meaning, I'd have Rick right where I needed him, taking my back. Something I planned to surprise him with later when I took him to the mess hall to meet the others.

"Man, I can't believe I missed your square-headed self!" Ricky laughed out while almost dropping me in the process.

"Dude, my head is not square. Yours is just round as all get out. Like that annoying orange character on that show."

Rick looked at me stunned for all of two seconds before his loud guffaws bent him double.

That was one thing I could say about my friend. Subtlety wasn't his thing. If he found you funny, you'd know it. Hell, the whole town would know it.

I tried to allow him the time to pull himself together so we could go, but patience was not my strong suit. Something my Dad always questioned.

"Bub," because that's what my dad called all of us, he didn't have the time or energy to remember the names of seven sons and four girls. And yea, he called the girls that too.

"How a body could be that laid back and goofy but still be as impatient and impulsive as you are, I will never know."

Finally, Rick straightened up allowing me to take a closer look. One I wish I hadn't taken. When I'd left, transferred over to the 3/7 or, "The Cutting Edge," as we call it, Rick's eyes had been full of life. Happy. I don't know, but definitely not whatever this was that I was looking at.

And, like most, I really wasn't in to helping my brother "process" his feelings or anything. I just said a silent prayer that my news would be good news for him and left it at that.

"Got some people for you to meet, man. We need to head back."

Rick frowned briefly before his almost dead eyes lit up and crinkles formed on the sides.

"You mean we're not heading over to your favorite place to catch some good old Jell-O-wrasslin?"

I couldn't stop my brow from bowing in when I crossed my arms. I could feel my mouth turn down in the scowl I normally gave my subordinates. Something I had to give up if I wanted to get going.

I decided to just do exactly that since Rick had not only NOT been intimidated, but he'd fallen over again, laughing his head off.

I hope he barfed up a lung.

"I hope you barf up a lung. Now bring your butt so we can eat. I got stuff to do and less than one week to get it done."

"Sir yes sir!"

"Smart aleck."

Grinning, while running to keep up, something I made him do on purpose (using my longer legs and fast gait to my advantage) because he'd just pissed me off, he all but yelled, "So who are these people you want me to meet?"

Jumping into the passenger side of his jeep, I waited for him to run up and jump into his driver side to turn the key. I could feel the smirk on my face and didn't bother to hide it.

At his side-eyed glance I made it even creepier by pushing my chin into my chest, forcing my brows in and letting the loose shock of hair (now that my cap was off) fall over my eyes. With perfect timing I intoned with my spookiest voice, "Your worst nightmare."

Rick's side-eye morphed into a side glance before he grinned and waved his hand at me.

"Whatever, man."

Too bad he didn't realize that I was not lying. While Minute aka Cheryl, the medic we brought back with us might be right up his alley when it came to Marine's that happened to be female, Balboa was going to give him a run for his money. I already had a bet with two of the guys,

Max and Sam going. A bet that Johnny, Sam's best friend, had elected to stay out of since he says he likes his teeth where they are.

Ricky had been more than just lifting weights since I'd been gone the last three years. He'd gotten so good at hand-to-hand combat that he literally had to register his hands as weapons. And having promoted up to corporal, he'd also been granted commendations as munitions and guns expert levels three through five with certification to train.

That had made my friend many things, one of which was cocky. And a little too sure of himself when dealing with the ladies, even those that were soldiers.

And then there was Balboa, a woman that sprung from a hardened kid growing up in the streets of Miami. She'd fought her way into one of their most notorious gangs, working her way up to lieutenant of the male gang leader, something unprecedented as far as street gangs went. Schooled in several types of fighting styles from the Israeli fighting style of Krav Maga to Aikido, Jujitsu, mixed martial arts, boxing and stick fighting, the woman was a weapon of mass destruction all by herself. So, when I told my friend it would be his worst nightmare, I was not exaggerating. And I was not wrong.

Chapter 4 – Storm Clouds

December 31, 2012 – Alton, IL
Reignor, Lee and Stratford Law Firm
Brainwaiver Reveal Gala

Delilah grimaced and grit her teeth until her gums ached. She refused to hit the floor at his feet again.
A standard that she could hold to since he didn't have time on his side to torment her at his leisure today.

They had a ballroom full of folks, a basement full of kids and a full-on breach of security in their building.

And the culprit was sitting right there in the middle of it all, wearing a dress that Delilah would kill for if she was into something as petty as clothes.

"Where are they! Security should have checked in twenty minutes ago!"

Delilah shrugged in the face of Lance's anger, earning another shock of pain that rattled her nerve endings from her neck down to her feet. But she didn't fall. She didn't even give him the pleasure of a grunt this time.

"Oh, so you don't care is that it? Like this doesn't affect you?"

Delilah deep sighed. *And here we go...*

"Don't you think for one second that anyone can save you. You are my property. You belong to me to do as I please. And after I'm done cleaning up this mess, I will be more than happy to spend the rest of tonight proving it to you... again."

Delilah rolled her eyes up into her head in a way that she was sure Lance would see before turning to walk off.

"Where are you going?"

She would have kept walking if he hadn't snatched her back, his hand clawed at her elbow like some horror film character. Wiping her face of all expression she said the first thing to come to mind.

"To the ladies' room. You know, to use the bathroom. That's still allowed isn't it?"

"Don't be smart! And hurry up, I need this breach under control now. I might have to leave our benefactors here to help, so I need you back as soon as possible. If I can't be here to give them what they need, I need you to be available however they need you to be."

"Got it, "she grunted, snatching her elbow out of his hand.

Delilah wasn't surprised when that little move earned her one of Lance's sneers.   And she didn't care either. Because she was over this. All of it.

One would think that, having been robbed of her own free will from the ripe old age of 16, she'd be settled into the life by now.

But she wasn't. Even with the thing they'd put in her head, she wasn't. Oh, she played the game they wanted her to play, flirt, draw them in, suck up to the right people, but that was all they got. They got her body, but they never had her mind.

Even when she was helpless and the only place that she could be herself was in her head, she saw that as a better option than being some mindless slave, choosing to obey just because they gave her a painful shock of pain from their cell phones.

In fact, Delilah felt herself reaching that same place of finality. A place where she could no longer be the empty headed, obedient slave; even when she knew she couldn't escape. That place where she remembered her dreams, remembered a hero. A hero that had convinced her that, just because she suffered didn't mean she had to take part in other's suffering. Just because she was doomed, she didn't have to just sit back and watch others be destroyed. The last time she felt this way, she'd lost. A girl died, another was taken goodness knows where and the last was missing.

It had been so long ago when all of that had happened. Almost another lifetime. But still, Delilah recognized the feeling as soon as she felt it.

This time the target was a corn-fed Midwesterner that was clueless about who her real enemies were.

A woman she'd just taunted not an hour before, flirted with her date even. A woman that Delilah could take one look at and know for a fact that she didn't deserve any of what was about to come her way.

And that's when that feeling of finality pushed itself forward, asserting its power of control over her legs and arms completely. Without conscious intent, Delilah found herself moving back toward the table where Celine Baltimore sat, sipping on her Champaign like she didn't have the foggiest idea that her guy and his buddies were currently pulling off the best breaking and entering that Delilah had ever seen.

"It won't matter you know..." Delilah blurted out, not even sure why she was saying what she was saying, but unable to resist the urge.

Delilah could see Celine assessing her, breaking her down to pure data from her head to her feet, mentally cataloguing her everything from her words to the look on her face. And Delilah didn't really know how she felt about that. All she knew was that she had to get this, whatever it was, out of her system.

And like a river, more words began to sputter seamlessly from her mouth,
"They have been on to you from day one you know. They know who you know, where you go, where you work, who you do and what you do."

Delilah watched Celine's eyes narrow and couldn't help but admire her. When she'd first met this lady, to Delilah she had the appearance of a tall cherub with curly ash blond hair and pink cheeks. Healthy and big boned as those in the Midwest say, cute in her own way but far from attractive. She looked like every mom cliché in the book. And Delilah would have traded thirty years off her life to be that woman instead.

But now, to look at her, Delilah had no clue who she was dealing with. While the piercing green eyes were the same, gone was the look of the hunted. A hunter now lived behind those eyes, with a svelte face and body to match. Delilah had been surprised at the transformation and, while suitably intimidated as anyone would be, watching someone go from a regular soft body to a hard body with cut muscles and a look that says, please do it – I want you to... still, somehow Delilah preferred the mom image.
 Feeling sadder than she had in a long while, Delilah exhaled. They'd succeeded in robbing this woman of that

spark of innocence that had remained despite being in her thirties; something Delilah regretted. It was a painful reminder of Tandy dying with her spark and Maria's spark fading as she watched Tandy go down. It was why she struggled to finish. But she had to. Because this woman truly had no idea what she was up against.

"They know every single minutiae of your little happy Alton life. And they won't hesitate to smash you and everybody you love into bite sized bits for their enjoyment."

SO, RUN. PLEASE GOD, LET HER HEAR ME... Delilah wasn't one to pray, but she was shouting that prayer in her head to a God that she hoped could hear her and convey her message. The lady had a kid for goodness sakes! She was right there in that room when Lance and Andrew had threatened that kid. It had made her sick to her stomach. A queasiness that invaded again now as Delilah tried to find the words that would convince Celine to take her family and go before it was too late.

But before she had a chance to say those words, her guy, Enoch Sampson had returned to his seat beside her.

"Babe, what's up with the alarms? Is the building on fire? Why is everybody standing around like pigs in a pen when it sounds like we should be clearing the building?"

Delilah knew it was all a ruse. She knew that they thought they made a clean getaway. And in her mind, all she could envision was Enoch dying, gunned down while

Celine watched helplessly, before she and her daughter were hauled away, her daughter suffering a life like Delilah's. And her heart broke.

Her heart broke for Celine, for Enoch and for that little girl. Her heart broke for herself because, at least Celine had once had an Enoch and daughter, even if she eventually lost them... at least she'd once had them, something that Delilah would never be able to obtain.

It was the whisper carried on the breeze in her head that reminded her where she was and who she was amongst. It was the whisper of wind that froze her pain and regret for her so that she could function. So that she could move forward. So that she could survive. No matter the machine that thought it controlled her. No matter the men in her life that thought they owned her. Despite all that, Delilah had herself and the wind. And the one word that the wind always whispered no matter how tough things got. SURVIVE.

Turning from Celine's table Delilah moved toward the double doors leading out to the hallway entrance to find Lance and report back to the old geezers his findings, she promised the wind that she would do exactly that.

One Week Later...

"No Weapon."

Those were the words she'd said to them. Delilah lay still in her hotel room, the last of her bags she'd packed days ago. She was ready to return to her nicely guarded padded cell in the heart of Hollywood, CA.

Ready to go back to a place where people thought she had it all. They didn't have a clue that they experienced more freedom in a day than she had since she was a kid.

She couldn't let herself think about that. She had to focus on surviving, not living.

But it was hard to focus when all she could do was remember the horror she was forced to witness seven days ago. A horror she was forced to take part in. One that she would cut her eyes out to prevent her seeing it if she could. But she couldn't un-see it. Worse, she couldn't un-remember it either.

It had been barely an hour after her attempt to warn Celine in a twist that even she didn't see coming. And that was saying something considering how long she'd been a witness to the twisted minds of powerful men.

After her reported summary of Lance's discovery – the missing children in the basement along with one of the neurologists from Baltimore we'd hired, I was told to hold onto the tablet computer that they handed to me and report to the ladies' bathroom when they told me to.

My first thought had been GROSS. Then again, gross was kind of the norm in my line of work. While I wasn't doing anything conspicuous in the ways of being sold like I had been with Zeke, I was still bought and sold every day on someone's golf course as arm candy for award shows, favors to men in power, or even (believe it or not) espionage work. The implant made me physically strong but that didn't do me any good considering Lance's ability to control me with it from his smartphone.

So, while gross had been a way of life for me in the past, I hadn't been on this side of "gross" in a while. Because that's what going into the women's bathroom with a tablet computer was. Disgusting to the max.

It was only when I'd seen Celine leave the ballroom and was directed to follow did I get an inkling of their plan.

I knew that there were cameras everywhere, including in the ladies' room. Which means that whatever they were about to say on this tablet, they were watching. This was going to be some sort of shakedown, I knew. And I was helpless to stop it.

Another instance where I hated being right. I'd turned on the tablet and watched, to my horror, as the old geezers also known as the devil incarnate after that night, spewed such evil, I felt like going to confession just for being in the vicinity.

In short, they were making her come in. They were making her take the implant. They were going to turn her into... me. And I saw in that moment that I'd lied to myself. That spark of innocence I'd thought we'd robbed her of earlier? That couldn't have possibly been the case. Because

I watched it die, right there in that bathroom. And I felt that like a punch in the chest. It hurt so much I didn't catch the tear I felt sliding down my cheek until it was too late.

And as they threatened and threatened and threatened some more; after they threatened her family, her daughter and all that she'd held dear, I prayed harder than I have ever prayed before. God had never been there for me, but that didn't mean he wouldn't be there for her. So, I prayed with all my heart that if God was real, if He was everything those Christians said he was, that He'd make himself BIG ENOUGH to keep them, her and her family safe. And that's when I heard her say the words.

"NO WEAPON."

It was like those words were on repeat. Even when I turned off the tablet, shaking my head in silence, hoping to convey to her somehow that I wish, I wished with everything that was in me that this wasn't happening, I heard her saying the words.

And then she looked at the camera and said something else.

"No weapon formed against you shall be able to prosper. Every tongue that rises against you shall be shown to be made in the wrong. This is your heritage as a servant of the Lord, and your righteousness is of me, saith the Lord."

And that was when I felt it. A streak of lightning burned through me, hotter than the hottest thing I've ever felt. My hands grew hot and I fumbled the tablet that was cool to the touch.

I felt like I was about to combust. I rushed out of that room like it was literally on fire and dropped the tablet on the registration table. I flew toward the exit past the security guys lingering in the hall and skipped down two levels of stairs. Reaching an exit to the parking lot, I gulped until my lungs filled with air and my hands started to cool down.

Those words had haunted my dreams ever since that night, a new addition to the silver eyed hero, both now whispering on the voice of the wind that this is not who I am... whispering the one word that said nothing and everything at the same time: *WAKE UP!*

And I always did. But somehow, I knew that my emergence from sleep wasn't the only goal.

Chapter 5 – Winds of Change

January 6, 2013 – Alton, IL
The Caves Nestled Below Piasa Park

Delilah watched Celine go at Lance like a bat out of hell. She'd worried for a second when Celine had broken his nose and Lance had given her that creepy smile. Delilah knew that smile. Lance wore it often when he inflicted pain on her with his smartphone controls.

But then Celine rallied, and it was like time stopped. Watching her fight, obviously using the implant to her advantage and, despite being a novice, winning – Delilah became a believer.

No Weapon. She'd been there when Celine had first said it, and now she was a living witness.

Celine's movements were almost graceful they were so melodic yet precise. She knew there had to be some training involved, but the speed? The power? All of that had to be the implant. But there was something else. Celine... glowed.

There was no better way to describe it. And that was not something the implant had ever had the power to do. It was like Delilah was seeing Celine; but she was seeing someone else too, superimposed over Celine as she fought. And no matter how many times she focused her stare, no matter how many times she blinked, Delilah saw the same thing.

What Lance hadn't realized was that Delilah had planned to sneak the girls out in the heat of action, the moment he was distracted. She might not be able to save Celine, but at least she could save her and Sam's daughters.

Delilah exhaled and, fighting the sense of deja' vu, pushed down the fear that her life was on "repeat". She couldn't afford to let these girls be taken. She just wouldn't. And now that she'd watched Celine and whoever that glow was fight Lance? For the first time she felt hope.

And then a hand snatched her backward by the hair while another covered her mouth.

Next thing she knew, Delilah was being hauled backward as the girls were hugged and pulled away by two other shadows.

Delilah didn't get to see the end of the fight as she was pulled through the tunnels toward cave corridors she didn't recognize out through a maze of tunnels that ended at a hidden shed on RLS' property.

She didn't wonder about how the fight ended or the explosions, nor feel an ounce of fear as she was loaded into the van and threatened not to move by the weapons contractor lady and a stocky black guy that looked vaguely familiar.

She just sat back and fought down the hope welling up inside of her. Other people escaped, never Delilah. The girls had made it out unscathed. Nothing could have made Delilah happier. But that was never the case for her.

They always found her, or at least, Brody did when she'd belonged to Zeke. The Brainwaiver chip made it impossible to run; it had a tracer program embedded within it. There was no "getting away" for her. Ever.

These were the words that she tried to beat down the well of hope with. But it wouldn't die. It kept getting bigger instead.

And then the van door flew open, four more bodies quickly piled in, two yelling, "Go, Go!" Right before another set of explosions rocked the ground.

Crowded into the back of a cargo van was hardly fun. But a sense of elation was threatening to take Delilah despite that fact. She couldn't believe that she was free. She refused to believe it. And each mile that separated the van from RLS fed her hope, no matter Delilah's resolve.

It wasn't until the van pulled into a place she'd never seen that she began to relax. It was an underground garage that was clearly under construction. And while she had no idea where she was, nor who the people around her were; it was the sound of a voice laughing that caught her attention.

Yelling to the stocky man up front, the guy with "the voice" jumped out of the van, opened the doors and helped each girl jump down before the weapons contractor grunted at him, "Move," and jumped out on her own.

Quickly following her was Celine and Sam while the guys in front, that is, the stocky and the tall guy, jumped out the driver and passenger sides simultaneously.

Belatedly, Delilah realized that she was all that was left. Well, her and "the voice". He snatched off his skull cap (her guess? It finally occurred to him how creepy it was he still had it on), and laughed again, his voice so familiar, the hair on her arms stood up.

And when he stepped into the meager light in the back of the van saying (in his best Terminator voice), "Come with me if you want to live," his silver eyes laughing and filled with excitement; the hope in her chest exploded, nearly knocking Delilah unconscious.

K.C.

I knew that I was corny. My friends knew that I was corny. Heck, all of Texas knew that I was corny. My favorite movie was Killer Clownz for crying out loud.

But that didn't give the humorless woman in front of me reason to sit there staring at me with her mouth open like I killed her frog and she needed to perform mouth to mouth.

I shrugged, figuring she must be all, "I am woman, hear me roar," like Balboa. Which was fine with me. Because I was hungry. And pumped. There were two things that a man did when an adrenaline rush like this hit, whether he'd been on the battlefield or working the range – food or sex. And if he was lucky? Food and sex. Since I didn't currently have a lady of my own, it would have to be food. A thought that brought me back to the lady in the back of the van.

I remembered the intel on her, Delilah something. Well I remembered some of it anyway. She was implanted, that I knew. And had been one of the enemy, something else I knew. So, I couldn't just leave her sitting out here unattended. A fact that was standing in the way of me and a really juicy burger.

"Ma'am?" I threw her my best non-threatening smile (because my mama trained me right) and tried again.

"Are you coming? I'd be happy to help you down."

I don't know if she just shook her head to clear it, to tell herself not to jump my bones or choke me out (she had been the enemy so...); whatever it was, she made a decision, put her hand in mine and let me pull her to the edge of the door to help her down.

I felt my smile double in size as I all but tasted that juicy hamburger I couldn't wait to order from Steak N Shake.

"Thank you."

She'd mumbled as was expected since I just helped her down, but I hesitated. I didn't know why, but a sense of deja' vu staggered me. Her head was down, and we were walking in the shadows, but I couldn't shake the familiarity of the moment.

It was my stomachs loud growl and her glance upward at me with a smirk that distracted me from my thoughts. And that wasn't all that distracted me. I was a man, so yep, I was looking. She was a woman, a fine one at that.

We made it to the stairwell to take the stairs up, the elevators didn't have power after hours. Walking behind her, hungry with adrenaline pumping through me, I couldn't help but look some more. She stood at about 5'5" or so but she wasn't some tiny fairy. She was a woman with a woman's curves and a woman's smell. Lavender and something else floated like a cloud around her.

Her blond mass of curls was caught up in a ponytail and I swallowed twice to ignore my body's reaction to the swing of her hips as she took the steps in front of me.

Like I said, she was fine. But as pretty as she was, her eyes told a story that carried a huge sign in red letters saying, "DANGER, DON'T TOUCH!"

I didn't know women as well as I would like to, but I knew animals and kids. Both had certain mannerisms that, if keenly observed; allowed you to see their past injuries (even if they've been healed). It was in the way that they walked, moved, approached or moved away. Some approached with distrust and at an angle, ready to fight at a moment's notice. Some wore a bleak expression of expectation coupled with an air of disappointment that suffocated them. Those were what I called the living dead. It took a lot to breathe life into an animal that had either of those conditions.

And this lady? Ms. Delilah? She was both.

For certain, I just wanted to grab my burger, hit my hotel and call it a night; but something told me that this lady needed me.

Not to save her or anything. I have a strong mom with strong sisters that would put me in a headlock just at the thought of trying to be somebody's hero.

Nope, my job wasn't to save her. That would have probably been easier.

In my gut, I had a feeling that I might have to show her how to save herself. Swallowing hard, I sighed. Because I was not looking forward to that. At all.

Chapter 6 - Blown Away

February 12, 2013 (current)
Baltimore, MD

Delilah

"Boy! Come on up here and give me some sugar! Now you know you been gone too long!"

   KC grinned before racing up the steps to the brownstone next door. The woman he embraced made Delilah think of every stereotype in the book when it came to black women.

   She looked to be in her late fifties and was around Delilah's height at about 5'6".

The lady looked like the word MOM would have her picture under it in the dictionary. She was pleasantly round wearing a flour smeared apron and the cutest cap on her head.

KC planted a loud kiss right on her cheek before giving her a hug and spinning her around.

The woman kicked up her feet and laughed joyously. It was a moment that pulled a grin Delilah tried to fight, to the surface. It was better than a hallmark card or one of those mushy commercials with pets or babies. It was a moment where people were good and loving and normal. Delilah soaked up every second of it.

"And who is this you've brought home? Why she look hungry? You gonna have the nerves to bring home a girl I haven't met and dare to starve her while you do it?"

K.C. burst out laughing and hugged the woman again before calling to me across the porch.

"Delilah, please meet my nosy neighbor and the only woman that owns my heart besides my mom, Ms. Delores Jenkins."

"Hush boy, and honey, everybody on the block knows me and calls me Mother Jenkins, Momma, Mama J or Ms. Dolores. I answer to any and all of those. Now come on over here and let me get a good look at you."

Delilah hesitated. Apparently really neighborly neighbors were normal. Since life on the Res or in the cities where she was held against her will hadn't prepared her for normal life, Delilah thought it best to take her cues from others.

On that thought, she hurried over to the other brownstone.

"Yes honey, come on here and let me see."

Mother Jenkins held her arms out to her sides then stepped back and motioned her finger in a circle, the universal symbol for "turn around."

Delilah tried her best not to scrunch up her nose as she did so. She really didn't understand what this was about, but it didn't surprise her that normal would feel weird to her. Finishing her spin, she dropped her arms and glanced at K.C. then Mother Jenkins with eyebrows slightly raised.

"Baby-girl. You need a sandwich!"

Unexpected. And funny. Which was probably why Delilah nearly fell over laughing. She tried to stop before they thought her weird, but she couldn't help it. Never, in her 26 years of life, had anyone ever looked at her and, after assessing her fully, state with such confidence, that she needed a sandwich. It was sweet. And normal. So normal and sweet that Delilah didn't realize she pulled the woman into a hug until Mother Jenkins was hugging her right back.

Delilah fought tears. She wasn't a crier; she was a survivor. But this entire encounter was blowing her away. It was telling that, with the life she'd lived and all that had gone down, her hard, toughened exterior was broken down by a kind woman's heartfelt offer of food.

Undone, Delilah tried her best to pull herself together before letting go. She had three weeks to get focused. That was the time limit she'd given herself after Dr. Larson and Max partially deactivated her implant.

Apparently, the implant she had couldn't be removed and many parts of it couldn't be shut down. Having the older version meant removal would require a couple of things. First, the surgery would be intensely invasive and require a long recovery period. Over two months to be exact. Second, because her body had adapted and incorporated much of the chip into her brain with false synapses that entangled with real ones, surgery would be very risky. Thus, the decision to go forward with partial deactivation (including the tracer and links to external devices).

After all of that, CeeCee had asked her the question all of them probably wanted to ask.
What would Delilah do now?

It was a good question. Delilah had had no clue.

CeeCee invited her to stay in her house in Alton. She and Sam (everyone called Enoch "Sam") were moving in together before the wedding as he'd vowed to not let her out of his sight. Delilah didn't blame him.

But she couldn't accept that. Delilah wanted to get as far away from RLS, Lance or anyone else that worked for those old geezers as she could. Just because the tracer program had been shut down didn't mean that they would make no attempts to recover her.

Despite having no money or resources, Delilah had been preparing to "hit the road," maybe find her way back to the Res. Until K.C. had come to her room in the compound (what she called their secret headquarters).

He'd looked worried. And since Delilah actually *was* worried, they'd been on the same page.

"How you holding up?" He asked softly, dropping down in the chair across from the bed she was using.

"I'm holding."

"I see your bag is packed. Where're you going?"

Her shrug spoke for her. Fear choked Delilah as her thoughts ran rampant. All the "what ifs" came rushing in, piling one thought on top of another. Like what if they found her, what if the tracer wasn't completely deactivated, what if Eli or Brody came for her, what if she ran into someone who knew who she was and called it in...

"So, I own a few convenience stores." K.C. grunted after clearing his throat.

Okay, Delilah thought.

"Since you don't have a destination or occupation in mind, I'm wondering if you can use the work?"

Ah. "Where do you live?"

"Baltimore."

"Maryland?"

"Is there another Baltimore I don't know about?" K.C. grinned, taking the sting out of his words.

Delilah's lips quirked in an almost smile before she asked, "Is that where you're from, like, where you were born?"

"Nope. Born and raised outside of Houston, Texas."

Delilah nodded, because that sounded about right. His accent was barely there but, for those who'd been down south as she had, it wasn't hard to pinpoint.

"You ever been to Texas?"

Delilah shook her head. Her folded hands rested in her lap. She felt awkward and strange. And a little queasy; she was in unfamiliar territory. Like someone who'd gotten lost but was afraid to ask for help.

Because Delilah had learned a hard lesson early; men could not be trusted. It was her self-preservation and that lesson warring heavily against her desire to go with K. C.

"So how come I feel like I should know you?"

Delilah almost choked before answering.

"I have one of those faces. Plus, I'm a box-blonde. So, you know. A lot of women have this exact same hair color."

K.C. nodded. Then he rose and stretched.

"Well, the offer is open. I realize that working at a convenience store isn't glamourous. But, it's a job. And an honest way to earn money while you decide what you want to do. So, think about it.

"I will," Delilah promised as K.C. let himself out.

And she had. She'd thought long and hard about it, which was why she was standing on a strange lady's porch, fighting back tears because she'd offered her a sandwich. This was obviously a delayed reaction to her former trauma.

It was no surprise to Delilah that Mother Jenkins somehow felt her pain, even though she hadn't made a sound.

Because one moment, Delilah was on the porch, hanging on to Mother Jenkins for dear life, and in the next, she was somehow sitting in the woman's kitchen at the table. While Mother Jenkins ducked into the fridge to find "sandwich fixins".

K.C. handed her a tissue while Mother Jenkins fussed.

"You've got to know the importance of feeding people, son. You can't just have women flying from place to place without feeding them some type of nourishment. It just ain't right!"

"Yes ma'am." K.C. answered dutifully, grabbing an orange from the bowl of fruit on the table before peeling it and popping sections in his mouth.

Glancing up and catching Delilah in mid-stare, K.C. grinned before eating another slice. It was a grin that she was coming to learn. Which meant that Mother Jenkins was about to erupt again in three...two...one...

"Boy, what are you eating! That orange ain't gonna be near enough for your big ole body. Sit on down here while I fix sandwiches for the both of you."

Mother Jenkins was still fussing, though Delilah couldn't hear it. All she heard was mumbling with an occasional, "don't make no sense," thrown in.

At that, Delilah couldn't help but grin back. And prepare herself to enjoy the first sandwich she'd ever eaten on the east coast.

K.C.

I tried hard not to laugh at Delilah's bucked eyes as she took in the size of the sandwich Mama made her. It would not be exaggerating to say that there was at least half a pig, cow and vegetable garden on that thing; wrapped in two huge pieces of French bread.

I probably should have warned her. Mama don't mess around when it comes to food. The bigger the better, the more to feed, the merrier. And this was just a quick sandwich, we hadn't even touched on Mama's food possibilities when it came to actual mealtimes.

Watching Delilah try to get her mouth around that thing was a comedy of errors. The girl was going to unhinge her entire jaw if she wasn't careful.

It was with that kind of consideration that, when I finished my monster Dagwood, I very politely offered to finish hers for her.

It was the narrowed eyes that drove home the recognition. I knew her. I'd seen this woman. I'd helped her once...

"Delilah! Get back here."

The guys voice had been heavy with a growl as he'd threatened her. I'd figured for the rest of my life that I would never forget that voice. And apparently, I was right. Which meant Ms. Delilah I-can't-believe-I-still-didn't-know-her-last-name had some explaining to do. And it was an explanation that I couldn't wait to hear.

Chapter 7 - Stormy Winds

"So, were you never going to tell me that it was you down in San Luis or what?"

Delilah blinked at me like an owl caught in a hen house. I blinked right back.

She wasn't much different than that time I'd first seen her, but there were obviously notable changes.
I didn't mention any of that though. Because my goal was not to make this easier for her.

"And by the way, since we *are* answering questions and all, what is your last name exactly?"

She blinked and swallowed this time. She was caught... and she knew it.

"After you finish answering those two very necessary inquiries, we can round this conversation out with, what the hell happened to you and who you are, really. Because I've put two and two together and I'm hoping with everything I got that I do not have four."

That was the same hope that had kept me from kicking her out the moment I realized who she was. I hated lying. Further, I hated liars.

And since the lie that stood like Andre the Giant between us occurred before this whole Brainwaiver debacle? Let's just say that "hope" was a force all unto itself. The fact that I hadn't thrown her out with all her crap without one word past GET OUT was a miracle all by itself.

Delilah deep sighed before walking around me to drop to my sofa. I didn't bother to look around. I knew what my place looked like. It was a bachelor pad, so it wasn't fancy. Yet I was a man with a mother and four sisters that liked to visit; suffice it to say, it wasn't trash either.

Grabbing the ottoman from under my table, I sat close enough for her to reach for me if she needed me, but far enough away to give her space. And I couldn't for the life of me figure out why I cared enough to do so. That was something you did for people that didn't lie to you. In fact, it was an art I'd perfected as a high school student for my four sisters that had experienced boyfriend troubles on the regular.

Time passed as she spilled. I felt no better after Delilah was done giving me the full story; Truth be known, I felt ten times worse.

Because my two and two had made four, but THAT four was so maniacal, I couldn't fathom it.

As a man that was taught by my strong women that I could be protective and still let a woman *be* strong and independent, I suddenly felt out of my element here.

Because this girl had not only NOT been protected, she'd been violated to the point that, in her mind, it was what she deserved; a thought process that I couldn't even fathom.

And I could tell by the cadence in her voice through certain parts that shame and fear had been her ruling emotions. While Mama Jenkins or other strong women would call her a survivor, I saw Mary Magdalene all over her. Not because she'd done anything wrong, but because the world sucked so bad that she *thought* she did, not even considering the true villains in the scenario.

It was then that I realized she couldn't possibly save herself. She didn't know how. She fought, lied, stole and cheated to save everybody else, but never herself. The concept of taking care of herself instead of others was completely foreign to her. And hell if I knew how to change that.

"So, Delilah Running-Wind. What do you want to do with the rest of your life?"

I could tell she'd been thinking long and hard about that. And now I understand why I hadn't gotten an immediate answer the first time I'd asked. This woman has never had the opportunity to be a kid. To dream about a future where she could be anything she wanted to be.

Which was another thing that made me sick to my stomach. I had nieces and nephews. I had family. I had little people around me all the time, coming into my stores, living on the block, visiting Mama next door. I couldn't imagine one of those kids being enslaved to the point where thinking about the future only brought more pain.

"I want to help girls; the girls that deserve a better life and had that opportunity snatched away."

And here we were, back to helping others again. Now, it wasn't like I was completely against helping other people. My take on that philosophy was simple: To help others, you had to first be able to help yourself.

I kept that thought to myself. We all had a different way of seeing things. The least I could do was help her narrow her goal down to an occupation.

"Do you mean like a social worker that helps abused and neglected women or starting something like a coalition that focuses on helping girls adapt after being caught up in trafficking?" I asked.

"The second one."

Delilah's response had been so quick that I blinked several times before nodding my understanding. Her beautiful blue gaze was on fire with passion and excitement, apparently just at the thought of it.

I couldn't help but feel a little... okay a LOT drawn to her. I hadn't felt this way since leaving Abilene over five years ago.

Which was why, instead of telling her how beautiful or strong she was and how I was amazed at her resilience and her ability to survive -- despite being pissed at her (because had she allowed me to help her that night, she could have possibly stayed safe... maybe), I hopped up to grab some notebook paper and pens.

"Here you go." I grumbled. I was trying not to give her a hard time; but right now, that was too much of a challenge. Huffing instead of fussing at her was the best I could do.

"What's this for?"

"For you to write down your plan."

She frowned. "What plan?"

"How should I know? It's your plan..."

"What," was her flat response. It wasn't a question, but spoken as more of an exasperation, like I would say – Really...

I grinned. Delilah's confusion made me feel like I'd gotten some justice for her offense of not allowing me to help her when I could have, so I let her off the hook.

"Write down where you are now at the top and where you want to be at the bottom. Then list the steps that you think will be necessary to get you there. Make sure those steps are time sensitive, realistic and specific enough in a way that you can hold yourself accountable. When you finish, voila! You've got a plan."

She stared down at the paper like it was a guy in jail waiting to beat her down in the yard. Then I watched her square her shoulders, clear her throat and reach for the paper and pens.

"Remember, you need money to live. So, whatever your plan is, you need a means of earning income to pay for the resources your plan will require."

I watched as she bit on the tip of the pencil for a minute before jotting things down. While she was writing, all I could think about was how unfair it was that some people who don't deserve to breathe prosper while others like Delilah didn't prosper at all.

Having no answer for that, I caught ahold of her bags and hauled them to the guest room, leaving the light on for her to follow when she was finished.

After having a quick heart to heart with my body to dispel the guilt of remembering how Delilah licked her lips when she was nervous, I yelled good night from my room and took a cold shower before dropping face first onto the bed, passing right out.

***

Three months later...

Delilah

Delilah grunted before handing the customer his change while pushing the case of beer he'd just purchased toward him.

"So, are we gonna do this or what?"

"Or what." Delilah responded in the same monotone voice she used when some random guy propositioned her. And just like clockwork...

"What? You think you're too good for me or something?"

Delilah tried hard to keep her eye roll in check while mentally going over the statistics homework she'd been assigned.

"DO YOU?!!!"

This was escalating quickly, and she had three more customers behind "Mister Can't-take-no-for-an-answer". Which was probably why the small chime sounding in her left ear wasn't a surprise. The Brainwaiver had self-activated, picking up on the threat to her safety. So, the punch that suddenly flew at her face was easily dodged without her even looking at the guy. And before she could say something sensible like, "I'll call 911," or "please exit the premises," the chips self-defense protocols kicked in. Her growl of frustration was very real as Delilah found herself leaping over the counter, placing her knee smack into the middle of the man's throat. Her right hand had flown upward with the palm out, ready to deliver a strike that would send the bridge of his nose into his brain.

Breathing hard, Delilah cursed and struggled, fighting through the haze to think of kittens, ignoring the applause echoing throughout the store. She'd found that thinking of cute little kittens and puppies was the only fool-proof way of forcing the chip to disengage. The present protocols would have her take a life dispassionately and with ruthless logic, without thought or remorse.

Gaining full control, she snatched away from the man as if he were on fire and calmly took her place behind the counter.

"Next please," she growled banging her fingers needlessly into the register to burning off some of the adrenaline coursing through her. It too was a byproduct of the chip and had been activated the moment her fight or flight instinct was triggered.

"Can you teach me that?"

Delilah blinked and looked up. Standing barely as tall as the counter was the most adorable tween girl she'd ever seen. Adorable and rude.

"Excuse me?" Delilah answered through gritted teeth.

"I asked, can you teach me that."

Delilah frowned. "Teach you what?"

"What you did with that guy just now?"

"You want to learn how to reject boys? Just say no kid, not that hard." She mumbled, focusing on the tags of the three items on the counter.

The little girl went up on her toes and crossed her arms. Apparently, she didn't find Delilah amusing.

Glancing up, Delilah sighed.

"What's your name," she asked, changing tactics.

"Destiny Willis."

"Cool name."

The girl smirked. "I like it."

"So, you're having boy problems Destiny?"

"Nope, I'm having a group of girls problems. But, if I can do to just one of them what you did to that guy, I won't be having those problems for long."

"How? By ending up hospitalized because they decide to jump you all at once since they can't beat you one on one?"

Tween hands went from folded in front of her chest, one to each hip as she prepared, Delilah assumed, to blast her with more teenaged logic before a quick glance out the window at the parking lot gave the girl pause.

"Hey, is that a news van?"

Glancing up from her book toward the window, Delilah bit back another curse. Because it *was* a news van. News vans, news people and news cameras were something that she actively avoided. Delilah had been famous once. TMZ would be thrilled to catch her working at a convenience store. The show she used to be on was one of their rivals.

"Do me a favor, Destiny. Put this apron on and get behind the counter, I'll be in the back." Delilah said, moving fast.

"But I'm too little! And only families can work their kids without a work permit."

"How old are you?" Delilah yelled from the back.

"Nine." Destiny yelled back.

"How do you know about work permits?"

"Shhhhhh," Destiny whispered loudly at the same time the bell over the door sounded.

Delilah could hear the mumbling voices of people talking. And her anxiety grew.

This was by far her lowest low, letting the kid face off with reporters instead of doing it herself. Even though she had no idea why they were here, the bottom line is that they were. And she couldn't let her fear of being discovered by the old geezers get in her future's way.

She had a plan. She'd written it down. And she was going to make it happen, old geezers or not. There were kids out there like Maria, Tandy and Maddie. Kids that didn't deserve to be snatched away from everything they knew and people that loved them.

Delilah was going to do whatever it took to make sure those kids got the help they needed; even if she had to face off against the media to do it.

Throwing back her shoulders and taking a deep breath, Delilah walked out into a bunch of flashes.

"There she is!" Some lady shouted.

Delilah groaned quietly. *Oh, For the love of...*

"Are you the one? Are you the lady that single handedly foiled a robbery here about an hour ago?"

Delilah gritted her teeth. And thought about all the puppies and kittens that she could muster. Because it was going to be a long night.

***

K.C.

I wasn't prepared for the crowd milling around outside of store 287. It was the 3rd store we'd opened on North Calvert Street. I say we because my father, Charlie Kilian and my Uncle Nevel were joint investors in my convenience store operation. We owned 7 stores in Houston and 3 here in Baltimore.

After five years of hard work and pushing to make our brand a household name down south, I had to get away and go anywhere but Texas. I'd chosen Baltimore because it was where Cheryl was. She'd completed her residency here and was making her name as a highly sought out Neurosurgeon.

My thought was, when Rick finally got his head out of his butt and acted on his crush, he'd be giving up running his brother's custom motorcycle and car garage near Abilene to move up here.

Speaking of a man and his crushes. I had to get myself into the store and quick.

Delilah Robinson, former television personality aka Delilah Running Wind, human trafficking survivor (and the woman that I was currently crushing on) was apparently being featured on the news. I could see the headline now: Sensational store clerk foils robbery attempt, single handed!

Which was probably only half the story. Cheryl had warned us after learning of Delilah's history that the Brainwaiver couldn't be completely shut down.

With no room on the lot to park I swung around the back of the store to my personal space where I found a news van illegally parked. If that wasn't bad enough, there were two more cars haphazardly parked in the alley, blocking the path to the back of my store.

Now I was irritated.

Before I'd just been freaked. When some little girl called me from Delilah's phone, I'd thought it was a kid pranking Delilah's stolen phone.

But then I'd heard the voices, the yelling, and the kid telling me to turn on the channel 9 news.

Which was when I all but lost my mind.

So, like I said, I'd been freaked. We'd found out the hard way that the chip could activate itself for self-preservation purposes when Delilah had been standing on the bus stop two months ago.

Some dude had run up behind her to snatch her purse. Next thing we knew, Delilah had snatched the would-be-thief backward into a right cross that made my eyes water. The purse hit the ground as Delilah executed a perfect left-right-left combination followed by an uppercut.

I'd winced in sympathy before I noticed Delilah's reaction. Her hands had started shaking and she was staring at them with big eyes, her mouth open wide in shock.

It was the horror that laced her blinking eyes that jolted me into action.

Cheryl had hurried down for an emergency examination however, having seen Delilah in action, I wasn't all that surprised by the diagnosis.

The Brainwaiver was still active though dormant until the program determined that action was needed. When it did, it triggered a response to the imminent threat with the adrenal rush that accompanied a person's fight or flight instinct.

If the fight or flight impulse is tripped, the chip automatically chooses "fight," accesses its programming and logically determines the best counter actions to eliminate the danger.

We didn't know what would have happened to that guy had I not been there to shock Delilah back into control by yelling her name, a tactic I'd learned in the deserts of Afghanistan.

It's what we used to combat what we called *Berserker* mode; when a soldier, fueled by bloodlust and rage was no longer in control of his body's responses. He or she would be in complete survival mode, a mere passenger in his/her brain with the body and will's drive to survive piloting.

Grab a soldier in *Berserker* mode and you could lose a limb, an eye or your life. We learned quickly to shout the soldiers name or key trigger words like NO or STOP along with their name to shock them back into the driver's seat of their psyche.

And because I didn't know how the reporters, flashing lights and cameras were messing with Delilah's head right then, I jumped out of my car and left it behind the cars and news van, blocking their exit, to run inside.

I didn't know which was worse; Delilah Robinson, former Hollywood and TV personality snapping on a bunch of folks in the store on camera; or her being located by the two masterminds behind Brainwaiver.

Sadly, I had a feeling that we were about to find out.

Chapter 8 – Tricky Winds

Nina Irwin
Clearwater, Florida
same day

Ducking the idiot's punch wasn't a challenge.

The truth was, Nina fought hard against the yawn threatening to make her boredom obvious. She'd been trained by the best. That being the case, fighting an overweight fat-head 5 times her size and forty times slower that telegraphed his punches?

Yeah, not her definition of a thrill. And normally, she'd just kick the man's butt for wasting her time and go about her business. Except today he WAS her business since she was on the hunt.

A bounty hunter for hire, Nina had been contracted privately to locate a vicious biker gang trafficking ring four months ago. And the trail had gone cold until last week. Her contact, an old army buddy now working for the Clearwater Police Department tipped her off to intel that linked a person of interest to the ring, putting her back on track. The trail, no longer cold but piping hot, had led her to this guy, the overweight non-champion of the world, and his brother.

Dancing out of his reach as the guy went for the wrestler's grab, Nina grew tired of stalling for time, hoping his brother would show.

So tired that she snatched the taser baton out of the back of her waist band, snapped it to extend it, and took a running leap at Damien Cabello (brother to Carlito Cabello, president of the Crimson Bones Biker Club - read gang).

And just like an amateur, the slow as molasses blowhard reached for her while she was in the air, hoping to catch her into his backbreaker grip and squeeze her into submission. He was so intent on that in fact that he didn't see Nina's arm raised with the sparking baton arcing down to connect to his neck. But his buddies did.

Amidst shouts of warning and running feet, Nina delivered thirty thousand volts of electricity directly into Damien's throat, not even pausing to look at his spazzing, drooling form as it hit the ground.

She didn't pause because she had four bikers coming right at her, one pulling a Glock from his waist band. Biker one rushed in for a direct attack. Short like Nina, instead of reaching for her with a punch or a kick, he dove at her, only to miss as she swung out of reach.

Reaching again to her own waistband, now armed with two batons Nina took out biker number two with a jolt from baton number two, then swinging backward in a downward slice with baton number one, she disarmed biker number three.

Ducking a wild swing from biker number four, Nina grinned at the scream that sliced the air as her left foot landed a sweet kick directly into his groin before she dove and rolled out of the way of biker three's left cross since he'd recovered.

Coming out of the roll with his Glock in her hand, Nina didn't have to worry about cocking it as it was ready to fire. And just like that, two sets of hands went up into the air from their pained positions while the other two bikers vibrated helplessly on the ground.

Still grinning and blowing her rainbow died tresses out of her eye. Nina kept the gun aimed while walking calmly in a circle to make sure all four bikers were will within the gun's sight.

"Thanks for the work out fellas. Now that that's done, since Carlito won't be joining us, you give him a message from me. Tell him I'm looking for Zeke and his boys. He's got one day to get that information for me, or I swear I will take all of you out one by one."

"Go to Hell!" Biker three snarled, holding tight to his injured wrist.

"Been there, done that," Nina snarled before stalking toward biker three until the muzzle of the gun was resting squarely between his eyes.

"I know you see the color streaks in my hair and figure I'm some punk kid that got lucky. So, you need to look at my eyes. What do my eyes tell you."

That's when the bearded biker that looked like he was desperate for another hit to get him high, swallowed.

And Nina didn't mind that. Nor did she mind that he took his time to figure it out. And because she smelled and heard his bladder release, she didn't mind filling in the gap for him.

"That's death you see bro. I don't threaten. I don't exaggerate. Carlito has that intel for me here, tomorrow night, or I come for your whole crew. And when I tell you that they won't have a clue which body part belongs to who when they go to bury you, I mean exactly that. Do you understand?"

The biker nodded, his eyes on the ground.

"The gun is mine. It's yours tomorrow when I get what I came for."

Nina called that out as she walked away, kicking the downed body of Damien as she approached her bike.

It didn't bother her that she'd done all that damage in less than ten minutes in the parking lot of a known biker bar where she was at a complete disadvantage.

It didn't bother her because she had a timetable to keep and a wedding in St. Louis that she needed to get to. It was that thought that had her take out her cell to check the text message that alerted her just before she tasered Damien.

Ignoring the two from Rob that came in earlier asking how she was and what she was doing, Nina focused on the one that caused a chill to run up her spine.

Delilah Robinson was featured on the news tonight, some kind of glitch in the chip. Before you head back for the wedding, I need you in Baltimore for damage control. Be careful and call for an assist if you need it. Sam

Crap!

"Change of plans. Don't worry. I'll be back," Nina yelled as she emptied the clip of the gun before throwing it back toward the parking lot.

Putting on her helmet, she got on her bike and took off.

She had a long trip ahead of her.

And sleep, normally her best friend, just became a memory.

***

Delilah

"If I catch that boy staring at your behind one more time, me and him gonna have words."

"Mama!" Delilah laughed and shouted at the same time.

"Don't Mama me. I've been trying to keep my peace, but I don't think I can much longer. I think you might need to move in here with me child, until you get your bearings and find your own place. It's not right, you two living under the same roof when he looks at you like that."

Delilah shook her head and grinned, head down to hide the fact that her cheeks had turned bright red.

"He doesn't think of me like that Mama Jenkins, trust me."

Mother Jenkins snorted as she shuffled around her kitchen grabbing her ingredients for the dinner that she was making.

Delilah grinned some more, turning the page in her sociology text to jot down the notes she needed for tomorrow's class.

"Doesn't think of you like that, you must be crazy..." Mother Jenkins mumbled as she bustled some more.

Delilah tried hard not to laugh out loud. The best she could do was cover the chuckles with a fake cough.

The truth was, she had no idea how K.C. looked at her. She had no idea because he avoided her like the plague. At the apartment if she was in one room, he was in another. If he was home when she came home from work, he would ask her how her day was, make a little small talk then leave for his room.

The only time they managed to see each other was at Mother Jenkin's house when she cooked them a meal, usually once a week. Even then, he seemed to look everywhere but at her.

Delilah wasn't stupid. She knew that he'd been less than happy with her about not owning up to their first encounter. And she knew she wasn't his type.

She knew that because of the two photo albums she'd found under his television stand.

Photo albums that featured pictures of him and a gorgeous caramel, curvy African American lady in uniform.

Some of the photos were beyond cozy, like the two of them cuddling in a restaurant or smiling in front of some store front.

That woman had been the exact opposite of Delilah. Not to mention that she'd probably never been a sex slave. All good reasons why Delilah felt Mama Jenkins was imagining things.

"And furthermore, I don't get why you can't see the way he looks at you. Do you not like boys or something? If you don't Mama don't judge honey, we all got our areas where we aint pleasing the good Lord…"

Delilah couldn't help it that time, the roar of laughter flying past her lips uncontained with no fake coughs to mask its presence.

"What I say?" Mama Jenkins cried out causing Delilah to face plant into the table in another fit of giggles.

By the time Delilah was done, Mama was placing the cut-up vegetables and other ingredients in her big roasting pan and placing it in the oven, shaking her head and mumbling how white people were crazy and needed prayer.

Wiping the tears from her face, Delilah was just about to respond when Mama's grumbles sent her into another laughing fit. That's when K. C. called out as he came through the front door.

"In here!" Mama called back, flopping down into the chair on the other side of her kitchen table.

And, as was his routine, he walked past Delilah with a mumbled greeting of," Hey Dee," before approaching Mama Jenkins with a huge grin and following that up with a big hug.

Delilah, before that moment, would have never thought of herself as a jealous person. Actually, that wasn't true.

She would have never thought of herself as a jealous person until the night she'd found those pictures of K.C. and the mystery lady.

Now, just like then, Delilah found the sour taste in her mouth and the ache in her chest disturbing.

The man had barely looked at her since the night they'd arrived. To say that they were like ships passing in the night while cliché, yes, it was also the truth. There was absolutely no reason at all that she would have proprietary feelings toward K.C.

And yet, the awful yawning ache in her chest remained there, unconvinced. At first she'd tried to tell herself that she wasn't jealous of them per se', rather the relationship that they'd had. But now, watching him show love to Mama Jenkins, smile and laugh with her about the benign happenings of her day; just plain giving her attention?

Delilah realized with a sinking feeling that this wasn't about envying being in love.

It was about her falling in love... with him. A thought that scared her beyond reason.

***

K.C.

Having greeted Mother Jenkins with her hug and getting the rundown of her day, I took my seat across from Delilah and pulled out my cell to pretend to check text messages.

I was pretending to check them because, as had been the case lately, I was about to lose myself in my new favorite past time, watching Delilah surreptitiously while pretending to do something else.

And like always, when watching her, I was mystified by the air of sultriness about her.

It called to me so much I barely slept at night, awareness of her presence just down my hall beating at me and turning me inside out.

What was worse is that this was more than physical attraction. Watching her now; her blond hair pulled back into a ponytail (while tendrils that refused to be tamed hung around her face), her chin resting in her hand and skin flushed a rosy pink made me wonder what she looked like in the heat of passion.

And all of that had nothing on my desire to hear her talk to me. A desire I was helpless to fight as I cleared my throat.

"How's classes coming Dee?" I'd already cleared my throat, but my voice was still graveled with the urges I was beating back and trying hard to ignore.

She glanced up at me, her gorgeous blue gaze skittering across mine before she answered.

"Pretty good. Still struggling with statistics but everything else is fine."

I waited for her to elaborate. Something that pissed me off. I hated the longing I felt. Her not saying more bothered me, for no other reason than I needed to hear her saying something. Anything.

Clearing my throat again, I tried for a normal tone,

"Cool. Uh, I know that this little vacation from the store is probably bothering you. Once the hubbub dies down and the media moves on to another story, you'll be able to return to work. Are you doing okay otherwise?"

And then the freaking sun came out. At least, that's what it felt like when, this time her gaze didn't skitter across mine; this time, she looked me right in the eye; a tiny smile resting on her lips as she did.

I felt my eyes narrow as other parts of me helplessly responded.

And that was when I realized something. I wanted this woman with something deep in me that I couldn't identify; that didn't have a name. I'm sure the shock that I felt was mirrored in my eyes as her smile widened before her gaze dropped to my mouth.

My stomach dropped as I admitted the truth (if to no one else, at least to myself), wanting her so much was freaking me way the hell out.

Chapter 9 – Invisible Winds

Delilah

No Weapon!

Delilah sat up, her mind screaming the words, her heart beating fast.

The nightmare had triggered her fight or flight response and activated the chip but, unlike times before, it couldn't identify the immediate threat.

The nightmare was the least of her worries. It had been three months since she'd been featured on the news. The story was quickly picked up by national stations and their affiliates, including the Eye network where Delilah used to work.

Everyday her anxiety had eased just a tiny bit as hope took hold. Hope that the old geezers were not concerned about her or looking for her.

While one form of anxiety eased, a different kind of stress steadily increased for a different reason.

She'd never, in a million years, even considered that she would be attracted to a man. She longed for something stable and special in her life, sure. Everyone did.

But for her, that longing hadn't been related to having a romantic relationship. Ever since that day, the "NO WEAPON" day, she'd longed for the faith, the assurance... the 'something else' that Celine had.

Delilah had longed for a relationship with someone that would never fail her. Someone that could always keep her safe. Someone that would show her who she should be and give her an identity. It was a longing that she tried not to dwell on as it begged the question, why would that 'someone' want to have anything to do with her? She'd been a prostitute. It didn't matter that she didn't choose that life. It was what it was.

And while she'd been tested for any sexually transmitted diseases twice since coming to Baltimore, she still felt... unclean. Used. Worthless.

Delilah hated that feeling in the pit of her stomach the most. The one that churned with every encounter; ensuring her that, whoever she was talking to could see right into her.

It was a feeling that sparked anger and resentment deep inside her where little Delilah Running-Wind still lived, thumbing her nose at death and everyone else.

Well, at everyone else except K. C.

Delilah had learned a lot about him since their arrival in Maryland.

She'd learned that his legal name was Mathew Killian and that he would be thirty-two years old next week on June 30th.

She'd also learned about his family, his marine days and his time served in Afghanistan.

More interestingly, she'd learned that, because he felt he wasn't talented, he'd decided to invest in a convenience store in Houston with his father.

Putting business acumen to work that he didn't know he had, one store became three stores. And then he moved to Baltimore, Maryland where he did the exact same thing.

K.C. wouldn't say why he'd moved; Delilah had a feeling it had something to do with that woman. But she didn't ask, and she didn't' judge. He deserved his secrets.

She had several of her own.

Like that she'd never been attracted to a man or anyone else before now. She'd never had a boyfriend or social interaction that allowed her to be interested in anything but survival. She'd learned how to manipulate clients for more money but never how to flirt. She'd learned how to catch a man's interest sexually and that was it. That had always been the end goal.

And now, survival was no longer an issue. With K.C. and Mama Jenkins' help, she was crushing that goal.

It wasn't until she'd started feeling some kind of security that all of those other needs, desires and wants started making themselves known.

If nothing else, her life pretty much proved Maslow's hierarchy of needs theory, a school of thought that she was learning about in her psychology and sociology classes.

The thought process behind the theory went something like this: Life is a huge triangle. At the base of the triangle was the most important and immediate concern for humans – survival.

Survival included food, oxygen, sleep and sex (procreation); the model summed these up as physiological needs. The next level up from the bottom was all about safety and security including physical safety and health, employment or resources, family, property/shelter and morality.

Delilah had been living for so long within the very basic rung of the theory, she hadn't even allowed herself to think about what she would do for a living or wonder if her dad was still alive... or morality. But she did now.

She thought about all of that now with a vengeance. Especially after what happened three days ago. Delilah had arrived on time, like always, to Mama Jenkin's house for their weekly Tuesday night dinner. Since Mama had given her a key several weeks ago, Delilah no longer had to wait if Mama happened to be out; she just headed right over as soon as her shift at the convenience store ended.

Seeing a rare opportunity to do something for Mama (who gave so much but received so little from others in return), Delilah straightened the few things that she saw out of place, finished up washing the dishes in the sink and was bending over in front of the door when she heard the tumbler click.

Everything else had happened so fast, she barely had time to look up before the door came swinging inward with a voice shouting, "Mama, where you at," before slamming right into her forehead and knocking her to the floor. The edges of her vision blurred.

"Crap!" was what she heard next, followed by K.C.'s knees hitting the floor on her left.

Rough hands gently grasped both sides of her face to turn her head in his direction.

And while he kept saying her name over and over, Delilah couldn't shake the haze that clouded her vision, or the tremors that K.C.'s touched initiated.

She did however notice two things: first, there was no fight or flight response; something that the entire situation should have generated (responses that would have disabled and could have possibly killed K.C.)

And two, his face was close to hers; very close. Like, so close that she could feel his breath on her lips.

"Come on Dee Dee, talk to me."

Delilah really would have if she could. Only, what little focus that she could muster now remained on his mouth; watching is lips move as if in slow motion. He had really nice lips.

"Help me out babe. What's four plus four?" K.C. asked, stroking her right cheek with his thumb.

He had nice thumbs too. In fact, his whole body was nice, unlike most of the men she'd seen.

His skin tone was tanned a medium shade and while muscular, he wasn't bulky with veins everywhere.

Delilah had always thought those guys were gross and false looking.

No, K.C.'s frame was perfect for his height, not too lean or too large.

She struggled to get her suddenly heavy breathing under control.

Was his mouth getting closer? Because she felt like it was. Apparently her rapid breathing was contagious. Soft puffs of K.C.'s own were wisping over her lips at a quickened pace.

It was when her vision blurred further because those lips were so close, that Delilah's gaze collided with his hooded silver one.

While she shouldn't have been surprised, the kiss shocked her system, taking her breath away.

It was a rule of thumb in her former life to never kiss anyone. Kissing was intimate; it made the sex act meaningful and significant.

So, no matter what, even when a John became insistent, kissing was a no-no. It was one of the rules that was brutally enforced; Brody made sure of that.

She was out of her league entirely here. The kiss, soft and sweet, unlike any encounter she'd ever had, drew her in.

Delilah savored the newness of it, memorizing every touch, the contour of his lips, his taste.

She kept her eyes open though he closed his, committing to memory every detail, from the passion that had burned in his gaze, to the enraptured expression on his face as they connected.

And when he angled her head further to the left to delve deeper, she was all for that.

Feelings assailed her that she'd never felt, and her body buzzed with energy she didn't know was possible.

She'd been unable to keep her eyes open any longer despite her desire to not miss a thing.

The explosion of feeling that swept through her the moment they closed, increased the pull and the power of each sensation – almost as if by depriving herself of the ability to use one of her senses, the others kicked into gear.

The world fell away. Never before had Delilah been so caught up, so swept away. She was so enraptured by these new powerful feelings that she didn't hear the loud clearing of someone's throat near the kitchen door.

Suddenly, where there had been a blanket of warmth and pleasure there was now a windy rush of cold air.

K.C. moved so quickly, it was like he evaporated and materialized five feet away from her prone body.

Delilah blinked several times, attempting to recover from a wholly unfamiliar experience. And even while she'd known that Mama Jenkins was standing over her body, her arms crossed and tapping her foot (and head angled in a way that Delilah knew spelled "attitude), she still took her time cataloguing what had happened.

Because Delilah knew how short life was and how rare these "in between" moments of sheer bliss were, she didn't feel bad about taking the time to do so.

The rest of the evening had been a quiet one. Mama sat at the table after serving her fabulous meatloaf, potatoes and broccoli and stared daggers at K.C.

Delilah hadn't been able to keep her face from turning red every time she looked up to catch K.C. staring at her intently.

His brow furrowed, and his eyes shadowed caused a thousand thoughts to run through her head.

Many were not good thoughts. There were those whispered reminders of her past and accusations of promiscuity. There were also thoughts that about how she would never measure up to the lady she'd seen with K.C. in those pictures.

Last, there were thoughts that told her she was cheap, dirty and worthless.

"Isaiah 54:17," Mother Jenkins grunted, interrupting the depressing mire Delilah was burying herself in.

"Ma'am?" Delilah asked hesitantly at Mama's pause.

Without looking at K.C. she sensed him shifting his attention from her to the only other person in the room.

"Remember? Yesterday you asked me where you could find the verse that says, "No weapon formed against you shall be able to prosper? I told you I'd look it up and we could talk about it over dinner. Well. It's dinner time. And that's where that verse is found, in the book of Isaiah."

"Oh." Delilah took a bite of her mashed potatoes and tasted ash. Between her growing obsession for the One who Celine had trusted in so blindly, and K.C., Delilah felt like she was losing her mind.

"I for one feel like people focus on the wrong part of that scripture when they say it," K.C. spoke into the dead air.

Delilah, jumped, her gaze blinking up in surprise at his announcement. Caught and held captive by his silver regard, she listened as he finished.

"Or I should say, its incomplete without verse 16 that explains how God is the one that created the destroyer in the first place.

It's like God is saying that he gave the destroyer a job. But no matter how good the destroyer is at what he does, God already stacked the deck against him. Nothing that he does against you will see him victorious in the end. It might look like he wins for a time, but in the end, it's going to be obvious that he didn't. And no matter what he or anyone else says or tries to accuse you of, because you belong to God, the destroyer will fail."

Clarity was a funny thing. Delilah had tried to read the bible on several occasions but could never get into it. All those thee's, thous and thuses only served to confuse her further when she tried.

Yet, hearing K.C. explain it the way he did — she understood it clearly. It made total sense.

There were many things in life that Delilah might not understand, but what she did get, was authority. She knew that, in truth, everybody worked for somebody.

Everyone was someone's slave. So, if the destroyer was a slave to the one who spoke — the creator, God, and everyone else was too, then even if he was doing his job, he could only be as effective as his master let him be.

In that moment, so many questions she had about God and who He was had been answered. And four times as many had formed in their place.

So now, laying in the middle of the guest room bed, sweating like never before, Delilah knew two things for sure. That she was gone for K.C. Like, head over heels gone in a way that she'd read in an old romance novel once.

And, she was running out of time. The heavy feeling in her chest telegraphed her bleak future in the same way it had so many times before when all hell broke loose.

Flopping back down onto her back, she used her hand to wipe the sweat from her brow. Closing her eyes as tiredness dragged at her, she did something that she'd never done for herself before, only for others. She prayed.

***

K.C.

"So, what was that about," Mama Jenkins huffed at me three nights ago after Delilah left her house to go to bed.

I didn't have an answer for her then and I didn't now. Which was probably why I've been spending more time in my basement weight room than sleeping in my bed.

I was either lifting free weights in front of the mirror paneled to my basement wall or running on my treadmill; all to accomplish one goal.

To avoid owning that kiss Delilah and I shared. And while I was at it, avoid coming to terms with my physical and emotional response to that kiss.

Because I'd never been one to avoid owning my mistakes or feelings, I'd figured that I would do so... eventually.

But it had been three days.

Not only had I NOT owned up to it and talked to Delilah to see where her head was at, I'd actively avoided Delilah, Mama Jenkins and making my rounds to the stores.

What was worse, I hadn't shaved, had barely eaten, and was running (right now in fact) on my treadmill as if my life depended on it.

It just might.

I had to work this out in my head before I could talk to anyone. The last thing I ever wanted to do was hurt Delilah.

Another pain sliced through my chest that had nothing to do with exertion as I realized I would be doing exactly that.

I wasn't ready, plain and simple. I'd done the engagement thing once. I'd auditioned for the part of loving husband, future father of 2.5 kids and a dog: yada, yada, yada.

Despite my expectations, I didn't get the role. At the last minute, due to a casting call I wasn't aware of, that part went to the high school sweetheart who'd been her first love and, (unbeknownst to me), her only love.

It had been a while since I'd even thought about putting myself back out there. I hadn't thought about dating since I'd left Texas.

Though, that part really wasn't on me.

I'd been busy on an op, helping Sam recover his son from those freaks that put a chip in his head. And then we'd had to save a whole bunch of other kids – and still we weren't done. We'd had to go back for Celine, get her and Sam's daughter out of an enemy stronghold, as well as rescue other people (also chipped in the head) like Delilah.

That said, things had been busy. It had been a year though, and life had calmed down. I missed Sam and Celine's wedding; I'd hated the sound in Celine's voice as I expressed my regrets.

I couldn't risk leaving Delilah alone, not after that news clip of her at my store aired nationally. And I couldn't have taken her with me, or she'd have ended up within arm's reach of those that we rescued her from in the first place.

I'd become so lost in my thoughts that I hadn't realized how fast I was going on the treadmill. Sweat poured down my naked chest and into my jogging shorts.

Slowing down the speed on the treadmill and huffing as I did it, I came to a conclusion; one I didn't want to accept.

I just had to man up and say the words that needed to be said, even if they cut holes in my chest as I said them.

Chapter 10 - Warring Winds

Capital Square at 400 Locust
Downtown Des Moines, Iowa

Lance sneered at Andrew's video image projecting from the big screen in Reigner, Lee and Stratford's conference room. At the behest of its largest, and for now, only client, RLS had relocated its main offices from Alton, IL, to Des Moines, IA.

With good reason. Most of the "test subjects" necessary to put the Brainwaiver chips' mass production back on schedule resided in Des Moines. And while the majority of said subjects weren't legally acquired, consenting or even adults, well, none of that really mattered did it?

What mattered was Lance having to listen to Andrew's sniveling, weaseling excuses for failure. That was the thing about failure; depending on the person, if you allowed them to continue unchecked despite their history of failing, they tended to take you for granted.

Apparently, Lance wasn't the only one that felt that way. Mr. Cypher, the more ruthless character of the two old men that pretty much ran the United States when it came to technology, thus the world, was communicating exactly that fact, making it difficult for Lance to continue to hide his smirk.

"Make no mistake boy," Mr. Cypher continued, "your being a blood relative does not exempt you from elimination. You can easily be replaced. That said, I have a difficult time here following your logic."

Lance hadn't realized that he was shaking his head from side to side in disgust. One piercing look from Mr. Louis, the other half to the evil duo, caused him to realize and stop that immediately. Because Lance had made a quantifiable error as well. While, in his defense, he hadn't been afforded all of the variables that should have been considered before their last operation, he knew that the two old men wouldn't care. Further, he didn't have the blood connection that would allow him to make more than one mistake, like some people. With his thoughts returning to said people, Lance tuned into what Andrew had been saying.

"...demand it sirs. I was humiliated. They messed with my head. All I'm asking for is a chance to make them pay. They all look up to the tough one. All I need is reinforcements. Not only will I humiliate her worse than how they humiliated me, I will crush them one by one, starting with her. Watching a recording of me destroying her will make it that much simpler to pick them off. And that will be the end of this nuisance once and for all."

Lance almost chuckled at the storm cloud expression on Cypher's face. And had the idiots plan not been of use, he would have been in heaven, watching Andrew cringe as his uncle lit into him with both barrels.

"Sir's," Lance interjected before Cypher could get started, "I realize that Andrew's uh, plan as it were, may sound counterproductive and like a waste of time and resources, I believe it is perfect for this juncture of the Brainwaiver project."

Cypher turned his piercing glare toward Lance and opened his mouth, Louis however raised his hand to stay his brother's response. Good. That meant that they were interested. And interest meant that Lance had a shot at redemption.

"This 6th generation chip meets all of the specifications of the desired hardware necessary to begin mass production and distribution. We've found fewer side effects with this version than any other and have completely solved the hemorrhaging problem. What we need now, in order to push this through the FDA as a cure to certain ailments with the American Medical Association backing our claims, is freedom to operate without hindrance from these yahoos."

Louis' raised eyebrow was Lance's only indication that he was growing impatient.

Lance outlined the rest of his argument hastily adding, "thus Andrew's plan is the perfect distraction. And if he manages to be successful and eliminates them once and for all, that's just icing on the cake."

Cypher grunted while Louis beamed, his smile making his weathered face look decades younger. He looked almost innocent. And had Lance not known the true evil that lurked behind that falsely pacifying exterior, he would have felt proud to receive such recognition.

"Wait, "Cypher hmphed, clearly not satisfied with his inability to chew someone out today, "what about the anomaly in the code? We still haven't solved that problem and every single IT professional on our staff is stumped by it."

Lance smiled. Because it was all about perception and perception could be manipulated rather easily.

"No worries there Mr. Cypher, the anomaly has now been configured into the chip's protocols. Brainwaiver may not be able to stop the anomaly from occurring, but it can manipulate how the chipped ones perceive the glitch. If we do this right, not only will we be able to track the anomalies anywhere in the world, but we will be able to get an accurate count of them and facilitate a false tolerance that will again serve our purposes by keeping them distracted."

It was Cypher's turn to smile.

"Alright Andrew, we'll get you your reinforcements. Lance, get that biker friend on the horn for the boy. Since Zeke's already had his boys chipped along with his inventory of females, controlling the operation and any information as it disseminates should be easy. Now, on to the next order of business. The asset has been located?"

Lance grinned his own evil grin as he answered, "Yes sir. She's living in Baltimore, Maryland with the blond jarhead."

"I too was a Marine once boy, "Cypher scowled and gritted, "be careful how you speak about one."

Lance deep sighed before saying something that he had desperately been wanting to say. Instead, he nodded his assent to those instructions and continued as if he'd never been interrupted.

"We've had a few of the chip designers and engineers ping her chip."

"And," Cypher almost shouted.

"And," Lance calmly returned, "we get a return signal but only when the assets heartbeat is elevated, as if she is running or exercising or something. The ping usually returns in about fifteen seconds. Murray, our tech in Abilene, believes that, while we can't control Delilah unless she were here with us, what we can do is shut down all vital operations to the chip; attached to her synapses as it is this should cause an immediate coma, one that she can't come out of without us turning it back on."

"Nice boy. Now I need a nap. Let us know when you get started with both projects. We want our asset recovered and that sorry excuse for a crew eliminated or out of the way, at least until we have the legislative backing to make the chip mandatory to all citizens." Louis was the speaker this time as he rose out of his seat.

While the old men exited, Lance pulled out his cell phone to give Zeke a call to set the stage. Lance smiled as he thought about how he'd add K.C. to the mix with this particular play. It was a spark of ingenuity so sinister that the desire to laugh like a movie villain or stroke a non-existent cat was hard to suppress. Plus, working out a plan to mess up people's lives was almost as exhilarating as watching Delilah suffer; something he couldn't wait to do again and soon.

Delilah

Friday mornings were always a bit laxer when it came to Delilah's schedule. Waking up for a morning workout and coffee usually jump started her day, followed by hopping the bus down to the library and getting some studying in. After that she'd normally head to Mama Jenkin's place for brunch, then kick back a little until she had to report in to work at 3 pm.

Only, this morning there was something, or someone rather, standing between her and her coffee after she came in from her morning run. The same "someone" that had been avoiding her for the last three days.

Quickly masking her surprise at seeing K.C. in the middle of his kitchen glistening with sweat in only his sweat shorts (that obviously used to be sweat pants but were cut off at the knee) and pouring a cup of coffee, Delilah cleared her throat to let him know that he wasn't alone.

Pretty sure that she was only mentally drooling at the tight muscled form of his back, Delilah forced her gaze away and plastered on her best fake Hollywood smile.

That smile had gotten her through many an awkward moment. Delilah prayed silently that it would get her through this.

Glancing back at her while he poured a cup of coffee, or sludge as she called it (because that is what it was when he made it) K. C. smiled and gave her the "chin up" gesture. It was a move she'd once hated. It felt like it was overly macho and pretentious. She was sure that men who did that were always compensating for something.

But not K.C. For him, the chin up greeting that acknowledged her presence fit perfectly. And made her stomach flutter. Like she was a schoolgirl with a crush.

Ugh.

Delilah felt her fake smile slip, so she hastened over to the cabinet above the sink where the mugs were kept. She had a schedule to keep. It didn't involve leering at K.C. and counting the sweat droplets that glistened on his back,. Or meditating on how the low waistline of his sweat shorts hung invitingly.

Double UGH!

This time it was K. C. that cleared his throat, a sound that preceded his gruff, "Hey."

"Hey," Delilah responded without turning around, focusing instead on adding a little water to the bottom of her mug at the sink.

She'd learned the hard way that if she didn't cut the sludge that he called coffee with water, cream and lots of sugar, her tongue would hate her for life.

"We need to talk. You got a minute."

Hell no, Delilah thought.

Because when people wanted to talk, in her experience it was always bad news. And she didn't have time for that today. In fact, were she a queen she would make a royal decree that she didn't have time for it *ever*. Bad news would officially become someone else's job. She'd make it a freaking law.

Since she wasn't a queen and had no power to make royal decrees or laws, she settled for responding in the negative.

"Nope, got to hit the shower then the library if I'm going to ace this test on Monday. How about we talk later tonight after my shift?"

"Your shift ends at eleven. You know I'm usually asleep by then."

Delilah turned to face K.C. but focused on the wall over his shoulder. She took a sip of coffee, eyebrows raised, and waited.

Her non-spoken "so what," resonated loudly between them. He was irritated. She could tell because the furrows on his brow grew deeper the longer she went without comment.

Too bad. She wasn't starting her day with this crap. If he wanted her to move out or to tell her that the kiss they'd shared meant nothing, he was going to have to do it at the END of her day. She refused to spend the entire day pissed off or depressed.

Her heart racing now, Delilah tried to dial down her attitude, but it was hard. Maybe if the loud banging in the background wasn't battling for her attention, she could focus enough to do so.

"Dee Dee..."

Delilah interrupted his "tired, placating, be reasonable" tone with, "And what is that banging sound? Are your guys making repairs on Mama Jenkin's house or something?"

Walking to the window on the other side of K.C. Delilah glanced out of it.

No one was there. However, the banging sound had been coming from that direction.

"Dee? What banging?"

Delilah turned quickly in a circle. The banging started again. And it was getting louder. It now sounded like it was coming from downstairs.

"Is that base? Do you have a stereo downstairs you left playing?"

K.C. frowned as he carefully placed his cup on the counter, his intense gaze laser focused on her.

"Dee Dee. You alright?"

Why hadn't she noticed how warm the kitchen was before she'd walked in. And it was getting warmer fast. Suddenly it seemed like a really good idea to take off her running jacket. She still had on her tank underneath, so it was all good.

"Babe, you're turning gray. What's happening?"

Delilah didn't hear him, but she felt him approaching from her left. She could feel his body heat reaching across the small space that separated them.

She felt like clawing at her clothes because suddenly she was burning up. Fisting her hand, Delilah looked down.

Focusing on moving one finger at a time seemed like a huge chore. It was so hot.

Her hand felt like it should be on fire. Causing her to wonder why it was gray instead of red? Shouldn't it be red?

"Talk to me baby. You're scaring me."

He called her baby. He'd been calling her babe lately, usually when something frightening was happening like when he'd hit her in the head with the door. But he shouldn't call her that. It made everything so much hotter right now. She needed not to be hot. She needed not to be burning up.

"Dee, quit taking your clothes off honey and talk to me. Explain to me what's happening to you."

Delilah turned her watery gaze in his direction. K. C. wasn't looking at her as he was talking, he was texting someone. She tried to form the words, pulling at her tank.

The tank top was trapping her. It wanted her to burn up. It wanted her to turn into ashes and be dead. Dead ashes like her mom. The only word that Delilah could get through that jumbled mass of thoughts, to her, said it all.

"Hot."

The banging that hadn't stopped but faded into the background became more insistent, increasing in tempo until it overrode Delilah's concern about the heat.

"Loud. Stop. Stop it." Delilah knew that she was whispering as she sank to the floor. She was melting. She was a puddle of banging, melting, hot goo. She was lava.

Hearing K.C. speaking urgently into his phone but not understanding a word, Delilah sighed before giving in. She honestly had no idea why she'd tried to fight it any way. It was a forgone conclusion. Death had finally found her. And just as she always feared she would be, she was powerless to stop it.

***

K.C.

"So, you're just going to leave?"

I grunted. It was the best response I could give as I grabbed my wallet and keys off Cheryl's office counter before heading toward the door.

I'd already had my cell in my hand. It was why I had to leave in the first place.

"K.C. did you hear me? Are you just going to leave her here like she doesn't matter?"

I grunted again, my teeth grinding in the process. Because I could hear that famous red head temper starting to ramp up, but I had no time to deal with it.

I'd barely had time to call Sam from Cheryl's cordless office phone (using Morse code to leave a message on the machine at their house). The first thing that I was going to do when I got back was get a hardwired landline in my place. Max had always told us going completely cell and VoIP was a mistake. Now I knew why.

Those bastards have been watching us and listening to us, right through our cell phones. In fact, they could watch and listen to us via any electronic device in the office.

Luckily, cameras in bathrooms were illegal or that call would have been an impossibility and I would have been at a loss.

Walking out the front door, I ignored Cheryl's Yiddish curses thrown at my back and headed for my truck in the parking lot.

Arriving home had happened quicker than I thought it would, so I made good time. Packing was the easiest part. I had to travel light but loaded. And since firearms weren't allowed on planes, I'd be driving across country. Fast.

I pulled my long storage case filled with several guns, my crossbow and ammunition along with a false flatbed cover from my hidden cubby behind the weight stack.

With one last glance around to make sure I didn't miss anything, I headed back upstairs to throw some clothes into my duffle bag.

In less than fifteen minutes I was on the road.

The text I'd gotten said they would kill her if I didn't get the job done.

But I wasn't going to let them. I didn't know the how. I just knew the Who.

Even while Cheryl had explained how dangerous the coma they'd put my woman in was, I had faith.

She was going to make it. There was no way that God would finally allow me to have a woman that needed me as much as I needed her, a woman that I wanted more than my next breath, to die on me. He wasn't cruel like that.

But for her? I would be. And yeah, I came to terms with the lie I was telling myself. No person is ever ready to be hurt again. But who says she was going to hurt me? Besides, I wasn't a punk. I wasn't afraid to live. So, I'd made the decision that, after I fixed this latest mess, we were done with games. She belonged to me. And I would put several bullets in whoever I had to to prove it.

Chapter 11 – Windswept

Delilah

Delilah had no clue where she was. Her gaze turned up toward the magnificent sky, she felt herself spinning in a circle, trying to take everything in.

The clouds were unlike anything she'd ever seen! White, wispy, and fluttering, they hovered just out of her reach.

Like, if she stood on her tippiest of tippy toes, she'd just be able to touch one.

Wherever she was, everything was so vivid. And white. It wasn't like a complete absence of color kind of white, more like all the colors in the world were reflecting into the bright whiteness of it all.

While Delilah didn't remember much about art in school, she remembered that all the colors mixed together made brown.

She knew this because her third grade Art teacher Mrs. Winter-snow had allowed her to mix them.

Delilah had declared rather confidently that she could make a rainbow by doing so. Mrs. Winter-snow, a scientist at heart, allowed her student to experiment and prove her theory.

Even though Delilah had learned that she was wrong, she'd also learned that knowing something in theory and knowing something from experience were two very different concepts.

It was a principal she'd based all her life decisions on. It was a principal that went hand in hand with living on the reservation, as a sex slave, and as a Hollywood puppet.

This place where she stood now, however? It was beyond her experiences. It was beyond anything that she could conceive or even dream.

There were people here. Tons of people. Just moving around through colorful nature scenes; like they were in the same place as she was but in a different part, though she could see them as if they were standing a few feet away.

The best way that she could make sense of it to herself was compare the place to a huge building with rooms that had invisible walls.

You could see through the walls into the different rooms and see what they see, hear what they say, or be totally caught up in the beautiful landscape that you'd found for yourself.

Her focus was so intent on making sense of such powerful beauty, that Delilah almost missed the little girl standing right in front of her. She appeared to have been waiting for a long time to get her attention.

Delilah's mouth dropped open. Because the girl was stunning! She looked to be about five or 6 years old. She had two beautiful ringlet filled ponytails, one on each side of her head, with a crown of multicolored flowers. Her dress was gorgeously white and multicolored at the same time, and her blue eyes shined with an essence that held Delilah captive. And then she changed.

Now she was a tiny Asian girl with brown doe eyes and long lashes. Her jet-black hair seemed to own the wind as it danced freely behind her in a breeze that Delilah couldn't feel or see. The flower crown remained as did the multicolor dress. But the child's visage didn't. She changed again.

This time she was a stunning black girl, with flowing locks of brownish red down her back. And while her eyes had remained brown, there were flecks of light in them that Delilah got lost in. And as she sank down into the bed of flora beneath her, her strength dissipating for no reason at all, she watched the little girl change again... and again...

and again. She became a gorgeous Latina. A beautiful Eskimo. A gracious Samoan. An Icelandic beauty. A ruggedly beautiful Australian. A strong-featured lovely Italian. A sweet round-faced Russian.

And on and on and on. And while she was changing, the little girl spoke without using words or her mouth. Several languages and tongues converged into one, all washing over Delilah's mind, imprinting on her that all these little girls... every single one of them... was her.

All these tiny versions of her had something that they wanted to relay. They had a story to tell. And before, she'd never given them the voice to do so.

Without moving, Delilah listened. She listened intently with an open heart to each story, intuitively understanding every one of them as they were all within her to begin with. Until she came to the last one whose visage was an exact match to her six-year-old self.

"You left me, "was all she said.

Delilah shook her head from side to side vehemently. She'd never left her. How could she leave herself?

"You forgot me," the little girl expounded.

Delilah covered her ears and refused to hear her.

"You believed their lies about me and left me there to die."

Tears burned trails down Delilah's face, but she refused to open her eyes or remove her hands from her ears to wipe them away.

"You stopped loving me when I did nothing to deserve that."

"NO!" Delilah's entire body shook with the scream. She screamed it again and again and again. Determined to burn away the accusations that lanced her soul.

Because she was guilty. She knew she was. She'd hated herself after a while, because of what they'd done to her. She'd hated the day she was born and the person that she had become. She'd been so filled with self-hatred that she'd stopped even trying to be free.

Delilah stopped screaming as she realized the most painful truth that she could imagine. Even while she'd been set free from the Brainwaiver's controls, even though the prison door of her painful past had been swung open, she'd remained right where she was; chained to the idea that she had become the very thing she'd been forced to do.

"Look at me."

The voice was different now. Delilah's curiosity got the best of her as she glanced up to find a man where the little girl had stood moments ago.

"You may have left me, *Ariela*. But I never left you."

It took a while for Delilah to respond to that. Reason being the appearance of the man that stood before her was far from the little girl that came before him.

He stood at about five feet, seven inches. His skin was a swarthy brown, the tone reminiscent of those that lived in

Africa or Southern India. And his hair was curly where it framed his face, trailing in locks down his back.

His torso was covered in a plain white tee with the initials, "WWJD," on it while below that it said, "What would Jeff do?"

His jeans were normal looking with a slit in the left knee and he had on a pair of Nike shoes.

His humor filled grin was that final anomaly that snapped Delilah out of her daze.

There was no way that this could be who she figured he was supposed to be. Maybe He was visiting the wrong dream. Didn't he call her by someone else's name? Delilah didn't wait to clarify.

"What did you call me?"

"Ariela. It was the name your mother wanted to give you. It was the name that I wanted you to have."

Delilah frowned.

"So, who named me Delilah?"

The man dropped down to sit cross-legged in the field of flowers, resting his chin on his palm, his elbow to his thigh.

He was positioned so that his focus remained intently on her, something that had her fidgeting uncomfortably.

It was like He could see everything about her; her past, her future, her failings, and her triumphs; all just from looking at her.

"Your father. He took one look at you and decided that your beauty could potentially be the downfall of the strongest man one day."

"But that's not who I am?"

The man smiled. Though half of it was hidden in part of his hand, it was no less stunning, bringing with it a rush of peace and a contradictory bubble of joy. Delilah felt like she was going crazy just watching him.

"Nope," he answered gruffly, "It's not even close to what I had in mind when I spoke your name."

Delilah could feel the rush building. It was a strong rush of emotions, a turbulent wind filled with wildness tumbling inside her. And she knew why.

So did He. Which was probably why He answered the question before she could ask it.

"Ariela means Lioness of God."

NO WEAPON.

It was in that moment that every puzzle piece; an instance of her life, fell into place.

"You are a protector. A fighter. My weapon forged against hate and corruption." He continued.

One tear started the rest, falling to her cheek though she hadn't realized it. Another dropped as He continued.

"You ARE a hero. I know it because I MADE you to be. The only person you failed to protect, the one that needed you the most… is you."

Delilah's hands shook. That is, until the strong brown ones reached over and grabbed hold to both. Even through the blurriness of her tears, she couldn't miss the ragged scars on His wrist.

Her gaze froze then jumped into His. And, like the girls before Him, He communicated without moving His lips, speaking in various tongues, all of which she could understand;

"You are a small reflection of me. How you see yourself is how you see me. How you love yourself reflects how you love me. And love my little lioness IS sacrifice. It is doing the best thing for those that you love when it is not convenient. At times it is painful, but the reward is great. If I have commanded you to love others as you love yourself, and you disdain yourself... do you not disdain others? Do you not disdain ME, the one that created you?"

Delilah had no words. She had none because before her didn't just sit a man. His visage was transposed with another figure, far bigger and far more frightening. And within that image was another that was almost feminine; softer, gentler, more loving... and then there were all the girls that she'd seen. Each image was transposed within the other, causing her to become dizzy at its funky funhouse effect.

And all of them were talking, saying the same thing with the same cadence, but in several different tongues and in several different voices.

Delilah had no idea how long they spoke. She'd long sense stopped trying to focus on each voice or image individually. She just accepted their collective counsel. They were all one, all a part of the greater visage; they all belonged to Him... and her. She was a small part of that conglomerate, but she had a lot to learn. And from what they were telling her, a short amount of time to learn it in.

So, when just the one visage again sat before her with his "What would Jeff do," shirt on and his glorious smile, Delilah smiled back.

She was no longer surprised by what He did.

Once He'd asked her to acknowledge that she was His (and she had), understanding Him and accepting Him (no matter how He presented Himself) had become easy.

It didn't shock her that it was time to go. He'd told her beforehand. And it didn't scare her to leave this place like she thought it would.

Delilah knew that He would be with her.

As they stood and hugged, she felt the strong power of his presence -- strength, hope, love, joy... everything she now understood Him to be, flood her entire being.

Right before her eyes snapped open and she was blinded by a different kind of light.

***

K.C.

I was exhausted. My being so exhausted that I could barely stand was why I left my truck behind. Rick had driven it up to Baltimore for me.

While it was likely an excuse for Ricky to flirt with Cheryl, I wasn't about to complain.

To say I'd had one hell of a week would be putting things mildly. I'd had to lie to my friends, avoid my family, and draw down on Balboa and Max; all after standing by as Balboa was kidnapped and beaten.

So, when I say I took pleasure in watching as Balboa beat the living crap out of Andrew, I do not exaggerate.

I hoped that concluded this current drama.

My friends were relieved to find out that I was still one of the good guys. I'd contacted my family to assure them that yes, I'm still alive and yes, I'm coming for a visit and yes, I'm bringing a special someone home that I'd better not get any crap from them about.

That said, it had been the phone call from Cheryl that had done what the other challenges failed to do. Brought me to my knees.

Delilah was awake. And based on all that Cheryl had told me, she'd regained consciousness with a vengeance.

I couldn't wait to see her. I couldn't wait to hold her. More importantly, I couldn't wait to tell her that she was mine.

Settling in on the plane, I noticed the passenger seated two rows ahead of me. He looked suspiciously like one of my former CO's (commanding officers) from when I was stationed in Afghanistan.

Too tired to be sure or even care, my eyelids made wondering a moot point as they shut out the world.

It was a rough shake to my shoulder that brought me back to life. Glancing around I saw my fellow passengers standing to gather bags from the overhead compartments.

I then realized that I'd slept the entire flight, completely dead to the world around me. I also realized that a very large and imposing man hovered above me.

"Matthew Killian?" A gravelly voice asked.

"Yep," I replied, yawning through the word as I waited for him to back up so I could stand.

"You don't remember me, do you?"

I couldn't help but grin at that. It meant that I'd been right about the passenger who looked familiar.

Instead of responding in the affirmative, I snapped into the attention military stance, saluted then blasted him with, "NCO David Smith Robinson SIR!"

The weathered grin I remembered from years ago appeared before he spoke, just as precisely as I did, "At ease soldier."

Laughing I dropped my salute and greeted David with a pat on the back before reaching up to grab my bag.

We exited the plane laughing, joking, talking about guys from our unit and reminiscing about the old days.

Promising to catch up later and giving him my contact info, I tried not to appear like I was rushing things... even when I was.

I was impatient to see her. Impatient to touch her.

Hell, I was impatient to tell her what I'd wanted to tell her a night long ago in front of the Jell-O wrestling bar.

Saying my goodbyes to my old CO, I hailed a cab to get home as quick as I could to do exactly that.

Chapter 12 – Summer Breeze

Delilah

She felt him long before she heard him.

Delilah had been in the kitchen brewing coffee and cutting up vegetables for lunch when it happened.

The room went from a normal temperature to feeling smothered and muggy in seconds.

And then she smelled his cologne. It was some knock off he wore called Captain America. She loved that cologne.

His presence, now heavy in the room, seemed to surround her. And still, the sound of his voice caused her to jump a little.

"Hey."

She shivered. Why, she had no clue. It could have been how deep and rugged his voice had sounded or how much she'd missed hearing it.

It could have been how close that voice was; so close she could feel his breath flutter over her ear as he'd spoken.

"Hey." A response she delivered shakily. She knew that she was shaking but she couldn't help it. It felt like he'd been gone forever. That she'd been gone forever.

And while she had no clue where he was at mentally, she was very confident in where she was.

So, she'd prepared herself for the little chat that they were supposed to have before things went sideways. Not only was she prepared, but she was okay. There was no fear, no anxiety, none of that. She no longer saw his acceptance as confirmation of her worth.

Gearing up for the showdown that she'd imagined would take place when K.C. walked through the door, she wasn't prepared to be snatched around and brought so close that she didn't know where he ended, and she began.

Nor was she prepared for his lips to possessively capture hers; awakening a passion that drowned every single thought in her head.

She heard a disembodied moan come from herself as the kiss went deeper. She'd had no clue that there even WAS a deeper.

Feeling his hand tangle in her hair, she exhaled as he pulled her head back, kissing her eyelids, her nose, and her cheek before finally burying his face at the base of her throat.

She felt him strongly inhale, his arms gripping her even tighter.

She wanted to make a joke or some light-hearted comment to add levity to the moment, but his groan as he held her tighter made her think twice.

It suddenly dawned on her that what she mistook for just passion was something else entirely. A fact that was proven when he took his face out of her neck and grasped hers between both hands.

His intense silver eyes burned with a light she didn't recognize but knew instinctively was all hers. And as he cupped the sides of her face, his eyes searching hers before taking the rest of her in, told her what his words wouldn't.

He'd been worried. Scared out of his mind for her.

She read all of that in the way that he peered through her, almost as if he refused to look away for fear that he would lose her.

The words that he spoke next told her how much she was not wrong.

Teeth gritted and eyes growing even more intense, Delilah was fascinated as she watched the harsh, grating words trip from his lips.

"You. Are. Mine. Do you understand?"

Transfixed, Delilah found herself nodding.

Yes, this unfamiliar version of K.C. freaked her out a little, but it also activated some long-buried instinct.

It was a desire-ridden instinct that honored and respected the man willing to do anything to secure his future with her because for him, there could be no other. And Delilah found that she was more than okay with that.

***

K.C.

I wanted to kiss her again, better yet, to devour her right there. I didn't want to talk because I didn't have the words. I just wanted to take. I wanted to take her into my room and show her for hours how she belonged to me and no one else.

I wanted to take my time with her; to own her. And I wanted all that yesterday.

But I did none of that. There was a protocol that I would honor first. My woman had been jumped on by men all her life. Someone had to show her that she was better than that. And that someone was going to be me.

So instead of doing what I wanted to do, I did what I had to do. Forcing myself to release her hair and let go of her waist, I stepped back.

My body all but screamed at the steady increase of space between us, but I beat it down and forced it to focus on what she needed, rather than what I needed.

It was times like this that I hated being the son my mother raised. It was apparent that Delilah and I were going to have to talk. And then some. Because I could only be a good guy for so long. Knowing that she was mine meant my body cared nothing about protocol.

"I'm moving out."

My breath left my body like I'd just been gut punched. Was she in my head or something?

"What?" Dumb response I know. It's not like I didn't hear her. But her declaration had come from out of nowhere and had thrown me for a loop.

When something like that happens, especially when my blood flow has been redirected to other extremities besides my brain (as it had been for the last ten minutes) automatic responses kicked in.

The repertoire of words for this form of communication was limited to, "what, who, why, huh and yeah."

"I said I'm moving out. There's an apartment two blocks away that's affordable enough. Mother Jenkins and I went to go look at it yesterday."

Huh. So, this is what Cheryl meant when she said that Delilah was coming out of her coma "with a vengeance." Apparently, my woman had done some soul searching while she was out.

Still in auto-response mode, I pronounced the next applicable phrase.

"Why?"

When she turned back around to resume cutting her vegetables, I thought it was because she needed time to best phrase her answer. I had no problem with that.

It took a minute for me to notice that her shoulders were shaking with laughter.

What the...?

It was her gasp for air that forced me to move forward and snatch her around. Why I needed visual confirmation of her laughing at me I do not know. But I had it as I watched her bend forward and clutch her stomach in a fit that should have, with good reason, pissed me off.

So why I stood there grinning at her like a big goof I had no clue. Possibly because, while I'd seen her smile or heard her chuckle, I'd never seen Delilah laugh before. Not like this.

I was undeniably proud to have caused the fit that still had her in its clutches, even if it was at my expense.

"I'm so sorry," she gasped out as the giggles finally wore themselves down to just chuckles.
"But you should have seen your face. You looked at me like I had kicked you between your legs, set your junk on fire and cursed out your mom, all at the same time."

It was my turn to chuckle at that.

"And to answer your question, it's because I've never had a place of my own."

That was an undisputed truth. I nodded but didn't interrupt. Something told me she had more she wanted to get off her chest.

"And I want to get to know God better. There's so much I have to tell you, beginning with what I'd learned while I was in a coma."

What I didn't do was say, let me stop you right there. I've had many discussions with Cheryl regarding this Brainwaiver thing.

I knew about the white room or some other stream of consciousness that linked them all. While I can't say I was a fan at the thought of some shared delusion for those who'd been chipped to meet up in, I knew I'd support her however she needed me to.

"Also, I'm going downtown Monday to file some paperwork. I want to legally change my name."

I subconsciously jerked back at that. I had no clue where that was coming from but, again, my job was to be supportive so I could handle that.

"What are you changing it to?" I asked as I reached around her to snatch a cut up red pepper off the cutting board before popping it into my mouth as I dodged her swats.

"Ariela; and stop stealing!"

I chuckled and dodged again as I came away with a green slice and devoured it.

"That's pretty."

"I know," she smiled before playfully growling and shaking the knife at me.

I didn't hesitate to wrap my arms around her and pull her back to me. I rested my chin on the top of her head as my eyes drifted shut.

Because this is what I wanted. More, she is what I needed. And if I had to let her live alone for a moment to realize that she would better appreciate living with me once we got married anyway? I had no problem with that. That was a discussion for later, in the meantime.

"By the way, we may be having company soon. I ran into one of my old CO's on the plane. He said he might stop by this afternoon before heading downtown to scope out some consignment shop, he'd been told about."

"Hmmm," was her muffled response. Obviously, she could steal her own peppers and scarf them down, but I couldn't.

I didn't care since the line of her neck distracted me.

Unable to help myself, I gave in to tracing it with tiny kisses down to her shoulder. An inner voice demanded that I get a hotel room with Ricky since he'd be arriving later tonight, but the man in me refused to give up its prize.

I reversed my trail of kisses until I got to Delilah's ear where I paused to exhale.

It made no sense that things were getting out of hand for me with just a few kisses. Frowning in disgust at my own lack of control, I jumped in surprise as my doorbell rang.

"I'll get it," Delilah grinned, head tilted back so her eyes could find mine.

I had no problem understanding why she offered. I wasn't the only one who noticed my struggle with control.

My sheepish smile was all I could muster as I set about locking it down and followed her to the door.

Because while I'd let her block my embarrassment by standing in front of me, she'd just come out of a coma due to a vicious attack from our enemies. There was no way that I would allow her to answer the door alone.

Shaking her head at what I could only assume she felt was my male ego asserting itself, she answered the door still grinning.

"Hi. Can I help..."

I felt her body tighten as the knife I didn't even realize she still had in her hand hit the floor.

My quick glance at the door told me that I had no need defend us as it was my old CO. However, Delilah's reaction said I needed to be prepared for anything.

I felt my brow furrow and my eyes narrow as I moved to push Delilah behind me. Was he one of the men who'd taken advantage of her?

That line of thought quickly dissipated as I focused on not just my old CO's presence, but his face.

His eyes were wide, his gaze filled with astonishment, wonder, fear and so many other things I couldn't name.

And they were wet too, like he was trying hard not to cry. As this was a man that I didn't think had tear ducts, to say that I was struck speechless by what I was seeing would be accurate, because I was.

The gurgle that I heard muffled into my back snatched my attention from David and placed it back on my woman. The same woman that clutched the back of my shirt as if her life depended on it.

"Baby? Is... is that you? Is that you Delilah?"

WHAT THE...

I was in my fight stance before I realized it. Apparently, this WAS one of those men that had wanted to steal her away and make her his own personal slave.

He must have wanted her so badly that he didn't even see how I was about to introduce him to the worst beating of his life.

When I felt the shaking behind me increase, I saw red.

Rage bled into my vision on every side, narrowing my focus directly on my target. I really wanted him to take that step that brought him over my threshold. All I needed was a reason.

Focused on my intent to harm with extreme prejudice, I missed it when Delilah had let go of me and appeared at my side. It was her voice that acted as a punch to my gut.

"Daddy?"

The man before me swallowed and the wet that I saw hovering suddenly drenched his face. I saw pain. I saw my own rage reflected there as he glanced at me then back at his daughter. I saw so many things. But more than that, I saw massive control as he stood right there and spoke the words that shattered me for the both of them.

"Baby. Where did you go? I looked for you. I looked everywhere for you. They said you ran away after Graycie died. They said you left after they told you I was on my way home to get you..."

When I felt her body shaking next to me, I had to grab hold to her. The gut twisting sobs that followed her father's words tore me to pieces.

And I watched the man across from me fight to hold himself in check. To keep himself from crossing over to the daughter that he obviously loved more than life, but thought had run from him. The daughter that he thought feared him so much, she'd left the safety of the reservation to avoid him.

I gritted my teeth as I held her shaking body. And forced myself to say the words that might lance open her wounds and shatter David's world. But I had to say them. He had a right to know.

"She didn't run away, Sir. She was taken. Your daughter has been a victim almost her entire life of human trafficking and has only been free for about a year."

Never. Never in my life had I seen such horror, such pain and such anguish completely encompass a man before. I felt it in the air, filling the atmosphere with its bitter twang. It's very nature, I knew, would have destroyed a lesser man. I found myself thanking God that it didn't destroy this one.

I watched as David Smith Robinson crossed over into my home, his steps sure, measured, and confident.

I felt Delilah's shaking adjust as she looked up to see what I saw. It was the longing I saw and love for someone he thought lost to him that got to me.

For that reason and that reason alone, I let her go. And I allowed him to take my place.

As I witnessed this father and daughter reunion, a mere man and his little girl finding each other again after so many years of not even considering the possibility, I couldn't help but think about something my mother always said.

If we, being evil, can love so hard and so deeply as this, imagine what it must be like every time God in heaven is reunited with one of his lost ones?

I couldn't. I could never imagine that. But I could imagine the next best thing. Giving my woman and her father the privacy they needed, I headed toward my bedroom.

Once there, I pulled the cell from my pocket and dialed a number so familiar, I didn't need to look down to do it.

"Hey, son." My father's voice was strong and confident like always when I called him. It was a voice that I'd taken for granted. A voice that I'd assumed would always be there on the other end, available any time I needed to access it.

A voice I'd never even imagined not being there.

As I chatted with my dad about everything and nothing, I made myself a promise.

We might have to fight the entire world one day. This Brainwaiver thing wasn't going away any time soon; I could no longer delude myself into thinking that this war wasn't my war; that it wasn't my fight.

This was about freedom and the right to choose. And one day soon, that right just might be taken away.

Therefore, I was going to spend every single day loving, living and appreciating every single gift God gave me.

Starting with my parents. Laughing at my Dad's corny jokes harder than I ever have before, I dropped back on my bed and lost myself in the sound of his voice. And his love.

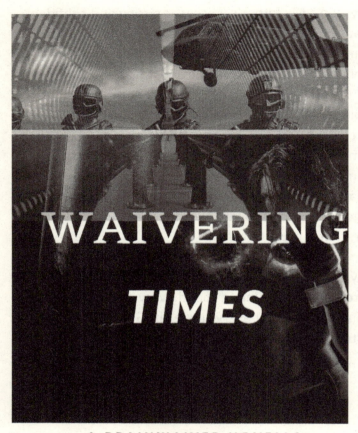

The kingdom of heaven (God's way of doing things) suffereth violence and the violent take it by force....
We are a generation not fighting for our right to party! We are fighting for our right to choose. We are fighting for our souls. – Mandy Same

Part One:

DAWNING TIMES

0

Chapter 1

The warehouse was huge. It was gray all around, like the standard issue warehouse – a steel building with metal plating throughout, it looked easily the size of a football field.

The gun point wedged into my back, forced me forward. Scanning more I saw that the grounds were littered with broken bottles and trash. What used to be a parking lot was now barren broken concrete with weeds growing out of it.

The place looked deserted. Surprisingly every window that I saw was intact. Each one was double-paned and there were at least two floors of them. One side of the pane held glass, the other what looked like some type of cork board material or wood.

Pushed forward into a garage door type entrance, I saw the inside was huge and told a different story. There was so much space – clean space. A sort of platform or stage was constructed on the farthest end. Music and sound equipment rested there like it was being set up for a concert. Slightly to the left in front of it stood some type of tent or structure, like those huge vendor huts you'd see at a country carnival or fair. I walked past miscellaneous types of tables and chairs. Some were wood, plastic or metal and many were so old, I wondered why they weren't collapsing while I watched.

I rubbed the bump on the back of my head and grimaced. At the grunt behind me I hastened my step to prevent being pushed (again cause that was getting old) to where Shae and I were obviously being directed, a stairwell near the stage structure on the very left side of the building.

There was obviously an upper level there and, while we couldn't see into it from where we were, you could see lights and sounds coming from that direction.

The cloth coverings thrown over the top railing and alongside the steps we were now ascending confused me. It was hard to tell what this place was exactly, but whatever it was, again surprisingly, it was clean.

As we reached the top of the steps, we were directed into a series of rooms that used to be the office part of this warehouse. The cubicle walls gave it away. We passed several of them, all also draped in multicolor fabric.

At the very end of the main row walkway is where we came to a halt. There were a couple of bean bag chairs scattered haphazardly with an ottoman or two, all sitting on a huge red shag rug.

"Sit."

That one word grunted at me was also getting old. But the man had a gun. So, I kept that thought to myself.

Instead, Shae and I chose a bean bag each and dropped into it. Mr. Polite was huge and stood too close for my comfort. I could barely see him slightly behind me, to my left, almost outside of my peripheral vision range.

"Mind telling me why we're here?"

The man didn't respond. Shae was shaking her head "no" wildly at me with wide eyes.

Channeling what I felt Balboa would do, because I lived by that creed, I snapped again when I didn't get an answer, "Yo! Hulk! I'm talking to you. I'll say it slow. Why... are... we... here?"

Channeling a tough chick persona was not something I did well. I know this because the flash of movement I caught out of the side of my eye right before everything went black, told me so.

And as always, when life was happening to me in the worst way, I dreamed. I was there again. My uncle's place in upstate New York, in the Hamptons. My dreams weren't so much as dreams as they were memories. And ultimately, they were the reason why I never went to horror movies. My life had been a real-life horror movie. So, I didn't need any reminders.

But when I dreamed, I had no control. I was back in that room. That unimaginable room. People dancing around in masks. Not like Halloween masks but like, animal head masks. Ana and I had been brought in blindfolded and laid out on tables. My uncle lied to us. His voice was smooth as butter when he lied. He told me and Ana that this was a family tradition and a party. It would be a fun party. We would have fun. It was a game, we liked games, right? But there were no games. There was laughing and people dancing around and singing. There was so much weight sitting on my chest that I wriggled until my blindfold slipped. I could see just underneath it with one eye. We were laid out on these tables in the middle of the room. The mask people walked by us, tickling Ana. Tickling me. Ana giggled. A normal reaction for an 11-year-old autistic child. I did not. I wanted out.

I called out to my uncle. In my dream I was watching myself do it, heard myself doing it, all while people walked past me, pointing, and laughing. And then the cutting started. They milled around us, Ana, and me. Fear and adrenaline coursed through me. I'm just now realizing that this isn't right. Well, not in the dream anyway. I knew it wasn't right the minute I started dreaming. But back then, back then, this is where the tide changed. The people in masks now had knives. Walking around me, cutting me, licking the knives. Ana's giggles became screams.

I screamed. Ana screamed. I heard her calling for mom and dad. My blindfold grew wet. I knew I should feel more pain from the cuts, because they just kept cutting and cutting. But I was too busy trying to get away. Watching myself in the dream, the part I dreaded most was coming; I knew it was coming. I was helpless to stop it, but I had to. I had to stop it. I refused to allow Ana and I to go through that again, even in this weird dreamscape.

Usually I woke up before I got to this part. But for some reason, I couldn't pull us out. I couldn't save us. I couldn't save Ana. I couldn't wake up. I heard, felt and saw from the side all at the same time, as my white gown was ripped to shreds with knives that cut and cut and cut. Hands pawed me. WAKE UP. Cuts, more cuts... so many freaking cuts! Why won't they stop? WAKE UP! No! Don't touch me!!! I screamed! I cried as hands moved all over me, wetness that must be blood from the cuts smearing as I screamed louder. What are you DOING! AMANDA ELIZABETH SAME!! WAKE THE HELL UP!

I felt a smack on my cheek, heard the resound of it echo as my eyes shot open.

***

I woke up with the mother of all headaches. My body screamed as I decided to take stock of what worked by moving one body part at a time. My mind went into playback mode. I remembered being in the small apartment I'd gotten off campus with my new roommate, Shayla, who insisted I call her Shae. We were discussing bills, while jamming 99.9 on the radio – getting ready to face our future as first year UMSL students together.

I'd met her a week ago when I moved in. The school social media page had been a great place to find a roommate near the campus who was also a first-year student. That's how I found Shae. After skype interviews and talking over the phone, her cool factor made her the perfect roommate. She was smart and cute but not gorgeous. Noticeable, but not exceptional – kindof like me

5

(as Balboa always said, a smart woman picked her friends carefully – not too pretty to make you disappear and not so insecure that they secretly hated you). That was Shae in a nutshell. Plus, she was funny; as in the girl was hilarious! Put my life under a microscope and you would totally understand why I had a special place in my heart for people with a sense of humor.

I liked her. She'd reminded me of a young Ms. Baltimore (now Mrs. Sampson), only Shae was black. Plus, she was my size which meant double the clothes and double the closet space.

The fact that she seemed to be all into Robert, my friend from Alton, after only meeting him for all of five minutes? I chalked that up to flighty but still fun. She didn't seem like a party girl and definitely didn't give me the "I'm rebellious and hate all authority," vibe.

But she'd been into something. Because two weeks after moving into our brand-new apartment, after I'd started my classes, kapow!

Kapow as in, the sound of our apartment door being kicked in, a bad-mammajamma walking through said door with a gun and escorting us out of the apartment then knocking me out when I fought back. I realized this truth when I ended up at this warehouse with water being thrown into my face before Shae and I are escorted inside.

All of which brought me back to the now. I'd taken stock of all my body parts. Nothing was broken, sprained or injured. I was sore though. Which didn't prevent me from getting up and moving out. Because I'd been much more than sore once. My hand went to my head subconsciously as I felt for contusions. There were two huge lumps. Great. Something else to thank the hulk wanna-be for.

I heard rowdiness and noise on the lower level. Revving engines, laughing and loud music. So, I didn't have to sneak up on anybody.

One glance over the railing and my trepidation gave way to rage. Which was a problem. Because several years of therapy and giving my life to Christ should have fixed that. I'd thought it did anyway. Which was why my brain possibly went numb with shock at what I did next.

I'd been tortured. I'd been beaten. And I'd been raped – repeatedly. So, seeing women being pushed around and kicked on that platform? Suffice it to say, was NOT my cup of tea.

Watching a group of rough necks cheer that hot mess on while the women stood around the room looking devastated? REALLY not my cup of tea.

Balboa, and all that she taught us, again, rushed to the forefront of my mind. She was a tough lady. And a gorgeous one. With Mrs. Sampson and the rest of the team, they'd helped me and my sister out three years ago. It felt like forever though. After all the drama went down, Balboa taught us a lot, her and Mrs. Sampson. Self-defense, Israeli street fighting (Krav Ma Ga), Tai chih, boxing and kubaton defense. One of those lessons stuck with me more than most. I could still here the words as if she were standing right next to me.

"Being female does not make you helpless. Or

7

hopeless. Even if they are bigger, stronger or outnumber you. Find a way to fight! Defend those who can't defend themselves. And doing all of that, get your exit strategy together while you work. See everything going in so you can fight your way out. Never EVER accept defeat. Make sure you train yourself to think like that every day and every minute that you breathe. It's the kind of thinking that might save your life one day."

It was that kind of thinking that had me catching sight of the small door on the left back side of the building when Shae and I were forced inside; the one with tables and crap piled up in front of it.

It was also that kind of thinking that had me stomping down the steps, snatching a pipe out of a startled biker's hand and running up behind the behemoth that was, watching impassively as three or four men dragged women around the stage by their hair.

I didn't think and I didn't assess which was what I usually did. I ran forward. And, putting all my weight behind my swing, I did my best to knock that giant, leather wearing, fake hulk into the next millennium. And I was no weakling. Me, plus rage was a force that a normal man wouldn't have been able to withstand.

To say it gave me pause when hulkazoid went down but only on one knee versus passing out, would be an understatement. My rage gave way to confusion when the behemoth's head turned from his bent position to look me square in the eye. His right eye twitched.

I was now standing face to face with a rage that rivaled my own. And something else I didn't quite

8

recognize. A decidedly blank stare. How someone could have a raging "blank" stare was beyond me.

I didn't have time to ponder that thought further since his bandana-wrapped head, wild blond hair and craggy mustached face loomed in my vision. Those piercing blue empty-raging eyes glared at me adding menace to what he shouted next.

"KNEEL!"

And like that, every woman in that room dropped to their knees. I blinked because, wow.

What the...? Did I just step into a scene straight out of the Avengers? This guy was no Loki for sure. He was built like a Thor, in fact, just nowhere near as cute. I glanced around the entire room, counting the men the behemoth had with him. It looked like seven. But there were ten bikes parked in the space.

Having catalogued all of that, my attention refocused on the largest obstacle in the room. That stared at me with expectation, like he was waiting for an answer.

And since I was never one to disappoint...

"No." It was something, a new habit maybe, I'd picked up from Macchio. Why use several words when one would do?

Not comfortable with a couple of his guys at my back, I circled around and backed up until I was now standing in front of one of the beaten woman with Santo tattooed on her arm, I kept the wall behind us and the enemy in front.

The giant still knelt with only his head now turned my way. And the other seven in the room hadn't moved.

9

The expression on their faces were synchronized, which should have been disturbing – as if they'd just tasted something sour. It was apparent that they were waiting for something. I just couldn't tell what that was.

I'd counted ten bikes. And I wasn't stupid by any means. So, it became apparent to me that they weren't waiting for something, more like someone.

When a shortish fellow wearing a skull and crossbones tee exited the tent-like structure and headed my way, I was not surprised. Think of the devil and he doth appear. This guy was all devil with no angel in him.

I could tell that right off because his smile was charming. Not the good kind of charming, the smarmy kind. Just like my uncle's had been.

His eyes were almost black they were so dark. While his hair was also covered with one of those bandana/hats that bikers tended to wear, you could tell that it was dark as well. He wasn't thin, nor was he fat. It was the glasses, however, that would throw a less observant person off. Which was probably his intent. To me, it looked as if he was that type of guy that pretended to be harmless – yet intelligent. But I saw what he was. It was in the way he smirked at me. I was looking at a snake in human skin. And I really hated snakes.

"What's this Brody?" Charming voice to go along with a charming face. But still smarmy.

The behemoth rose then like a puppet on a string. He crossed his arms and smirked as well – an expression almost identical to smarmy pants. I catalogued this too. For some reason I knew that it would be important

10

information to have.

My hands tightened on my pipe. Otherwise my stance didn't change and nor did my expression. And I waited. At twelve years old I'd been fascinated by the book The Art of War. And I'd learned a few things about strategy. Misdirection and deceit were two principles as a Christian, I would normally frown upon using. But I remembered God blessing the midwives of Israel in the Old Testament. That when the Pharaoh wanted to kill every male child under two, the women lied and said that girls were born instead. Lying for the sake of lying was wrong, no doubt.

To save lives? I had no problem with that. So, I watched, and I waited. *Your move, smarmy.*   I didn't need to fill the silence. Because people like him loved to talk and loved attention. I didn't have all that long to wait.

"And who might you be, young lady?" Ick. I could literally feel snakes slithering over me at the sound of his voice.

"I don't know you. You don't get to know me." I must have tried channeling Balboa again. My voice was confident and strong. All tough sounding.

"Fair enough."

He circled to stand directly in front of me, though still fifty yards out. No one else moved. Not the women that were still kneeling all around the building; and not the men whose arms were crossed as well – all their stances nearly identical.

And I waited some more.

"It seems as though we're at a standoff huh?"

He must have thought I was stupid. I was one girl with one pipe. There were eight men in the room including him, one of which was huge as all get out. There were at least two others that I couldn't see, a bunch of cowed women and a beaten one behind me, my only possible allies. We were not at a standoff. They could have rushed me and overpowered me at any moment.

But if he wanted stupid, that's what he would get.

"Looks like it." I spoke with bravado and slapped a bit of a tremor on the "it" at the end. I also let my arms shake a little.

The widening of male smirks all around let me know that they'd taken the bait. I quickly scanned the room again, but this time I did it as if I were scared and looking for a way out. This next look gave me a weapons assessment. Three tables on the east corner of the room covered with semi-automatic weapons. Some had ammo – several clips, boxes of bullets and a few casings. None of which had been there when we'd come in.

"Let's take this outside then cutie. I'll even let you have your pick of who you fight. That is, if you think you can handle it."

And there it was. The arrogance that probably assumed I would try to get outside and make a run for it.

Good thing he didn't know me.

"You first." Again, with the shaky voice. Chuckles all around. Muscle bound but clueless.

Yet I knew better than to underestimate them as an adversary. It didn't take much intelligence to hammer a nail into a wall. At the same token, it wouldn't take much

12

for brute strength to overpower me. I had one chance to get us out of here. A bunch of women, an injured one and an unconfirmed exit. Balboa would be so proud (not).

I guess I'd sounded pretty scared since the men proceeded to the raised garage doors without looking back. They had no doubt that I would follow. I coughed and sniffled a bit. To them it sounded weak. But to the person I needed to hear it, it was a call to arms.

Shae and I didn't know each other all that well. But we knew enough. That must have been the case because at my signal, she raised up. Eyebrows high in question, she was night and day from the subjugated slave person she'd seemed before.

I quickly nodded toward the ropes and locks at the garage doors. A quick grin and her quietly going around, tapping all the other girls let me know that she understood. I didn't know what had gone on before I'd gotten there, but I knew what would happen now. We were getting out of here. And we were taking the girls with us.

Brody the behemoth and his smarmy buddy could have this warehouse. But they would never get their hands on these women again. I hoped. God had my back, I reasoned. How could I possibly fail? Isn't that why He called me back to St. Louis, in the first place? To save these women. And my mom?

14

Chapter 2

6 months ago; Seattle, Washington

I checked out my group of gal bikers and thought to myself, "I could get used to this."

Riding a motorcycle was something I thought I'd never do... never need to do. But a weird sing-song poem from my sister two years ago and voila – I was not only taking motorcycle class; I'd become a biker.

I loved the wind, flowing freely over my skin. The speed of the ride, exhilarating from the word go, seemed to eat up stress and exhaustion as I chewed away at miles and miles of black top. They say that a true biker becomes one with the wind. I couldn't say that I was a true biker, but I can say that the wind and I... we were mates of a kind.

And right now, with no word from the crew about Mom in the last month and having lost granddad before we could bring mom home once and for all, there was only one thing to do.

Lose myself in the wind.

"Are we doing this or what chick?"

Dana Dee, also known as D.D.'s rough voice cranked from her chest with a sound similar to the turning of a rusted doorknob. The voice of a smoker and a drinker, it was well worn and aged to what Dee considered perfection. And when you heard it, you loved it and hated it at the same time.

Like sandpaper on the nerves, that voice ground away at the eardrums of those in hearing range. When you didn't know her, your first instinct was to head in the opposite direction anywhere away from that sound, quick fast and in a hurry.

But once you got to know her, and on the off chance she became your friend... your family; that voice came with a powerful feeling of peace. There was no one in the world quite like Dee. A rough woman standing at over 6'4, Dee could bench press over 400 pounds and knew several different types of wrestling maneuvers that could take down just about any man in half a second.

So, when Dee became your family, she had your back. And if Dee had your back, woe to any being in the universe save God himself that would dare step to you with attitude. Dee could throw a punch, take a punch, and ride a mechanical bull like nobody's business. Most of all, Dee loved me. And she loved my sister. We were family.

"You can't rush perfection old lady," I laughed because she'd already sneered a warning at me. It was a look she gave all her gals to get them rolling. It probably

16

didn't speak well of me that I was proud to be a recipient of that look.

The SC's – that's short for Slick Chicks, were not well liked. No that's not true. They were hated and despised. Hated and despised far and wide throughout Washington State. They were constantly harassed by law enforcement for being a public nuisance, they were often blamed for crimes and the destruction of property that they hadn't even been in the vicinity to commit... and they gave no thought or care to any of that.

They were who they were. A tattooed bunch of women who'd banded together and become a family, all of them having been the victim of some type of a physical or sexual abuse. Even Dee.

The Solomon House, a shelter for battered women is where I'd first met Dee and the gang. I'd quickly learned that a part time job working with kids before and after school wasn't my gig. I liked kids, loved them even. But not in that setting.

Working at Harbor Latchkey put an employee between a rock and a hard place, no disciplining the kids! But at the same time, you were expected to encourage them to do the right thing. It was like sending a man to war with no weapon. Kids were geniuses that sensed weakness and sniffed it out with the determination of a bloodhound. When they realized that there was nothing you could do to back up what you say? Well... "It's all over," a trite and anticlimactic phrase, explained the situation perfectly.

I knew that if I still wanted to have my own

children one day (which was debatable) then I'd better get out of there pretty darn quick. I found the position at the shelter on Craigslist. And having found it, I found a key to my future.

Dee and I hadn't started out as best buds right away. In fact, when she'd heard me talking to one of the residents about my faith, she'd lost it on me right there in the hallway.

"Keep your God and your religious crap to yourself! Folks in here learned the hard way that if they have no one to watch their backs, then they are Fu-barred. Your God ain't *been* helping her, he ain't gonna start to help her now. She has to learn that the only person she can trust is herself. Not you. Not God!"

And just like that, I'd become Dee's enemy. It wasn't an overt thing either. It was a quiet animosity that built in strength for the following reasons. A. I didn't listen to her and kept doing what I'd been doing, talking about God and how He has always been there for me. And B. I wasn't afraid of her.

This was something Dee couldn't understand. I stood all of five feet and six inches. Her being almost a whole foot taller than me with forearms that were bigger than my thighs, you'd think I'd be frightened to death of her.

But the thing is, I'd seen worse. I'd seen the monster under the bed, the bats in the belfry and the life sucking banshees that inhaled the marrow from your bones. So, I wasn't afraid of her just because she was big. God was bigger. That was something I'd learned two years before.

And it was something I held fast to, when her and the girls subtly tried to put the fear of Dee in me… then not so subtly stalked me to make sure I knew that my days were numbered, all up unto the day of the fight.

The day when the Director of the shelter, Mrs. Mulberry left town for a conference and left it in the hands of Judy Deimeke, an honorary member of Dee's club despite her degree in social service. I was in the middle of praying with Destiny, a young mother of three that left everything behind to escape her abusive husband, when I was yanked away and thrown, yes, *thrown*… by my ponytail.

Ouch! It felt like she'd pulled my brains right out of my head and swung them around for good measure before stomping on them and slamming them back into the hole they'd been snatched out of!

When I'd landed, the scraped knees and palms I'd experienced were the least of my worries. I barely managed to raise my head and my vision swam with tears; so much so, it was hard to make out the huge brunette coming at me full tilt, the knife scars on her cheeks whiter than they'd ever been within her face, red with rage.

Remembering that clear as day I still shook in the awe of it. Her oversized fingers had approached my neck with the intent (at least in my mind) to choke the life out of me, when; I promise you, I heard Balboa's voice in my head say, "Pinky."

Telephone chats with Balboa and CeeCee along with training videos I'd been sent to Washington with had

19

continued the self-defense, MMA, and strategic warfare training she'd started with Anabella and I years ago when our lives depended on it. And, before this day, I'd never had cause to use any of it.

Having deep breathed to slow my heart rate in the time that it took Dee to reach me, I grabbed for the weakest body part that wanted to grab hold of me, the pinky fingers on both of her hands, and jerked up, pushing them back with all of my might. The *SNAPS* were loud, and the air stilled as a roaring silence-filled tension crashed into that room, in concert with Dee, crashing to her knees.

Knowing these were women who'd been abused, knowing that she was no stranger to pain, I quickly let go of her fingers and circled away until everyone in the room was at my front, the wall at my back.

But she didn't get up. Dee stayed there on her knees, breathing so hard I thought that her chest would collapse. Her eyes were squeezed so tightly I was sure that she would crumble into dust from the force of them. I could see her pain and, despite having experienced my own, regretted being the cause of it.

I had to make a choice. Either I was going to try to walk away, letting my actions speak for themselves. Or I was going to try for one of the greatest strategies in war I've ever studied – make my enemy my ally.

Since I was the type of girl that was all about strategy, making Dee my ally was the way to go. And there was only one way to do that. I had to tell her my truth.

"It was at least 6 men that night, when they raped me and my sister. "I spoke to the room at large. And I kept

20

speaking.

By the time I was done, every woman that had been standing was sitting, and there was not one dry eye in the room. I hadn't realized that, even I'd been crying as I shared with them my shame.

But what I will never forget is how that story ended.

"And because God rallied a woman who thought she just wanted to be left alone, a fighter who'd grown bored because life had lost its ability to challenge her, a man whose heart had died over-seas along with a group of ex-soldiers, a doctor, two girls, and two boys... because He chose in that small town to take down a huge conglomerate with people who were considered nothing and nobody; I can say this today, *despite* my shame – I am free from fear. I am not alone, and I am not afraid of anyone or anything. Because if God stands for me, who can dare stand against me."

On that day my enemy died, and an ally was born. Dee had gotten up and walked off. I thought she was leaving for good at first; that maybe my strategy had failed. It hadn't. She'd gone to bandage her broken pinky fingers and tape them up before coming back into the room.

Her approach should have made me wary. I had to fight every instinct not to go into my fighter stance. It was her gaze that told me a different story. Wide and accepting. Caring. And before I could react, I was enveloped in a hug so tight, I forgot that I even needed to breathe.

As moving as it was, the hug didn't hold a candle to what Dee said next.

"I've been wrong before, " she'd whispered, agony lacing every syllable, making her rough as nails voice more rough, "and I got no problem with admitting that."

Her grip on me had tightened to the point of pain. But I didn't pull away. She needed something more from me and I'd had no clue what it was until I heard what came next.

"I owe you. Not for the broken fingers, not that. I deserve what I got and take it as it's due. But I owe you for my life. My daddy was a preacher. He'd warned me long ago that I couldn't run from God. No matter how hard I'd run, no matter what foul business I entrenched myself in, God wouldn't be letting me go. Not now. Not ever, he'd said. I fought my daddy's prophecy with every breath I took, from the boyfriends I picked to becoming a biker chick. And only just now, hearing your story did I finally accept the truth. I ain't been running from and fighting my dad. I've been running from and fighting God. That ends today. It ends now, little sister. THAT is why I owe you."

I'd broken down, crying even harder and hugging Dee back until neither of us could breathe; and soon collapsed wheezing and laughing to the floor.

That was the day we became sisters. It was the day I realized that God knew what he was doing, despite my questions and misgivings. Though I may never need to know about the inner workings of a biker club, their wacked code of honor or how twisted their view of the outside world is, I knew that I could never have too many allies. Not ever.

It was with that memory that I kicked my bike into gear, rolling the throttle to feel the hum of vibration take over, starting at my feet and working its way up. I answered Dee's smirk back at me with a nod, silently letting her know I was ready as we filed out into the street and into formation.

It was time to ride the wind and lose my troubles. I'd worry about destiny tomorrow. But today, it was all about the wind.

Present Day,

St. Louis, Missouri

"So, that guy with your uncle, he's your cousin? Because, and, don't think it's the trauma of the last 24 hours talking, that dude is HOT; with a CAPITOL hot!"

I shook my head at Shae's pacing enthusiasm. I hated pacing. But I didn't stop her. I couldn't blame her considering we both had every reason to be nervous. Which was why I desperately tried to hide my shaking hands under my arms. I didn't want to telegraph to Shae just how freaked out I was! Though I don't know how she couldn't know that, all things considered.

And Cruz Arpaio, Max's brother was hot. He just wasn't hot enough to make me forget my colossal failure.

Max and Cruz had followed us to the old Sampson headquarters in Kirkwood, Missouri. Just over twenty-five miles out, on the back of that hog with the wind in my face, it was like time stopped. And for twenty minutes, in my mind, I was back in Washington, riding with my crew. A crew I didn't realize I'd missed all that much, until now.

The old headquarters had been ground zero. All Brainwaiver-ites had been brought here for Cheryl Larson (also known as Minute), the team neurosurgeon, to disconnect and shut down most of the chip in every child that had received it. Along with a few adults.

While the team no longer used the site for formal meetings, having dispersed and gone their separate ways after completing their mission; Sam's construction company had bought the business for Max and Ricky to store massive amounts of technology and weapons (I'm sure the government and local authorities knew nothing about).

I'd parked the hog on the very bottom level of the garage and waited. I knew I wouldn't have to wait long. I was pretty sure that one or two of the team had been following me out of that warehouse district. And I didn't even want to know how they knew I was there in the first place. Though, I did know. Max was a computer genius. So, it didn't take a genius to guess that somehow, he'd found out I'd gone missing. But Max and Cruz hadn't been the only one there. Balboa had been there. How she'd found out was anyone's guess. One thing was for sure. Max wouldn't have told her.

26

Chapter 3

I blinked several times to clear my vision. My eyes felt like they had been filled with sand, as they should since I'd only had about three hours of sleep, according to my cell.

The thumping of my racing heart had nothing to do with my limited hours of rest, unfortunately.

It was another nightmare. Another memory, I should say, of what had happened two years ago in Alton, my hometown. Of Brainwaiver.

A time of terror that my dream forced me to relive, I could see myself hiding in that attic storage inside my youth pastor's walk-in closet. Men in suits searched all over his home for me. Not just "men in suits" though, it was the FBI; looking for little old Amanda Same, a simple run away.

I could feel the winter cold biting through my light jacket nights later as I hid inside an old condemned apartment building. With just my one packet of tuna and a fruit cup.

I was terrified. So terrified, I gave the thought of suicide a long hard look. Until I remembered Ms. Baltimore.

I'm not sure what woke me up this time, but whatever it was, I thanked it and God. My vision cleared, but all of that blinking couldn't blink the memories away.

After everything had gone down, from Ms. Baltimore hiding Ana and I with Mr. Sampson's family to the RLS explosion; what I didn't get was how that could be the end? There was no public blow up about the Brainwaiver in-plant or missing kids, no lawyers on television offering to represent those that had hemorrhaged like my sister … no mention of the families of those who'd died from the experiments.

RLS, the law firm had exploded (mainly due to Sam blowing it all to crap), had been spun by the local media as having a gas leak; with the firm's new partner (Andrew something or other) determined to rebuild a bigger and better RLS in Granite City.

The only mention of Brainwaiver after that had been the commercials that continued to air about this newest technology and the benefits. "A neuro-net processor that could access the internet for you – right from your own mind, changing negative thoughts and behaviors, increasing strength and agility, yada yada yada."

No mention, however, of the controls, the social programming, brain washing, or physical harm that resisting the programming caused.

Every single perpetrator of the horrible crimes visited on those kids and their families had not only gotten away free and clear; they still continued to make money by the loads, watching (probably with glee) as their DEATHWARE spread stealthily through the masses. With the masses consent.

Legislators had turned a blind eye to our letters. Those written by me, the Sampsons and the Alton community (many awakened to the truth despite the media subterfuge).

Every effort we'd made, including Cheryl's and Ana's new doctor in Seattle (a colleague of Cheryl's), known experts in their field of neurology, had failed to gain national attention.

Feelings of helplessness increased as we watched ecstatic, relieved people leap into this horror story, thinking Brainwaiver was the answer to all their problems.

Like the same helplessness I was feeling now as I tried to calm my shaking body by taking deep, cleansing breaths.

I was back in my dorm room with Shae.

A Shae that still slept like the dead, regardless to her being kidnapped just a day before.

Feeling myself grow warm, I knew that he was wide awake, his gaze, burning a hole through me.

Cruz.

After our scene and my embarrassing mini tantrum at Balboa's, Cruz had refused to let Shae and I out of his sight. Which was fine by me. I just wish his "sight" wasn't so... disturbing.

"You alright?"

I shifted, my own gaze reluctantly meeting his. That would have to be answer enough. I didn't have it in me to lie. Because I was not alright, but there wasn't a thing he could do about it.

"Hungry?"

His eyebrows were raised in question, but there was a knowing look in his eyes. Like he'd read my mind, gotten his answer, and moved on to the next immediate concern.

I blinked a few more times, noticing the melted color of his eyes. Had he looked this good yesterday? Memories of hearing him call me "Bellissima," as I struggled with Balboa's harsh words assailed me. I'd unashamedly leaned into his comfort and his strength. He made a promise that he would help me look after Shae and bring the motorcycle gang to justice. It took everything in me not to fall in love with the guy right there on the spot.

I could tell that he must have gotten cleaned up. His hair was wet, and he looked shiny new, even though he was still wearing his same clothes from the day before.

Opening my mouth to answer that I was, having no idea what I was hungry for, my attention was snagged by a groaning Shae as she rolled over, loudly, in her sleep.

30

Shae snored. And snorted in her sleep. I hadn't realized my mouth had dropped in awe as I heard her break wind, snort then settle and snore some more.

Hearing his chuckling from much closer then where he'd stood moments before, my narrowed gaze shifted back to Cruz. His eyes crinkled even more in humor upon seeing my full embarrassment for Shae, complete with a burning face and slack jaw.

"Sounds like she's got sleep apnea. And gas." He chuckled out after approaching and sitting beside my prone body on my bed.

His laughing eyes had been on Shae as he said that. But then they shifted. And they were no longer laughing. They looked hooded, intense.

"How you doing?"

He was concerned. I could hear it in his voice as the tone softened, making my heart skip a beat.

The man was filthy in every way a man could be. Filthy, slang in Washington for "good" was the only word that echoed in my brain so hard I must have said it out loud.

"Who? Me?"

My jaw dropped again as the sexiest man I have ever seen sniffed under one arm and then the other, right there in front of me before focusing again on my face, his eyebrows drawn.

"Not filthy babe. I just got out of the shower in fact."

Babe? My mind stuttered. Who said "babe" anymore"? What did that even mean from a guy like him?

31

His sniffing the air surreptitiously broke my mind out of its stutter, allowing my mouth to take over.

"Filthy means good... it means good in um..." I stopped. I'd swear his eyebrows had their own language as they both rose high at my words, clearly indicating he doubted what I was saying. Ignoring that, I pushed on.

"Filthy means good, in Washington, where I've been with my Grandma and sister for the last couple of years. So... um, its good... not stinky or dirty, like it means here."

His eyes narrowed. That was my only warning as he shifted, his left arm stretching over me into a power lean as a formerly acceptable distance between us lessened to the point of intimacy, his face just a few inches now from mine.

I desperately wanted to scoot backward. But that would smack of cowardice. Forcing myself to remain stiffly unmoved, I don't know how much time had passed before Cruz spoke.

It was enough time that I nearly jumped out of my skin when he did.

"You talk in your sleep, you know that?"

His breath hit my lips. He'd brushed already, was my first thought as the scent of mouthwash and toothpaste hit me. Trying not to wonder on where he got a toothbrush to do so, I focused my gaze over his shoulder after a brief glance told me what I didn't need to know.

There was apparently something fascinating about my mouth since his eyes seemed to be locked there. I felt

32

my face heating up again as I fought to find words that would move him away from me.

"I do?" was all that I could muster, breathlessly forced out of my lungs and tinged with nerves that had me biting my bottom lip as I heard my own voice.

A mistake I realized too late. That melty chocolate gaze of his grew even more intense when I did.

Blipping fantastic. Freaking, I mentally corrected, remembering folks here don't recognize Northwest slang.

I needed to do something fast to distract us both. My face wasn't the only thing that was heating up at an astronomical rate.

"Um," I cleared my throat, fixating on the one subject that was on my mind all the time.

"Are you heavily connected to FBI sources? Like, people that will give you intel without asking questions."

Bingo. That worked.

Shifting backward, Cruz's gaze jumped to mine.

"What?" He barked.

Shae shifted, groaned, and broke wind again.

I couldn't help it as my nose crinkled, cause REALLY?

"What?" Cruz asked again, this time softly as he refocused on me, his eyes now laced with humor.

"I need help. My mom. I need to get her away from my dad."

I cleared my throat again as Cruz tilted his head, his brow furrowed. After a few moments of that, he startled me by hopping up while grabbing hold of my hand, all but pulling me out of the bed.

33

"Get up. Get dressed. We'll head to breakfast, then to Max's. I need to change. While we're there, I'm sure Max can get you what you need."

Grunting, I straightened up, shifting my shoulder to see if the guy pulled my arm out of the socket. Because it sure as heck felt like he did.

Next thing I know, my whole body is being propelled toward the bathroom, the bossy so and so moving me PHYSICALLY as if I were an invalid.

"Um, HELLO? I CAN walk, you know. All by myself. Been doing it since I was eight months."

I couldn't keep the snark out of my tone. I needed Starbucks bad. A true slick chick never started her day without being loaded up with unleaded. I was desperate for a cup. Or two. At least.

"Good, then you've had a lot of practice. Do it faster so we can get moving. I'll get Shae up while you're in the shower."

Rolling my eyes, I detoured over to my armoire to grab clothes before stomping toward the bathroom and slamming the door.

I almost giggled as I heard Shae shouting nonsensically at what I guessed was Cruz's normal "bed side" manner.

Warm water hit me in the face, filling me with vigor.

Trying not to think about all those women I'd left behind at the warehouse, or Balboa being mad at me and my being mad at her, I set my mind on doing what I came back to St. Louis to do.

34

Saving my mom.

36

Chapter 4

Rolling my eyes at Shae, I shifted my attention back to the two brothers as they argued.

It was hard to believe that these were men. Grown men, arguing like puppies over the coffee that Cruz brewed; coffee I desperately needed.

"Get over it already!" Cruz yelled in his brother's face, "you throw it out, I buy another one. I'll hide it just like I did this one!"

"And I'll throw that away too," Macchio groused as he played keep away with the liquid gold in a cup that had me salivating.

"Give it!" Cruz gritted through clenched teeth.

I almost didn't see the laughter in Macchio's eyes as his arm stretched further away from his body, enraging his little brother as he did so.

They were worse than me and Ana!

It was Cruz grabbing what looked like a container of protein powder and dumping the open can toward the sink that was my salvation.

Macchio, with lightning fast reflexes, released the cup that clattered onto the counter and tipped, to grab hold of the canister before any more of his precious powder spilled out.

Cruz, just as quickly, caught the teetering coffee cup, spun under his brother's reaching grasp, then danced out of the kitchenette exit, sipping out of the cup first, before holding it out to me.

Grinning at me like a triumphant five-year-old, I couldn't help but laugh. At least my laughter was composed.

Shae was nearly rolling around on the floor with hers.

Rolling my eyes at her again, I ignored the fact that dude had just sipped from my cup. Closing my eyes, I almost clicked my heels three times, desperate to open them and see my Starbucks in Washington, just around the corner from the shelter.

Only that didn't happen. Still. Cruz made some good Joe.

What I did open my eyes to, was a frowning Macchio whose head was swiveling back and forth between me and his brother.

Oy veh.

"And before you start, that's not on me, "Cruz fussed, heading back toward the kitchenette, "that woman

38

had coffee on her brain and tongue the minute she rolled out of bed this morning."

Not the smartest thing to say. Macchio went from frowning to thunderous.

Double Oy. Double Vey.

"What the...!" Max shouted, moving at a speed I'd never seen toward his brother.

"Wait Max wait!!! He was keeping us safe! Standing guard! That's all!" I shouted before I knew I'd spoken.

I don't know exactly when Cruz's safety became important to me. But it had. That was the first time I ever called Macchio by his given name. I heard my breath escape in a huge rush as Max's glare transferred from Cruz to me, his body now completely under his control.

Slowly, I exhaled.

The room was all but silent, littered with nothing but our heavy breathing.

Clearing my throat, I spoke succinctly.

"He stayed all night, but on the floor. Shae and I slept in our beds. He woke us up and got us ready. Nothing happened."

"Man," Cruz interrupted, disgust lacing his tone, "are you seriously standing there thinking that I would do that? She's barely out of high school for crying out loud."

"She's legal." Macchio grunted.

"So." Cruz countered.

"She's barely off her training wheels. I chase women, not teens. Get a clue." He concluded, turning to

39

pull out another filter for the little coffee maker and fill it with coffee.

Ouch. My pain was mental, but I dismissed it immediately... almost.

Yeah. Cruz was fine; as in razor sharp fine. But I didn't do schoolgirl crushes. Besides, he was only five years older than me. It wasn't like I was twelve or anything, which, was neither here nor there. I didn't' want to have anything to do with him anyway. Sort of.

Macchio continued to bicker with his brother as I redirected my attention to Shae.

It looked like she'd seriously fallen asleep on the floor where she was rolling around on it moments before.

Hoping she didn't' break wind again, I focused on Macchio's next words.

"... here for, anyway?"

"Baby girl's got questions." Cruz shrugged.

"Don't call her that?" Cruz blinked at Macchio's grouch.

"Call her what? Baby girl?" He asked, eyebrows raised.

"Right." Macchio grouched, his arms crossing tightly over his chest.

Uh oh. My gaze shifted back to Cruz, picking up on the matching thunder in his expression. Obviously, brothers as they were both extremely easy on the eye, I wasn't ashamed to let my eyes have all the candy they wanted. Though Macchio was more like an uncle than anything, he was still hot.

40

As both thunderous expressions shifted to me, I realized something else, my face turning bright red. Shae, who I'd thought was asleep was again, rolling, laughing, and choking this time.

Apparently, I'd said that last part out loud.

Oy veh.

Cruz

Resisting the urge to punch his brother in the jaw, Cruz focused on loosening up his face. Hearing Amanda say his brother was a "hot uncle" shouldn't have bothered him. She was barely driving, a kid, wet behind the ears, really.

Only it did bother him.

Everything about Amanda Same bothered him. Blonde, chocolate eyed, trim athletic barbies were not his type. He was into curvy, ethnic, dark women. Like Balboa.

Shae, while young also, was much closer to the kind of woman that Cruz liked than Amanda.

Yet and still. It was something about her.

A dark edge he couldn't put his finger on. While slightly naïve, he saw something hard, intense, and powerful occasionally shifting under the surface of those somber mahogany eyes.

Starkly oxymoronic from her apparent nature, the anomaly intrigued him. Cruz had caught himself watching her sleep (something he found so creepy that he would walk-run quick, fast in a hurry from anyone he caught doing it).

But in his defense, she talked in her sleep. No, that was wrong. She didn't just talk in her sleep. She spoke with fierce, vibrating power in her sleep. Her voice, deep and clear, hardly sounded like her as she spoke out vitriol words in a foreign language.

Cruz hadn't realized he'd gotten up and had been standing over her bed, spellbound by her complete lack of facial expression as the strange words flowed smoothly off her tongue in a powerful, authoritative voice.

He would have been standing there all night if her eyes hadn't popped open suddenly, focused as if she had been awake the whole time, boring into his with an energy he didn't recognize.

She'd kept right on speaking as her gaze held him hostage for several minutes.

And then her eyes shut suddenly as the flow of words stopped, like someone had hit a switch.

Cruz, not realizing he'd been holding his breath, had exhaled with relief. Frightened, fascinated and feeling somehow exhilarated by it all, he'd backed away and returned to his small cot on the floor.

And dreamed about that voice. Those eyes. Her words. Wondering why, as he faded in and out of rem sleep, he felt as if his very life had been fundamentally changed.

Chapter 5

Balboa was on her way over. I don't know how Macchio knew it, I just know that he did.

Rushing Cruz, Shae and I to the door, he slammed it on our heels, propelling me forward and directly into Cruz.

Halting my forward momentum seemed easy for him. Not so for my equilibrium.

Easy on the eye and dangerous to my senses summed up all that was Caruso Arpaio.

Caruso. Macchio had called Cruz by his full, government name during one of their spats. I savored the sound of this new name in my mind. It was hard to gather myself off him as I did so but, if nothing else, I have learned to control my fear and hold my composure through the worst of situations. Happy I had this skill in my repertoire, I turned to the sound of Shae calling my name.

"Girl! I'm hungry! I heard this Delmar loop over here has some good food. We're stopping to eat first, right? Did I mention that I'm starving?"

I felt Cruz giving us the side eye and hesitated. I mean, we did need to eat so...

"What'd you have in mind?" I asked, hoping it wouldn't be a big deal to convince Cruz.

"They've got this Mission Taco here just down the street..."

"NOOOO!" Cruz and I nearly shouted at the same time, eliciting the most comical run-jump reaction from Shae I'd ever seen. I tried to choke back the giggle itching at my throat. Hearing myself snicker I knew I was failing in increments.

"What! NO? Why?" Shae asked, her hand to her chest like we'd scared the living daylights out of her. Which we probably did.

I didn't answer. Biting my lips, I looked to Cruz imploringly. I figured being rude was his wheelhouse so, you know. He could just fire away.

"Helloooooo?" Shae echoed, her eyes squinting as her gaze bounced from me to him.

I bit my lip. Could I really do that? Tell her that she was gassy and didn't need taco's in her diet? I didn't want to embarrass her, and I didn't want to embarrass myself. Besides, I had bigger problems. Like the intel Macchio had hacked into about my family. Getting my mom away from my dad was going to be a lot harder than I thought.

Caruso Damien Arpaio, however (as I said, full government name courtesy of Macchio), was not stepping

44

forward in any way to help. Clearing my throat, I prepared for extreme embarrassment, when my cell phone rang.

Grabbing at my phone, fumbling, and catching it in the air twice before I could glance at the screen, I saw the name that made my day. Ana.

I know that "saved by the bell" was the biggest cliché ever coined. Even so, that's exactly what my heart cackled as I took the call with a sigh of relief.

"Ana – girl, what's going on?" I said it so excitedly that Cruz burst out laughing beside me in tune with my sister as she laughed on the line.

"Busy?" She asked, finally getting her joy under control.

"Never when it comes to you Ana-Banana?" I smiled, loving her genuine giggle and relaxed. The world could wait when it came to Ana. I was lucky that Shae, and the whole world knew that truth. And Caruso would learn it too. Family and God always came first. Period.

***

Four weeks flew by like minutes. Precious minutes that ticked away more of my life as I wrestled with a mission that, for all intents and purposes, seemed to be failing.

While I'd had to get back to "life as usual" as it were, my frustration at the events of the last two weeks made it anything BUT...

Here's the run down.

Along with faithfully attending class, this time from a completely different apartment that Max and Cruz had somehow arranged for me and Shae to move into (don't ask me how), I'd started my internship at JOY 99.9, a Christian radio station in St. Louis County.

Pretending that life was normal, I had to put up with a Shae that was growing more agitated by the day, a suddenly distant Cruz that was now acting as if I had leprosy for some reason (to the point of avoiding being in the same room with me at any time; an obvious behavior considering the small, three bedroom apartment we were now staying in) and a worried Ana.

A worried Ana meant a calling Ana. As in calling several times in a day, Ana. Autism came with a heightened focus and awareness that most "normal" folks didn't possess. Apparently, I was that new focus for my little sister. And for the life of me, I couldn't fathom why.

Ana and my Grandmother had no clue what I was up to, at least, I didn't think they did. Ana spent a lot of time in a weird place called "the white room". It was a mystical place if you believe in that kind of thing. A strange type of mental reality that many former "Brainwaiver-ites" would gather and meet.

While many of those having undergone surgery felt the place was heaven-like in appearance, thus set aside for them by God as a reward for resisting the Brainwaiver programming; I had my doubts.

Cheryl, limited by lack of surgical resources and equipment, with Macchio's help, had been able to deactivate the Brainwaiver chip in most of the recipients, but she had been unable to remove it.

Fact is, for many, the bio-genetic wiring had become accepted by the body as part of the brain itself, making removal extremely dicey and, most likely fatal.

So, while the recipients had been freed from all Brainwaiver controls, they still had the hardware installed, receiving certain benefits that came with it such as enhanced strength, senses (sight or hearing; for example, folks that needed glasses before could see perfectly without them), and faster healing abilities. Like mutants from an X-men movie or something.

That said, this white room situation weirded me out to no end. The "other reality" was off-putting on several fronts. First, according to Danny, my friend and Mr. Sampson's son (a former Brainwaiver-ite and the focus of Mr. Sampson's mission when he went missing), everyone appeared older and more mature, including Ana.

Why would something supposedly representing heaven make anyone look older?

And then there was the fact that everything was stark white there. I'd always imagined heaven or something "heavenly" to be filled with vibrant colors and beauty; not sterile or boring; which is exactly how that sounded.

There were other small details that seemed to be "off", but I couldn't really put my finger on why.

One thing I did know for sure, is that Ana knew things that she probably wouldn't know if it hadn't been for that place. Things that made her seem downright prophetic at times. Ergo, while I hadn't shared my true

47

mission in returning to St. Louis, it was a good possibility that Ana knew, hence the frequent phone calls.

It wasn't the phone calls that threw me for a loop last Saturday, however. It had been Shae coming up missing AGAIN, news I'd learned from Cruz upon arriving home extra late Wednesday, the week before last. I'd stayed late to help Cindy with prep for the next day's broadcasts.

"Where the hell have you been!"

Shouted right into my face as soon as the unlocked door swung open before I could turn the nob, I blinked several times as I was snatched over the threshold before realizing what was happening.

"I called the radio station, no answer! I've got Robert and Danny calling around trying to find you and Nina on standby! You haven't been seen since you left the campus this morning and I didn't spot your bike when I drove by the radio station!"

My bike. Well, not my bike, more like the bike I'd kinda stolen; it had been appropriated, painted, and made to look completely different by Cruz and a few of his friends. Friends he said I didn't know. And according to Cruz, I didn't wanna know.

I had asked Cruz after leaving Max's why we weren't going to the police with all this. I'd been concerned about those women. Praying that God would see them safe felt like taking the punk way out of what should have been my responsibility. I'd also asked why he, as a United States Marshall, wasn't handling any of this

48

through those particular channels considering his investigation of the chumps that had abducted us.

And was basically told to shut up and mind my own business like a good little female. His actual words being, "Let me worry about my investigation. You worry about Amanda."

It was because I had to worry about "Amanda," and more importantly, Amanda's mom that I'd grudgingly accepted that answer.

Cruz had been standoffish ever since that conversation; something I already had an attitude about. So, being snatched into the apartment and hearing the door slam behind me didn't help put me in a sharing mood.

"Touch me again like that," I gritted through clenched teeth arm, sore from his grip, "And you will taste scrotum for the next month, that's how hard I will kick you."

Hands on his hips and breathing like he'd run ten flights of steps, Cruz went incredibly still, before closing his eyes and exhaling loudly.

Feeling my face grow a little less tight, I dropped my backpack by the door and went to hang my purse and keys on the coat tree near my desk.

"Shae's missing."

I heard it. I heard him say the words. But my brain, for some reason, couldn't grab hold to the concept.

I headed into the kitchen instead, where I washed my hands with dish soap before going to and opening the fridge.

49

I could tell Cruz had followed me when I heard him speak from the kitchen doorway.

"I'm sorry. I've been half out of my mind looking for the both of you. The sat phone I gave her is off radar and yours was left here on your desk."

I refused to feel the sympathy nudging me as I watched him rub both hands tiredly over his face and into his hair. I know that I should have been freaking out, running around, and trying to find out what was happening. Instead, only God knew why, I was pulling out bread, lunchmeat, cheese, and mustard to make a sandwich.

Maybe the whole kidnapping thing was getting old. Maybe I'd become desensitized to the drama that was my life. Whatever it was, it came with a strange calm that I don't have words to describe. A calm that registered my physical needs first apparently. Because, you know, the sandwich.

"So, please tell me, where have you been? And have you heard from Shae?"

He was closer, probably a few feet behind me as I stood there at the counter spreading mustard on bread.

"No. And Radio station." I murmured, so quietly I barely heard it myself. Tomatoes. I needed tomatoes. And lettuce.

"I told you, I did a drive by, your bike wasn't there."

"Parked in the garage across the street," I mumbled through licking mustard from my finger before putting the lid back on the jar and turning to open the fridge.

50

He was quiet, but I could tell that he wasn't done.

I knew he had a ton of questions and probably more bad news, but I must have heard the worst of it already.

At least I thought I had, until what he said next floored me.

"Jorge, a friend of mine looking into the sitch about your parents called. Your dad had a stroke. He's at St. Luke's hospital in surgery. And your mom's in the waiting room having coffee. Alone."

52

Chapter 6

"Amanda Elizabeth Same! Explain yourself."

Those were words that meant my mom was beyond livid. As she should be. She had just been snatched out of a hospital waiting room by strangers, chloroformed, and dragged who knows where, only to wake up to her daughter she thought had been missing for over two years.

Did I happen to mention that my Grandmother had been harboring Ana and I away from her and my father's family in secret? Because that happened. With Macchio's help of course. It was good to have guardian angels that were also computer geniuses.

Since our departure, my parents had moved onto land secured by an entry gate and for some reason, had hired a security company that included round the clock guards on the premises. Getting to my mom in those circumstances would have taken a miracle. I sent up a silent prayer of gratitude at that thought. God had taken care of the hardest part for us.

And now Cheryl was on a flight headed this way from New York. Rick, having just arrived from Houston, was sitting on the table behind us, grinning. A mechanic and weapons expert with huge dimples and perfect brown skin, his wiry muscled frame hardly seemed capable of lugging around huge car parts and even bigger guns. But it was.

K.C. was here in St. Louis too, or at least, that's what Rick said. Neither of us had any idea why, though.

He'd returned home to Baltimore right after RLS went down, taking a particularly famous Brainwaiver-ite with him when he did. Cheryl had commented on "the charity of southern gentlemen," being the cause of K.C.'s compassion toward the lady.

Rick had chuckled at the time, as if he knew something no one else knew. Since he and K.C. were both from Texas and served in the same Marine's unit, he probably did.

Back to my mom, the woman pacing this room that had been insulated, padded, and wired to cut off any communication, especially the tracking or controlling kind.

"I mean, honestly! TWO YEARS! Two years we've been looking for you and your sister! Two WHOLE years and not one phone call to tell me that you were alive and well!"

"Mom..." I tried, walking toward her only to stop quickly as her hand flew out to ward me off.

54

"No! Don't MOM me. You have no idea what I have gone through! The police! The FBI! Do you even know who else has been looking for you?"

"Mommy..." I whispered it, seeing the tears in her eyes as they echoed my own; filled with pain.

"I thought you were DEAD, Amanda." Her voice caught.

And that was all it took. There wasn't a force in the world that could have kept me from her. Or her from me, in that moment.

We collided and cried, gripping each other like we were afraid that the other would dissolve into air at any moment, holding tight to what had been a vital part of ourselves gone missing.

It was heaven. And it was hell. A joy to be reunited, and heartbreaking considering my next words.

"Daddy knew, Mom."

Still sniffling and wiping at her eyes with the tissue Rick had handed her, she smiled through more tears that refused to stop.

I was holding her right hand to my cheek with both of mine, savoring the touch of the one person, besides Ana, that had been completely innocent of wrongdoing in all of this.

"Knew what baby?"

My eyes were clenched tight. I prayed for God to give me the strength to say the words that would break my mother's heart and shatter her world.

"Uncle Devin. He knew."

My heart broke again as she snatched her hand away from me.

Her eyes were wide. She was backing away from me, her hair flying from side to side while shaking her head no. I could smell and feel the fear emanating from her as her gaze flew from Rick, to Cruz, to Robert and back to me.

"Who are these people?" Her whisper was the kind of whisper that reminded me of horror movies. The whisper victims of horrendous, bloody crimes spoke in right before they went missing and were never seen again.

"Mom," I hesitated... the situation was beyond fragile. We had no idea of how the programming would respond to her finding out the truth. And like a fool, I barreled into full disclosure without thought. I should have waited for Cheryl. But time was a luxury we didn't have. Shae was still missing.

"What have you done to my Daughter?" She shouted savagely, her hands contracting into claws as her focus intensified on Cruz.

I stepped in front of him so that her focus could return to me.

"Momma, I need you to hear me... please."

I begged because the rapid side to side motion of her head had steadily increasing in force as I continued to speak.

"No, baby," she confirmed, "these people; these "church people"; they've brainwashed you..."

"I'm not brainwashed, Mom." I interrupted.

Her hands had gone from clawed to her armpits as her arms crossed. She paced again, still shaking her head no. I'd expected shock. Or some type of resurgence of the programming that had been used to keep her docile over the years. But this? I don't know what it is, this intense denial, but I had to get through to her. We had to disable that chip and remove the controls before my father's mother, currently in route, got to town.

"Mom, look at me."

She was mumbling now as she paced, clearly trying to shield herself from my words. Her arms were still crossed tightly, almost as if she were hugging herself or wearing a strait jacket.

And she wouldn't look at me. Or was it the simple fact that she couldn't look at me?

"Mom..." I swallowed hard. "Did you know?..."

The mumbling got louder. Loud enough for me to hear her words. Loud enough to hear her arguing with herself vehemently.

"No, they wouldn't do that, not to my babies. Yes, they would! They did it to you, they will do it to them, you have to stop them! NO! No, Edward isn't like them! He is! NO! LISTEN TO ME... NO!"

My heart, racing faster than it had ever been, felt as if it were being squeezed to death in my chest.

And tears of rage clouded my vision. Because my mother was obviously traumatized. Away from their Brainwaiver controls she was clearly experiencing the mental break of a person that had not just been mind controlled for years... but had been the victim of their

57

brutality herself. An experience she was now forced to relive through her children.

***

Cruz

"That's one hell of a status report." Max grouched through their cell phone connection and Cruz's earpiece. He couldn't help but agree. And what was worse, Cruz felt absolutely helpless in all of it. A state of being that Arpaio men didn't handle well.

"And Shae?"

Cruz unclenched his teeth to answer, "that's the thing; Amanda got a strange phone call from a pay phone outside of Georgia yesterday, right before Minute took her mom into surgery."

"And?" Max gruffed, his voice muffled like he'd shifted the phone away from his mouth.

Cruz hesitated. And what?

And... he couldn't tell his brother that he was, at that very moment, fighting with Amanda about travelling to Florida to pick up the trail that would hopefully lead to Shae.

Or that Amanda was so determined to go with him that she'd threatened to follow him down there on her bike if he didn't take her.

Last, he couldn't tell Max that, though he'd assured them that Amanda was not his type; he was wrong. She

58

was strong, vibrant and matchless in her womanhood already, despite her youth.

Her shrewd mind, quick intellect and obstinate nature had only increased the powerful attraction between them. An attraction he'd been fighting with a kung-fu grip since the day he'd seen her navigating the streets at high speed on that bike.

Cruz would have never described himself as hungry for a person or for affection from an individual. It was confounding and beyond confusing to admit the truth of where his desires lay.

But he wasn't a man to lie to himself. That kind of habit was self-defeating. Reality checks were a consistent exercise of self talk where his life was concerned.

Like the reality that, while he was a United States Marshall, his assignment regarding the Notorious Ones Motorcycle gang had been the last thing on his mind for at least three weeks. Then there were his "less than lawful" activities. Born and raised in the heart of Miami, Cruz had friends that were gang members and cops alike. He knew the streets like the back of his hand and still did very well on the education front, from college, to the academy, to his appointment as a Marshall.

Thus, Cruz had no problem "coloring outside the lines" when it came to problem-solving. Like how Amanda's bike was considered "evidence" and as such, supposedly in police custody in an impound, stashed away. Only it wasn't. Because it suited his purpose for her to be mobile. And beyond spending every minute of the day with her transporting her everywhere, there was no way he could ensure that she could be mobile with a fast escape out of danger without said transportation.

Plus, baby girl was good on that bike. Good in a way that he respected as someone who rides, and as a man. There was nothing sexier than a woman on a motorcycle. Just seeing her mount the thing gave him chills.

Since he couldn't tell his brother ANY of that, he settled on revealing the information closest to the truth that wouldn't have Max hunting him down to kill him.

"I'm investigating. The site where the girls were being held has been cleared, no evidence found other than what could have been a drunken rave. It's a dead end with no hint to where the gang relocated. Boss agrees with me that, for now, Shae's our only clue. So, I get to follow the breadcrumbs and see what happens."

Max was quiet for a moment, probably processing the second part of that message, the first part – that the gang had relocated, being something he already knew.

Finally, when he spoke with his usual gravity, it left Cruz more unsettled than before.

"Take care of yourself. I've got a bad feeling. Check on your mother and the girls before you head out. Love you."

Disconnect. The disconnect was the usual Max. But the rest of that message? Not so much. Though they shared the same mother, Max had been at odds with her for years. He never mentioned their mom. While they consistently checked in on their sisters and younger

60

brother, mom was always conspicuously absent from any of their conversations.

Staring at the phone for longer than he realized, the push from behind brought Cruz's thoughts hurtling back to his present, frustrating situation.

"We doing this or what?" Said a leather clad Amanda; her Barbie going biking outfit complete with Raybans in hair caught up in a ponytail. It was a good look on her. A look that called to the man in him. Praying silently to God to somehow rescue him from this, Cruz tried hard not to stare.

"This is not a good idea. Stay here. I promise, I'll stay in touch and keep you posted."

POP. Cruz rolled his eyes. Really, with the bubble gum? Trying hard to forget how in love he was with Nick at Nite as a kid, thus his many fantasies about Pinky Tuscadero from the show Happy Days, Cruz mentally cursed. She was going to be the death of him. And sadly, he knew that, just with one taste of her, he'd die happy.

"Don't get on my nerves." Is what his conflicted mind settled on announcing before hopping into the driver side of his black Charger.

It was her answering grin as she slid in and closed his passenger side door that told Cruz everything he needed to know about this trip. He was a dead man walking.

61

62

Chapter 7

Amanda

"Calm down and tell me again what she said."
I deep sighed, trying to compose myself before Cruz came back from pumping gas. Still not sure where I stood with Balboa, I'd called the next best thing to help with the fact that Shae's trail had gone cold.

"Nina, I told you three times already..."

"And you were about to tell me again, this time calmly, instead of wasting time telling me what we both already know."
I tried hard not to roll my eyes. But I knew what I'd gotten myself into when I'd called her.

Nina Irwin was a five-foot two dynamo that lived life according to her own rules. Much like Balboa, she was attitude-on-steroids. Unlike Balboa, Nina was rarely moved by compassion. Her cynical outlook on life most likely resulted from her dishonorable discharge in the military.

I'd overheard Ms. Baltimore mention something about her decking her CO once. Whatever the case may be, while Nina was not nearly as easy to talk to as Balboa, she was a mobile arsenal. Dangerous in the extreme, folks that knew her handled her with care. Having settled on investigator and bounty hunter as her chosen field, she was also the best resource out there when tracking someone down, next to Max.

So, I swallowed my frustration and repeated my tense phone call with Shae for the third time. Reliving it, yet again.

"Mandy I'm lost."

"What do you mean lost, where are you? I'll come get you."

"NO! I just need you to get me to a highway... I need to get to Miami."

"What's in Miami, give me the address where you are!"

"Sanctuary. I have to find sanctuary. I'll find it in Miami if I... Crap, they found me, I have to go..."

"Wait," Nina shouted into the phone, nearly busting my ear drum, "last time you said safety; that she needed to find safety. Was it safety or sanctuary?"

"What difference does it..." I started and was cut off.

64

"You're wasting time again. If it didn't make a difference I wouldn't have bothered to ask. Now was it safety or sanctuary?"

"Sanctuary," I gritted through clenched teeth, "I'm pretty sure it was sanctuary."

"Texting you an address; your contact there is Lace. When you get there ask for her and mention Balboa. No, wait. Give her Balboa's legal name, Denise Ferry. Tell her Niecy sent you."

***

The old church was huge. I mean HUGE. Situated in Little Havana or, as the locals called it "Calle Ocho" (assumed inspiration for the name of Balboa's old gang, the Latin Ocho's) it sat at the corner of Southwest 8th Street. Once an old Presbyterian monolith, the dusty peach tinged building loomed over the block like the nuns of old, ruler in hand, ready to pounce on the smallest infraction.

Miami, Florida. Far from like the Midwest where farmland was the scenic route outside of urban cities, beauty and culture exploded on every corner.

There was the terra cotta artwork, mud adobe housing and graffiti mixed in with beautiful floral palm trees, amazing modern architecture, and glass high rises closer to downtown.

And then there was the Miami Beach. I remember how my mom laughingly talked about a rap song when I was a kid by Will Smith, Welcome to Miami. She'd sing and giggle quietly to me and baby Ana. My dad's family frowned on such things; but Mom had always been down to earth. At least until she wasn't. My tenth birthday had been the last time my mother giggled with us in secret.

It had been the last time she had really been herself. Until now. Anxious to get back to her after a successful surgery, I wanted Shae found quick, fast and in a hurry. That said, Cruz must have felt my agitation, seeing as how we were going at least ninety miles an hour the entire way here.

Yes, I exaggerate I'm sure, I don't really know how fast we were going, but it FELT fast, and that's all that mattered to me.

I blinked realizing that, while I gathered wool about the strange building, Cruz had exited the driver side and was halfway up the steps.

"Dude," I fussed, hurrying out of the passenger side, almost killing myself as my purse caught on the window edge as I'd slammed the door.

"Crap," I yelled, reopening the door to grab my purse.

Hearing Cruz snort, my eyes narrowed. I made my way quickly up the steps just as the huge wooden door opened.

"Yeah?" Asked a saucy brunette with eyes so hazel they were gold. Eyes that looked Cruz up and down twice before landing on me with a grin from their owner.

I felt my face tense but fought the reaction. So, she liked what she saw. It wasn't my business, was it?

But it felt like my business, a fact that her grin told me she didn't miss.

Feeling another gaze burning through the side of my face, I glanced at Cruz. And didn't get it.

His stare was intense, like he was gauging my reaction. A reaction that I carefully schooled my features to hide. This was something that frustrated me to no end, also something we didn't have time for.

"Looking for Lace, "I barreled ahead, shifting my attention back to the woman; trying desperately to ignore my face heating under Cruz's continued scrutiny.

Dude, look away already! My brain shouted.

"Who's looking," The brunette asked, her arms crossing over her chest. The smile was gone from her eyes; they were narrowed now, and I could feel a different kind of heat singe the air.

"Names Amanda, tell her Bal – Denise, Denise Ferry sent me. Niecy sent me."

"Wait here." The brunette snapped before slamming the door in our faces.

"Nice going champ."

I gave Cruz the side eye before completely ignoring his snark. He'd taken to calling me champ on the trip down, a reference I didn't get at all. But it was better than baby girl. That sounded way too intimate to me.

"Why'd you turn all pink?" he asked next.

Apparently, the side eye didn't send the message I wanted it to. This time I turned a blank stare to the man I was coming to love to hate, blinked twice, then turned back to focus on the ugly wooden door.

Don't ask me how I knew, but I just knew he was laughing at me in his head.

Before I could turn to confirm my suspicion, the old door came flying open.

On the threshold now was a dark eyed, curvy Latina, standing well over six feet four inches. A FROWNING dark eyed, curvy GIANT Latina was probably a better description.

Any person with sense would have taken a step back out of range from a woman that looked like she juggled kegs in the air for entertainment.

We didn't have time for common sense, or fear for that matter.

"You Lace?" I asked, ready to get this done and find Shae.

"And you are?" She asked back, her voice melodic and calm, a complete oxymoron of her appearance.

Still, we were short on time, so I didn't allow that to give me pause.

"Niecy sent me to you; I have a friend, a runaway that came here looking for Sanctuary. We're trying to see if she found it."

"You mean found us." Lace stated, her stare narrowing.

I looked to Cruz on this one. I was thrown why the distinction was made and communication wasn't my strongest skill beyond being direct.

"Si, mamacita," Cruz responded, garnering Lace's full attention.

"This is Sanctuary, right?" Cruz asked, his smile all charming and adorably icky. It made me want to barf.

"Si, Cabron." Lace responded; her eyes gone from narrow to wide in wonderment at Cruz's smile. My stomach turned as my mind urged me to focus.

They were speaking now in fluent Spanish, something I'd never mastered past greetings and numbers. So, fighting the urge to glance off into nothing like someone intruding on an otherwise intimate moment, I did what I never do. Be rude.

"Does any of that mean you've seen my friend or not?"

The abrupt silence of Cruz and Lace was my first clue that all was not well in Miami. Cruz's snort was my second.

The third was an ugly wooden door slamming in my face.

I don't know why I was surprised. One look at Lace and I could tell, despite the deception of a calm voice, she had more attitude than the law should allow. While part of me didn't blame her because, I too have that kind of moxy as my Granny calls it; the other part of me stubbornly asserted that she was rude first, leaving us on the front porch and flirting with my... with Cruz, right in my face.

I was two seconds from banging on the door rudely and surely compounding one mistake on top of another, when I heard Spanish arguing coming from the other side.

The door began to creep slowly open as the brunette with laughing gold eyes waved us in with one finger over her mouth, her gaze telling me that she was more than amused.

The arguing got louder as Cruz and I stepped over the threshold and caught sight of the arguers in question.

Lace loomed over a dark-haired woman that could have been biracial yet there was definitely Latina in the mix. Amazingly, completely unfazed by the looming, the gorgeous brunette with gold streaked hair caught in a sleek updo jabbed her finger right into Lace's face, shouting, "Silencio! Not another word or you get bathroom duty for the next two weeks! Think it's a game, Laciana! Keep trying my patience with your foolishness and I will snatch. Your. Throat. OUT!

Oy Vey! The two startled gazes of said women flew in my direction, making me bite my lips. Hard. Because I'd did it again, hadn't I? Apparently, I'd said that out loud.

Chapter 8

Chara Hernandez, also known as Coco, led Cruz and I into a surprisingly swank conference room on the second floor of the old monastery.

I say swank because, not only did it look like a conference room in one of those fancy hotels, at the east end lay three tables decked with goodies and the life giving elixir that I could not get to fast enough. Carafe boxes with Starbucks logos danced before me like a siren call.

So enraptured by the call, I missed the first five minutes of conversation between Coco and Cruz. And would have missed more as I moved on autopilot, mixing in my creamer and Splenda, then sitting next to Cruz, eyes closed, with the cup to my face just allowing the aroma to take me to a better place... until I heard...

"Don't mind her, she's been jonesing for coffee for two whole days now. Coffee snobs like her think gas station coffee is akin to poison."

My eyes popped open at that. And narrowed into a venomous side-eye as I took my first sip. Only to close again. I refused to let the heathen ruin what was obviously God's gift to all of creation.

"No problem, I've been there myself. Believe me, everyone here knows not to even speak to me before I'm on my second cup. This room stays equipped with fresh coffee and pastries all day long. Sanctuary don't do things halfway."

Grinning at a newfound sister in the club of Starbuck-oholics, I took another sip. Oh man. I wondered if she would let us take a box with us.

Cruz was summing up our search for Shae and what led us to Sanctuary as I took time to simply enjoy my coffee and observe.

A people watcher since I was way young, very few people fascinated me these days. Chara Hernandez made the cut as one of those few.

Dressed in a fitted button-down silk blouse the color of eggshell and a gray pinstripe pencil skirt, the woman exuded class in an earthy fashion that somehow came off sexy and calming at the same time. I needed to take notes. My current fashion tastes of black leather for bike riding or jeans and tees for everything else could definitely use a come up.

I think it was the sleek updo that gave her such a professional appearance, while her chocolate brown gaze was full of welcome and warmth. Coco was obviously the boss around here, confident in ways I longed to be. She reminded me a lot of Balboa in fact. Only, without the same edge... Balboa was a whirlwind that came to town, wrecked the place, then, with a wink and a smile, barreled out; leaving you to clean up the damage, somehow feeling like you were blessed by her presence and should be honored.

Coco was like a calm and soothing rain. She exuded peace. It was easy to relax in her presence. It was into this lull of tension that Bette Jimenez (Bet) and Ramona Oaxaca (Rho) entered, immediately changing that vibe.

Obviously, enforcers, as Coco introduced them, the ladies meandered calmly to the table for goodies and cups of coffee before taking their seats across from Cruz and me.

Feeling Cruz tense, I immediately took stock of the doors, windows and potential weapons I'd noted upon entering the room. Then I took another sip and focused on the threats.

Bet was about five feet, nine inches. Like Coco, she was a brunette but with extreme gold and blond highlighted tresses tied back with a bandana "painter style", big hazel eyes clearly seen behind a set of librarian style glasses, and a cupid nose complete with a bow mouth that probably drove men crazy.

Buxom and hippy, her hourglass figure went well with the tee she wore that had SANCTUARY scrawled across the front atop black jeans. Her feet were clad in a

73

pair of Lebron James sneakers and the only jewelry she wore appeared to be some type of smart watch.

Rho, however, was a slim five feet seven inches. Her hair had an auburn tinge (at least the tendrils that fell along the side of her face did) and was mostly hidden under a black ball cap that said "Sanctuary", matching what appeared to be a uniform of the same outfit Bet was wearing. Eyes so brown that they were black, there was a shrewd look about her. As her fingers were sporting several rings, all big and clunky; I took her for what she was - a brawler. Probably their weapons specialist, she reminded me a lot of Nina. It was easy to envision her handling guns, knives or just about any weapon you could think of.

While Bet sat up straight, at attention almost, like she had military training, Rho slouched back in her chair. Confidence exuded from every pore of her. Weapons specialist was a definite in my mind. I would have bet my entire savings that she had at least three knives and a gun on her right then.

"You mentioned Niecy referred you us, tell me... how do you know her, exactly?"

Coco still maintained her calm and professional mien, but I saw that question for what it was. She was testing us.

Confident that Cruz could charm his way out of anything involving estrogen, I relaxed and took another sip. We didn't have any nefarious intentions here, so, as far as I was concerned, we had nothing to worry about.

"She and my brother are in a relationship, sort of. It's complicated," Cruz finished as I choked on my coffee because what? Balboa and Max? Since when?

A grinning Coco leaned back, her gaze shifting left and right between Cruz and me.

"You disagree?" She asked me, her chin up as she asked indicating to me that it was my turn to speak.

"Uh. I... ," clearing my throat, I settled on the truth and full disclosure; I didn't know why but, despite the open threat in the room with enforcers sitting right across from me, I really didn't think these people were out to hurt anyone that wasn't out to hurt them.

"To you she's Niecy. To me she's Balboa. Like, my mentor and a mother figure. If there is a relationship between her and uh, "my side eye to Cruz noted his grin before I continued, "Max, it was probably kept hidden from me. The truth is, she's not very happy with my choices right now and warned me about Shae. She wouldn't like to know that I'm down here searching for her."

"Ah." Coco leaned back and announced through her smile, an act that somehow sent a message I couldn't translate, one that caused the entire room to relax. Feeling the tension dissipate, I took another sip and realized my cup was almost empty already. Dang.

"Thank you for that. Please understand, what we do here is extremely sensitive and we are very private people. Before we could discuss anything, I needed to know that you could be trusted with privileged information. That said, I won't ask how you know about

Sanctuary when it's obvious that you haven't spoken to... Balboa, right?"

I relaxed again in my seat, not realizing how tense I'd just become. Glad she didn't ask about how we knew to come here, I didn't realize my head had tilted in question to "privileged information" until she further explained.

"Bet here ran facial recognition software on you, Amanda Same. She found you in several data bases including the FBI which was interesting. She also found you registered as a student at the University of Missouri in St. Louis with Denise Ferry listed as one of your emergency contacts. I know Niecy well. Mentoring and training is her thing. The way you took in the room as soon as you entered, noting the exits and possible weapons all but confirmed that relationship. Your explanation suggested that you could trust us with the truth, therefore I feel like I can trust you with who we are."

"And who are you, exactly?" I asked, curiosity getting the best of me. Probably because I was annoyingly out of coffee.

"Gangsta Nuns." Rho interjected, with a half grin. My jaw dropped. Because what?

"Uh..." My gaze skittered from Rho, to a fully grinning Bet, back to a Coco who was rolling her eyes, then back to Rho again. "Gangsta what?"

"Nuns." Rho repeated. I felt Cruz's bouncing body next to me, an indication that he somehow found this explanation hilarious.

"First off, we are not nuns," Coco stated, her voice edged with exasperation, "Gangsta Nuns is what the kids just call us around here. By around here, I mean Calle Ocho; it is the former home of the Latin Ocho's gang we were once part of. Said gang that is now a 501c3 organization long since turned from tearing down the community to building it up.

We had Niecy to thank for that. Denise Ferry was one of our former lieutenants. She did what no other could have accomplished before or after her – put the Latin Ocho's on the path. A path that God has kept us on ever since.

So, we aren't Nuns. We are, however, sisters that own and operate the same apartment building smack in the middle of the hood. The building is known by the locals as Sanctuary because it used to be an old church. But we like to live up to the name. They also call it sanctuary due to the resource center for the youth in the basement where we conduct bible studies, leadership classes and sponsor youth basketball, volleyball, and indoor soccer leagues.

Last, they call it that because the people (especially the women in our community) know that if there is ever a problem, ever a situation where they find themselves in danger, they can seek shelter here.

Law enforcement works with us to keep our community and our most vulnerable citizens – that's women, children, and the elderly - safe. But there are times when the law has gray areas. It's during those times that we get a little... creative. Which is why the kids call us Gangsta Nuns. To them we are old G's or "original gangstas". Not because of our former gang affiliation but because if you mess with our people... if you even think about coming for them. We come for you first. We will start the fight and finish it. If the law can't help us, we will help ourselves. In the name of Jesus, of course."

"Of course," Cruz laughed.

Wow. My mouth was probably hanging open. I know for sure that I hadn't blinked since Coco started explaining. Did I say I wanted to be like Balboa when I grew up? Because I totally wanted to be like Balboa! These women were my tribe! Much like the Slick Chicks, it was obvious that they had their own code of honor and they took care of their people. While the Slick Chicks "people" were limited to the women at the shelter, Sanctuary had taken on an entire community.

It was like sitting in a house full of Balboa's! Was I wrong to want to stay here forever?

Chapter 9

Cruz

"Are you sure that was her on the video?" Cruz sighed. He hated repeating himself.

"I said it was, Max."

"So, she found the place but didn't enter. Just got into some random car and drove off? Is that what you're telling me?"

"That's what I just said, yeah. You need to tell everyone to be on guard."

"We stay on guard. Sam and CeCe just got back from their honeymoon. I got this. I'll put a trace on that license plate and see what happens."

Cruz grunted. "You telling Balboa?"

Hearing his brother's tired sigh through the phone made Cruz tense.

"She's got enough to worry about. What did Mandy say when she saw the recording?"

Cruz shrugged, forgetting that his brother couldn't see him over the phone, then responded.

"Nothing. She kind of just... shut down."

"Explain." Max's voice was gruff. And Cruz knew why. His brother allowed very few people to enter his sphere of control. Those entering it usually owned his heart. Amanda and Ana Same were a few of those people, along with the team, their kids, Cruz and his sisters. A former FBI intelligence specialist, Max knew ways that people couldn't fathom about how to track people or cause them harm. And worried every single moment he drew breath for those he cared about because of it.

"I really can't. But we're on our way back so I'll keep you posted as soon as I get there."

That convo had taken place sixteen hours ago at a rest stop just outside of Georgia. As the crow flew, he and Amanda would be hitting St. Louis City limits in a couple hours.

Cruz's phone buzzed with an incoming text, a relief almost from the roaring silence coming from his passenger seat. Frowning, he glanced at Amanda, taking in her blank stare out her window and fisted hands. She had him worried. And Cruz was not a worrier. He was a doer and a fixer. It had been a long time since he'd run up on a problem or person he felt he couldn't help.

Amanda was quickly becoming so many "firsts" for him. From the beginning, the moment he saw her in that garage, Cruz felt as if Mandy was his responsibility. That

80

she was his to take care of. As such, not knowing where her head was at was more frustrating than it would be if it were the average person he couldn't read.

Checking the text, he accidently jolted them, having hit the brakes on reflex. The text was from Sam. MOS it said, right before listing Max's address.

MOS meant Military Occupational Specialty – it referred to the best job a soldier was suited for, verbiage Max used frequently requiring Cruz to do his research just to understand what his brother was saying. Cruz's specialty was, of course, his connections, being a United States Marshall. Whatever was happening, there was no way he could get there in time as they were just passing over the Illinois border. Quickly firing off a text denoting he was "out of range", Cruz hit the gas.

Praying silently, he gunned it, his odometer hitting ninety.

"Everything okay?" Amanda asked, her voice wooden and without inflection.

He didn't want to lie, so he shrugged. Thankfully, she wouldn't know what that meant since she wouldn't have gotten the text. None of the "kids" would have. Any member of the crew under twenty years old was off limits for calls to action.

Grip tightening on the steering wheel, Cruz prayed again. Because the bad feeling that Max had been complaining about, was all but choking him and, somehow, his gut confirmed disaster just rode into town on a hurricane. And his brother was the target.

81

***

Cruz couldn't believe what his eyes were seeing. He'd gotten back to town a day late and a dollar short, apparently.

As such, the still very beautiful but also very injured Balboa sitting on his brother's couch cuddled in blankets blew his mind.

Had anyone ever asked him, he would have told them that Balboa was immortal or something. Untouchable. The reality that she was anything but, however, was hard to ignore as he mentally digested all that had gone down.

Strung up and beaten, somehow the woman had taunted her captor into letting her down, completely thwarting Max's planned rescue as he walked in to find her kicking tail. With a broken rib no less.

And finding out that KC had been there because he'd been blackmailed, his lady friend having been put in a coma somehow, had Cruz shaking his head in more disbelief. In the end, miraculously, K.C. had gotten the call that his woman was somehow healed right before he was called upon to act against Balboa or Max. Not that he would have, anyway. K.C. was solid; he would have found a way to circumvent the situation, Cruz was sure.

Relieved that he'd dropped Amanda at the new safehouse (he wasn't taking any chances because Shayla could be friend or foe so they'd relocated again) along with arranging for her mother to be moved there as well for a much needed reunion.

At least that would be keeping Amanda busy while he figured out how he was going to break the news to her that Balboa had been hurt. She was going to be crushed. The last words between them had been filled with pain and betrayal. Amanda was the type that internalized everything. There was no way she wouldn't blame herself for this, though she couldn't possibly have done anything to prevent it.

Having already passed on another tip about the motorcycle gang and trafficking ring he'd received from his boss to Nina before they'd gotten back, Cruz breathed a sigh of relief. At least his investigation was being covered by someone who had his back.

Because the fact that there was more shocking news, this time about Ana, had him deep breathing to keep from being completely stressed out.

Apparently, Ana was no longer "autistic".

"Faking it." Max declared, taking another bite of his apple as he gingerly sat next to Balboa and took her gently into his hold.

It wasn't hard to read Cruz's expression considering Balboa had just dropped that particular bomb literally one second before.

Amanda was going to lose her mind.

"The whole time?" Cruz tried to confirm, a lump of disbelief wedged in his throat.

"Just from the time after she'd received the implant." Balboa confirmed, snuggling deeper into Max, again.

His brother had finally pulled the plug out of his behind that had kept him from claiming the woman. Max was gone for Balboa for as long as Cruz could remember him wanting anyone besides the girl he'd loved when he was barely twenty; a tragic story Cruz never allowed himself to fully think about.

Balboa's life being at stake had been the catalyst. And Cruz didn't blame him one bit. If Balboa were his, after that little misadventure, he wouldn't allow her out of his sight, not for a minute, not for a day.

Which is why he had to remind himself sternly that Amanda was NOT his. It was acceptable for him to leave her at the safe house with her mom, especially when no one else knew where he'd stashed her. But he didn't feel like it was acceptable. Thus, his anxious pacing while he listened with fascination to everything that he'd missed.

"Where is she now?"

"Who?" Max asked, his attention fully on Balboa as he gently moved her hair out of her face.

Oh brother. Cruz strained to keep his eyes from rolling.

"Ana. Where is she now?"

"At Balboa's."

Nodding, Cruz asked the next question that would affect the one woman who had somehow, in the span of weeks, become his world.

"Does she know about her Mom yet?"

Max's somber gaze collided with his in a look so knowing, Cruz swallowed hard to keep the lie of his feigned unconcern from slipping.

"She does. Not because we told her though."

Brow furrowed and arms crossing, Cruz asked the obvious question.

"Then how?"

Max shrugged, while Balboa, appearing to nap answered instead.

"Girl's a freaking genius whose IQ rivals Max's. She's been literally charting our every move and then some."

Cruz said it before he realized that he'd officially taken on Amanda's bad habits, "Oy, Vey."

To whit Balboa nodded and sleepily mumbled, "Exactly."

Part TWO: CHANGING TIMES

Chapter 10

Amanda

"So, what, you're not going to open this one either?"

I could feel my teeth grinding as I walked past the room filled with my sister and residents, past the dining room table where a small pink gift box sat with a gray bow and card beneath it, into the kitchen and out the back door.

He'd done it again. No matter the many times I refused them from the postal person or, in last year's case, dropped it off at Max and Balboa's without saying one word (just my chicken scratch on the unaddressed side of the envelope expressing my sentiment on the issue. That sentiment being, "TELL HIM TO LEAVE ME THE HELL ALONE," in all caps); he kept at it.

Today would make six years. It was my twenty-fourth birthday. And, despite what they say about time healing all wounds, this one hadn't gotten any better.

Falling into the porch swing Rob and Danny had installed for my girls, I tried to lose myself in the back and forth motion. Rob was still my best friend, if a little distant lately. Graduating one year before me, he'd received his degree in Journalism from UMSL. Inquisitive by nature and way too direct for his own good, Rob had found the perfect vocation. Danny (Daniel Sampson), or Dan, as he demanded we call him now, had returned home from Mizzou, a University in Columbia, Missouri, to enroll into Washington University's School of Law. Currently a six-year student, he would be completing all coursework this fall and take the Bar exam. As Dan and Rob were also best friends from way back, I figured that my not seeing Rob much these days had something to do with Dan's return home. Mentally, I shrugged. I never considered myself a possessive person, so that thought didn't bother me. Except when it came to Cruz Arpaio. Which brought my mind in a full circle, back to that box. I tried to distract myself again and meditate on the devotion I'd read this morning, but that little pink box was insistent.

Probably because last year it had been blue with a brown bow. The year before that, yellow with a green bow. And the year before that it was a red box with a black bow. I had every year memorized, etched into my mind like the statue of David was etched in stone.

Receiving each one had been more painful than the last, a constant reminder of the day my soul was shredded to pieces.

I shook my head, still amazed at my own naivety. What did I think would happen? Did I think he'd marry me? Move back to Seattle with me? Give me a son with hair so black it was blue and caramel colored eyes just like his dad? It wasn't like I was anything special. I was Amanda Elizabeth Same; my last name, somehow, a prophecy of my status in life. I didn't stand out. I was not exceptional. I was just me. The same as every other average person. Even Ana dwas some uber-genius that would give Max a run for his money in a brain race. She, like Balboa, Celine, Max and, even Cruz, was truly exceptional.

"You need to forgive and let go."

My thoughts had conjuring her presence somehow. Ana, my baby sister. She'd been a constant at my side these last five years as co-founder of the project closest to my heart. Her words echoed in my head as she dropped to my side on the swing to lay her head on my shoulder.

I snorted then felt her body shake beside me. Knowing she was laughing, I bounced my shoulder, jiggling her head.

"Get off me." I growled, not really all that serious about it. The truth was, I loved it when little snippets of her former innocent nature peeked through the genius she'd become after receiving the implant.

Of course, she would be the one to urge me to forgive. Considering my rage upon finding out she'd lied to me for over two and a half years, she understood better than anyone how I could hold a grudge.

It had taken almost a full year and endless nagging from mom and grandma (both happily relocated after my return to the Colorado mountains) to talk me around.

I took my sister's profile in with a side eye and begrudgingly accepted that my Ana was full grown. At twenty-one, her white blonde hair was shorn into a curly pixie cut that framed her gorgeous face perfectly. Wide sienna brown eyes, a slightly upturned nose just like mine and mom's, and a full set of pink lips had turned her kewpie doll persona into a full-blown hottie. Not to mention how she shot up ten inches during her fifteenth year, putting her four inches taller than me. Another change I found hard to get used to.

Amazingly enough, no one could have ever told me before Ana was exposed that I was one to hold a grudge.

Year nineteen had been the age of discovery for me.

I'd found out a lot of things about myself. Things that God would no longer allow me to ignore with excuses.

Seemingly reading my thoughts, Ana continued as if I'd just spoken out loud.

"All of that unforgiveness is eating you up inside. I hate seeing you like this."

I shrugged, bouncing her head again, not trusting my voice. Pain clawed at my throat like a wild animal. I deep breathed to keep calm.

Using facts that I knew would regain my equilibrium, I focused on the events of the past. Events that gave me this job and our new home. Sanctuary Sorority House.

You could say that my trip to Miami was pivotal to my future aspirations. Meeting the "Gangsta Nuns" and observing their management of the beautiful low-income housing facility that doubled as a community center woke something up in me.

Upon my return to UMSL, my major changed from communications to Social and Behavioral Sciences. Not social work. Social Sciences. I needed to understand how our society could allow such atrocities to exist in a day where technology could literally solve almost every problem.

I needed to comprehend the beast called "world systems" that would purposely institute false dichotomies of social class to reinforce and strengthen an already failed system's narrative. And I needed to obtain some kind of closure about the ritualistic practices of European family lines, how such practices had come to America. And why Ana, mom and I had to be victims of it.

Reasoning that the more I understood all of this the quicker I'd heal, I threw myself into my studies. It was in my second year, in August, that horrifying events in my city led me to another change.

The senseless killing of Michael Brown in Ferguson, Missouri. A killing that occurred less than 10 miles from my apartment complex.

Our apartment complex. Hurrying past that thought and the painful knoll it clanged in my chest, I remembered instead, the riots, the city-wide protests and the senseless burning of a small municipality.

Balboa and Max had come home early from their honeymoon. She'd seen on the television what those of us sitting right here had completely missed. That some of those stirring up trouble and rioting possessed the right eye twitch associated with Waivers – unliberated Brainwaiver-ites (now called BWs)

Max, also a recipient of forced implantation, had a unique perspective and gift other BW's didn't have. Like Ana, he could see stuff in code. It would take Ana to explain the science behind it all, and even when she did, I still didn't get it. All I know is that some dude he knew when he worked for the government had implanted him for the sole reason of harvesting his memories and knowledge. Whatever had transpired due to that procedure had made Max a totally different kind of BW.

Again, it would take Ana to explain it. All I know, is that Max was so good at predicting odds, he could predict future events with ninety seven percent accuracy. Creepy, yes. Useful for college sophomores that insisted on being a part of the protests with Rob and Dan (who'd left his first year at Mizzou to be closer to home)? Absolutely!

We didn't get arrested despite attending several protests, including the one at the Galleria where a bunch of folks were taken into custody. It wasn't just about protesting though. It was recon and reporting on the Waivers present at the rallies. Once we reported our findings to Max we were told to leave immediately.

I'm still not clear on what he, Balboa, and the Sampsons did with that knowledge; I didn't know then and I still don't want to know. Whatever it was, it required Cheryl and Rick to grab hotel rooms in Richmond Heights until both could arrange for long term accommodations.

Watching our justice system and the farce that ensued, much like with the Trevon Martin case had motivated me to make another change in my major. I switched to Criminal Justice with an emphasis on Racial and Minority Justice. Social reform wasn't going to happen in a day, I knew. But between the rampant human trafficking that I saw with my own eyes in my city, and the racial injustice that Mike Brown's situation opened my eyes to, I was determined to throw my hat in the ring, so to speak.

Enrolling in an accelerated course of study that spring, I obtained my Bachelor's degree in two and a half years. My Master's Degree in Social Justice only took a year to complete online at Clairmont-Lincoln University. Two weeks ago, I defended my dissertation on identifying and purposefully disbanding racial injustice in the Midwest.

And during all of this, my newly opened eyes saw what my time in Alton and Seattle allowed me to remain blinded to. The downtrodden, the hurting; the souls within societies walls also known as misfits. The numbers for disenfranchised students at UMSL alone were staggering, with Midwest statistics rating off the charts.

I had to do something. I volunteered at shelters and food pantries. I started organizations at church that would take us from home to home, meeting needs and ministering the love of God. I worked in food lines, with seniors in nursing homes and adopted families for holiday gifts and provision.

Still, it wasn't enough.

Three years ago, I was awakened out of a sound sleep by absolutely nothing. No outside or inside sounds that I could tell. Just me in my bed, sweating. One word rang in my psyche over and over, calling me to yet more action. SANCTUARY.

It was a word that became a mission. A mission that had led Ana and me to founding the first ever national college organization that catered to struggling college students.

Sanctuary Sorority House. My haven, my heart and, feeling the cool breeze kiss my cheek I closed my eyes as I realized, my hope for deliverance from an empty, numb life.

"So, we're setting the house on fire now cause of an ATTITUDE?" yelled from the kitchen in Destiny's high, screeching voice was all it took to catapult me and Ana out of the swing and running toward the back door.

Oy Vey.

Chapter 11

Seven months, two days later...

I stared at my computer screen trying to catch my breath.

"You there?"

Chara's voice was steady and calming as it reverberated from my cell in speaker mode from my desk.

"I'm here," I breathed, forcing the words out of my throat past some invisible blockage.

"That footage is from last week. I got a call from a very agitated Maximillian Caruso this morning giving me deets on his missing brother and an ultimatum to find him."

I almost choked on my next breath. Chara, I remembered was like a calmer Balboa in most aspects.

Except probably one. Neither of them did ultimatums. Something Chara went on to confirm, sounding miffed.

"I don't have to tell you how much I don't like it my ex-lieutenant's man is calling me about his missing brother, almost accusing me and mine while doing it, only to wrap up said call with threats, do I?"

No. No she didn't. The fact that Max called them without Balboa running interference as these were, her people, meant one thing. Balboa didn't know. This was tantamount to waving a red flag in front of a bull. Chara was the bull. And her sights had just landed on me.

Which lead to another concern that caused fear and pain to zing through my tight chest. Balboa's pregnancy had been a difficult one. Remanded to bed rest for the last few months (a command she hardly obeyed), she had been ordered to take leave from work and avoid stress at all costs.

The threat of miscarriage was so great that Max had done the unthinkable; and I don't blame him.

Max didn't normally keep things from her. Not just because he loved the woman like bears loved honey, but because her mind for strategy was unmatched. It had to be for a 12-year-old to fight for (and win) a status position in a gang, work up the ranks, then shift the primary objective from victimizing the community to helping its people. That being a whole other story, I had this mess to deal with.

I was going to need all hands-on deck for this one.

"... care what you need to do to figure this out and find him, but you need to do it. Or I'm making that call.

And it won't matter, whatever the reason that he doesn't want my sister to know what's happening; she'll know. Unless there's something you wanna tell me?"

I bit my lip and blinked. If I told Chara what was up, she'd be less upset and more likely to work with me to get this done. But Balboa would find out. Don't ask me how. I just know she would. Then I'd catch hell like you wouldn't believe. A hell that might stress her out putting her and the baby in danger.

Something that I had no doubt, beloved unrelated uncle or not, Max would kill me for.

My silence spoke louder than a resounding no, so I let it answer for me. Chara's deep sigh from the other end of the connection indicated her recognition of that fact.

"Find him Same. Get this done. If I have to, it won't be pretty." Click.

I had no doubts of that. In fact, I had a sneaky suspicion that Chara had downplayed the threat.

Staring at the video footage of Cruz, arms folded and in the face of some woman, probably a lover or something, I snarled. I'd heard of his womanizing over the years. Tales that poured salt into the open wounds he'd left behind.

Moving to shut down the video clip feed, I jerked when a sudden hand movement on the woman's part, her finger now jabbing in the direction of Cruz's face, gave me pause.

Leaning closer to the screen, my suspicion flared into full recognition.

Shae. I didn't have long to wait for what happened next. That hand was snatched and pulled away by a man appearing out of nowhere. As it was black and white footage, it was difficult to make out the hair color or anything distinctive about him, other than the fact that he was gigantic.

My memory stirred again. Pulling Shae away was obviously his intent, however what happened next would have blown my mind if I wasn't so pissed. The once passive and friendly Shae not only snatched her hand out of what had to be an iron clad grip but executed a perfect right hook on the guy. Cruz, who'd been moving to help her apparently, stopped suddenly, his mouth hanging open. I didn't blame him. Mine was too.

And Shae wasn't done. Following her punch with a well-placed knee, dude went down like a struck tree in the woods. I couldn't stop the grudging admiration building in my gut. She'd survived. And learned to protect herself. With that came the sense of relief that Balboa (more importantly I) had been wrong all along. Even so, my anger was oddly fueled by this realization.

Sadly, Shae's defense skills didn't include taking on multiple attackers. She and Cruz were swarmed by several men, obviously Caucasian sporting leather and bandanas, similar to the first. Pulling away from the computer screen I almost missed what happened next. In fact, I would have completely missed it had Chara not zoomed in with a close up from one of their perimeter cameras.

Big man hadn't stayed incapacitated for long. As the camera zoomed into a close up of him getting up and stretching like a cat awakening from a nap instead of somebody who'd just gotten kneed in the gonads, I felt my jaw drop a second time.

His head had turned slowly with his gaze lifting to where he obviously knew a camera, or someone was watching him. His right eye twitched. And then he grinned.

Full recognition hit me. It was the behemoth from the warehouse. Six years faded completely as a new and real fear clutched my chest. And that fear had a name. Brody.

My reaction sounded distant, like it was miles away. Yet and still, I could feel my quick inhalation of shock segue into a snarl, ending as a growl through gritted teeth.

"I overheard. Help's on the way."

Rage clouded my vision as I glanced toward my office door where Ana now stood.

My nod was quick and tight, my neck stiff as I turned to refocus on the screen.

Ana always seemed one step ahead right when I needed her most. Which was good. Because we were going to need all the help we could get.

***

Anabella Same
Just outside of Sanctuary Sorority House
2 hours later...

Ignoring the liquid bronze – gold eyes burning into her back, Ana greeted Rob with arms open, receiving a mighty bear hug for her efforts. She grimaced, hiding her gritted teeth in his chest. Having gained at least thirty pounds of pure muscle over the years, his bear hugs were no longer "cute and cuddly".

Pulling back to draw air into her tight ribs, she hesitated on just this side of rude before turning to acknowledge the bane of her existence.

"Do I get a hug or what?" She settled on, her hand on her hip with attitude. Ever since he'd found out that she wasn't autistic (long story) Dan had been avoiding her like the plague. It was obvious by the closed look on his face that today would be no different, despite his quick pick up when she'd called him in.

Ana just didn't get it. She, Dan and Rob had been through so much together; shared so many experiences that God must have handpicked the three of them for. They knew her inside out just like she knew them; did it really matter that she could talk without singing everything? Did it matter that he could no longer treat her like the happy puppy dog he adored every time he saw her?

Shaking her head at his refusal to move, Ana stepped forward herself to wrap him in a hug that , just like the last two times, she knew he wouldn't return.

She missed him. Missed his quiet reassuring voice. She missed the calm wisdom he possessed for one so young. Standing at over six feet three inches with a wide barrel chest much like his dads, Dan was no longer the cute, brotherly Danny he'd been.

And just like the time before, she felt an electric buzz zing through her when her cheek hit his chest. Her arms sliding under his still ones at his side, she wrapped them as far as they could go around him and squeezed.

Her heart screamed for him to let it go and forgive. It had taken her a whole year to get through to her sister so, to be honest, she was exhausted. Tired of begging and tired of explaining that her pretense had been to their strategic advantage, she swallowed through a tight throat and sighed. It's fine, she thought. Because she was done begging.

It was as she was pulling away, her head turned to hide the wet in her eyes that she felt his muscled arms close her in and squeeze.

Then completely embarrassed herself by soaking the entire front of Dan's tee.

Praying silently her gratitude, she cried and squeezed harder at God's grace. A little because she'd give just about anything for Dan not to think badly of her; but mostly because it was almost done. That was two obstacles down and only one to go. And that one, not having shared any type of bond with her like her sister or Dan, was going to be the hardest of all.

Daniel Sampson

Life, it seemed, was full of surprises.

Seeing Rob get out of his GMC pick-up at the same time he pulled up wasn't one of them. They were oddly synchronized whenever they all came together, it seemed. Grinning, Dan had tried hard not to appear eager to see him. They'd been to the other side of hell and back together, having come out with a bond no one could break.

So, despite their schedules differing so much and the guys rarely saw each other since he'd been back, Dan knew things would be no different. That said, he'd still missed his best bud.

Sure that Rob's incognito status had more to do with a certain "someone" than it did with their schedules, Dan's grin had widened.

"Good to see you, man. I guess being a big-time reporter keeps you too busy these days to call a brother. Or is it someone... I mean, something else, keeping you busy"

Throwing in the wiggling eyebrows was probably overkill, but that had never stopped him before. Dodging the half swing directed playfully at his head, Dan had laughed and danced to the left, almost missing the whisper of a presence he felt down to his soul.

A presence that had just thrown itself into a bear hug from Rob. A presence that had been lying to everyone for years about being autistic. A presence that, with one look since being outted, flooded his bloodstream with testosterone.

The stark contrast of her peaches and cream skin tone next to Rob's flannel shirt stood out in the orange glow of twilight.

He'd fought to keep his expression blank and tried to force himself to remain calm. The thing was, he couldn't. A seventh-year law student at Washington University, Dan knew pressure, recognized it, identified it, and in every instance, he beat it. For BW's, it didn't take much to win mental battles, all they had to do was focus. There wasn't a test he couldn't pass, a quiz he couldn't master, or a project that could shake him.

To the other students he was Mr. Calm, Cool and Collected. On dates, at the DMV, even standing in line at the post office; no one could ever accuse him of losing his cool.

Except Ana.

Ana the now twenty-one-year-old, buxom, tall, techno-genius that had plagued his thoughts from the day he'd got home and clapped eyes on her again.

"Do I get a hug or what?"

The question had dragged him to the present. He'd been so caught up in his thoughts that he'd missed her finishing up with Rob only to turn his way.

She'd stood there, a mere foot away, acting like she wasn't looking like sex on a stick.

Hands clenching along with his jaw he employed an old trick his father taught him and directed his attention over her right shoulder.

Forcing himself to relax he'd purposefully blurred his vision with a determination to get this done and over with.

The thing is, he couldn't move. Worse, it felt like he couldn't breathe. It was like he was locked into place. And, except for the fact that the little girl he once thought of as the most innocent being in the world was so compelling it hurt to look at her, he was completely in the dark as to why.

Then she hugged him. He fought it; that overwhelming feeling of ownership and protectiveness toward her. He fought it with all his strength and BW enhanced control. In the end, he couldn't stand against such an onslaught.

Dan finally admitted the truth to himself. He was tired of fighting. Time stopped. He'd taken one last breath that flooded his being with her scent of vanilla and jasmine. And caved, pulling her into him where she fit perfectly. Like she belonged there.

Man, Dan thought, rolling his eyes. Ana was turning him into a girl. Next, he'd be reading the crappy romance novels he saw her carrying around and crying in his soup.

Chapter 12

Cruz

"Quiet. Sleeping Beauty over here is back with us."
Cruz's jaw tightened, however his eyes remained closed.
"Get on up Hoss. I know you can hear me."
Teeth grinding slightly, Cruz forced himself to relax. Sight
wasn't the only sense one needed to get their bearings. A
deep draw of breath and familiar scents told him
everything he needed to know. Opening his eyes to
confirm, Cruz was blinded by the overhead light and
decorative neon placed sporadically around the room.
Hearing the raspy chuckle as his head swiveled
from where he sat strapped down somehow, in an old
barbershop chair, Cruz allowed his head to fall back with a
groan.

"Yeah, figured you couldn't resist checking out the place. Brings back memories don't it?"

Way too many, Cruz silently admitted. Ignoring the surging pain at his temples, he forced himself to relax.

"I told them you wouldn't give up. Gotta say though, to be honest, I started to have my doubts."

Hoping his vision had adjusted and would cooperate this time, Cruz allowed himself to peek through his eyelids to be sure. He needed more information; a clue to guide him. He knew WHAT he was in... it's the WHERE he was that begged to be answered.

"Meeting you in person, I can't say you're as impressive as your brother... but then, it's clear that number two son Caruso Arpaio AKA the fired US Marshall turned private investigator works hard not to be."

Cruz cursed a blue streak in his head. This guy had done his research.

Hearing someone else enter the room to his left, Cruz allowed his narrowed gaze to shift.

Benny. Benito Gutierrez.

It had been that kind of day was the only explanation for why Cruz wasn't surprised.

Ben smiled shamelessly, baring a mouth full of gold teeth. It was the only thing that saved him from being a Dave Navarro clone, down to the tats and stretched ear lobes. An odd thing, since he claimed to hate the man.

Ben hadn't changed much over the years. Cruz needed one look to take him in completely from head to toe. From the dark hair and goatee, to leather apron, Ben had hardly aged a day since their teenaged escapades.

"Amiguito," Ben chin upped at him, his eyes somber and lips tight.

Cruz sighed. Obviously Ben was being sarcastic since they hadn't seen each other since Ben's arrest when they were sixteen, thus they were hardly close friends.

It looked like his past, as always, was coming back to haunt him. The unnerving look on Ben's face all but confirmed that. However, it was the sinister phrase his captor spoke into what had to be a headset (probably the person he'd told to be quiet earlier) that set Cruz's teeth on edge.

"Not yet. I'm waiting on his little girlfriend to show first. We'll prep them together and I'll make him watch. It should be fun."

***

Amanda

"Eyes here, Ana. I need you focused." I sighed, frustrated.

Then rolling my eyes I steadfastly ignored the eave's droppers aka my house residents that kept peeking around the doorframe and whispering annoyingly.

What should have been a quick briefing that allowed me to be on my motorcycle and hitting the road had somehow turned into almost two hours of interrupted breakdowns.

I didn't have time for this. More importantly, Cruz didn't have time for this. And for every second that we lost, fussing over details, feelings of dread threatened to overwhelm me.

"Sorry," Ana mumbled through her chewing gum, her monotone setting my teeth on edge.

I forced myself to deep breathe and remember that this was a generation of cell phones, hyper texting, and limited focus, even for geniuses, and especially for twenty-one-year-old one's.

"Let's just go, already. I'm bored." Nina yawned, slightly more irritating than usual.

I felt my lips tighten and again, forced myself to relax. We needed a strategy. To get that, we needed to know our enemy and as best we could, ascertain their motives. I had a nagging feeling that we were missing something huge.

Ignoring Nina for now, I focused again on the white board in our cute little conference room that used to be a dining room area before our renovation.

Fact one: Human trafficking had grown rampant in my city over the past ten years. Truth was, within the United States it was more pervasive than indicated by statistics. Skewed data because prosecutors were hesitant to indict due to an ambiguous understanding of human trafficking and lack of precedence, resulting in lost cases was part of the reason. So, the public (namely me) had been lulled into thinking this wasn't a big issue in our country until I experienced it firsthand. I still had nightmares about that warehouse full of women that had just collapsed for no discernable reason. Getting police and the legal system involved was obviously out.

Fact two: Involuntary responses (i.e. passing out) to situations as simple as walking outside of a building hinted at external controls. And smacked of Brainwaiver modus operandi. Which meant we hadn't just been dealing with biker-thug human trafficking sicko's... we'd been dealing with something more. After what had happened to Max and Balboa (on their wedding day no less), it was agreed that we were outmanned and outgunned. We'd settled down to strategies like building awareness, forming organizations, and human trafficking legal reform instead of facing the IT conglomerate Lewis-Cifer head on. We'd decided to lay low, live normal lives; thinking doing so would ensure our families safety; that we'd be left alone. All of us except Nina, anyway. Besides that, apparently we'd assumed wrong.

Fact three: Cruz had no business in Miami meeting up with a known victim of human trafficking. It would have made sense if he was still a Unites States Marshall. But he wasn't which was something I know only because my sister was the best hacker in the known universe. Given the opportunity to "resign" when he'd acquired evidence against Zeke and his ilk (the motorcycle gang people had names; Zeke, Brody... evil incarnate) against protocol while chasing down their scent, Cruz had turned in his badge and relocated to Houston, Texas. Without so much as a goodbye note or text message.

My head throbbed as I forced myself to skip over my memory of that time to focus on the fourth item listed on the white board.

Why Shae and why now? There wasn't much I knew about her other than what I'd found out right after we'd rescued ourselves from Zeke. Shae'd had a sister; Candicia.

Gorgeous and only a year older, she was Shae's best friend too. They did everything together; Shae, her sister and one other friend of theirs, Maria.

Born and raised in California, their parents had been liberal about freedom, letting the girls do pretty much whatever they wanted as long as they stuck together. It was sticking with Maria and, for some reason leaving Shae behind one day, that had gotten Candicia into trouble.

Trouble that resulted in her sister not coming home that night. Or the night after that.

Long story short, Shae had never given up on finding Candicia. Fact is, I don't know if she ever did. It was her amazing survival story that had distracted me from finding out her sister's fate.

Having been captured herself while looking for Candicia; she'd escaped at a truck stop where a trucker had come to her aid. That had been the part of her story that astounded me the most. Apparently, farming these poor girls out at truck stops was a big part of the trafficking business. Truckers were lonely, tired, and usually, not particular about age or cleanliness. So, they partook. Often.

Then again, there were those truckers that were fathers, brothers, uncles, and grandfathers. Truckers that had looked into those girls' eyes and SAW their own.

Truckers that had decided enough was enough, their hearts breaking every time they saw a fellow trucker take one into their cab.

To combat this injustice, they'd formed an organization. TAT, Truckers against Trafficking.

Filling their trucks with literature, the men laid out cards at truck stops that other truckers could pick up along with fliers and pamphlets.

Shae had happened upon a trucker that had picked up a card. She'd given him the scripted greeting, "Hey buddy, looking for a date?"

When she was asked, "how old are you?" She'd responded, "old enough." Usually that was enough to get her into a cab. Her alternative was to keep walking or get beat down by her captors.

This trucker, however, knew the play and had a play book of his own. He'd invited her into the cab, blasted his radio, and got down on the floor with her to ask a series of questions.

Shae's responses had led to him calling the 1-800 number on the card and giving the representative their location. The Highway Patrol raided the truck stop not 10 minutes later, leading to Shae's freedom and induction into the Illinois Child Services division. Apparently she'd been shipped within the two years of her captivity from California to Illinois. Having told the authorities that her family was dead and that she'd been a runaway from a foster home, they didn't bother to check into her story.

As far as Shae had been concerned, she couldn't return home without her sister. The reason, I'd assumed she was looking for the Gangsta Nuns. Until I saw her get into that car and drive off.

Now I didn't know what to think.

Which meant, again, I had no strategy, no plan of attack, and no idea how to get the facts I needed to pull one together.

Balboa would be ashamed of all of us, if she knew that we were about to go off into a situation blind.

And, despite my irritation with Nina, I couldn't help but agree that it was time. The way I saw it, we had no other choice. Cruz's life depended on it.

Chapter 13

Three hours. That's how long it took everyone to settle on a game plan. It was sketchy at best, foolish at worst, but at least it was a plan.

Nina had gone ahead of all of us despite Roberts protests. I wasn't privy to the conversation that I saw them having, a heated one at that, on the back porch after everyone packed up to head out, but you didn't have to be a mind reader to know what was going on there.

To talk about the weirdest friendship in creation was to talk about Robert and Nina. Crushing on Nina since we were teenagers, Rob had followed her around metaphorically like a puppy dog. Balboa laughingly described it as him "bullying" his way into her tiny, Grinch sized heart.

To be frank though, Balboa was not wrong. Rob had been tenacious in his determination for Nina to acknowledge him as, not only a part of our clan, but as a viable part of her life. And, as we'd matured (somewhat) and grown older, it was as if the roles switched.

Nina was about five years older than Rob and Dan. As someone raised around Dan's family sort of like a cousin, Nina had been the big sister type that Dan and I had looked up to. She'd tried to be the same thing to Rob. That did not happen.

Now it was Rob, towering over all of us at six feet six inches, that acted like the older sibling; dogmatically and emphatically, where Nina was concerned.

I shook my head and chuckled as I shut down the conference room lights and locked up.

Because Nina was so NOT receptive to that. Even Balboa knew better than to think she could tell Nina what to do. The quietest one of our little clan, Nina was, in my mind, the most dangerous.

To be a bounty hunter, process server and bail recovery agent at five feet two inches, you had to be all kinds of dangerous. Nina was approaching her tenth year. And unlike Balboa and Mrs. Sampson who preferred Muy Tai and Krav Maga fighting styles to disarm an enemy, Nina was all about the guns, knives, Kubatons, brass knuckles, etc, etc., etc.

Realizations that had me shaking my head and laughing some more. Because it was clear that Nina "let" Rob get all up in her grill in the back yard, point his finger in her face then cross his arms while she laughed at him.

Like, she LAUGHED. Nina NEVER laughed. Tell a joke? A really funny one? Nina's response would be a blank stare or, at best, you'd see a little twinkle in her eye, maybe even a cheek twitch. But she didn't smile. And she never laughed. Except for with Rob.

There was a part of me deep down that wanted to be jealous. To feel like she'd stolen my bestie from me. But the truth is, I loved my people; every single weird, cracked up and crazy one of them. So, if they had a friendship that was unique and special apart from me, who was I to begrudge them that?

No one, that's who. Besides, I had bigger fish to fry. Fish that had migrated from Houston to Florida to being God knows where. Determined to get to my room and pray this one out before I got on my 5 a.m. flight out of Lambert in the morning. I walked the bottom floor to make sure all windows and doors were locked down before heading upstairs to pack a bag.

It was when my foot hit the bottom step that I heard the knock on the door. A quick glance at my Apple watch told me that it was 9:18 pm. The girls could have company in the lounge area until 10. I tried not to grumble at whoever was cutting it this close. Hearing Victoria answer the door I determined it must be for her and began my jog up the steps to my room.

"Hey Mandy," Victoria, apparently still at the door, yelled through the house.

I felt my face get tight. They know I hated that. Because really? That's what we do? We yell the whole house down?

"Yo," I yelled back, tired of it all. If they didn't care why should I?

"You got a visitor! It's your Dad!"

Thinking it must be Sam because Edward Same had been dead now for about three years (the third stroke finished the job that the first and second had started), I hurried back down. Did Max call him in on the Cruz situation?

Since Vick would have taken him straight to my office I headed that way down the back hall. My mind scrambling, trying to find the best way to tell Sam we had everything under control. Focused, I turned to close the door and engaged the lock against possible snoopers before greeting him with a fake smile of assurance plastered on my face.

"Well look at you, all grown up. Happy twenty-fourth birthday, sweetheart. You got a hug for me?"

Ice cold fear and fiery rage assailed me all at once, from within and without.

"Hello Uncle Devin," I responded, my voice surprisingly calm, "when did Hell let you out?"

***

Nina

"What's the deal with Dan and the Liar, anyway?" Nina asked, grunting as she tossed her saddle bags on the other full-sized bed in the hotel room.

"I'm really gonna need you to let that go." Rob sighed.

Grunting again, Nina let her silence speak for itself, flopping back onto the empty bed, exhausted.

Sighing again because he knew that was the end of that, Rob answered, "Like I said, you need to let that go, and I'm not sure. At first I thought it was stubborn unforgiveness like with some people I know but won't name." His pause was telling.

Nina ignored it.

"But..."

"But what?" She prodded. She had about two minutes to choose between the shower or just going to sleep before the bed she was splayed out on chose for her.

"I think now, maybe not so much."

At his hesitation, Nina opened her eyes, and promptly rolled them.

"Because why?" She asked, trying her hardest not to let her impatience leak into her voice. He had one minute.

"Today at Sanctuary junior, she'd done her usual, hug me, remember how cute I am thing she does..."

Eyes rolling again at the stupid nickname they'd given the sorority; Nina fought a lip curl and growl. He'd somehow pick it up through the phone, she knew. The man had dog ears. And she was not in the mood for another lecture on being nice. She wasn't nice; and wasn't ever gonna be. Period.

On her second count to five he continued thoughtfully, "Normally he'd let her get it out of her system then walk away and completely ignore her. Something I thought was much better than threatening looks thrown at her occasionally, by the way. This time though, he hugged her back. Hard. They had a whole "moment" right there in the front yard. In front of God and everybody. And you know how private Dan is..."

She did know. She'd known Dan since they were kids and played hide-go-seek together. She knew his patterns, his habits, even his worst nightmares.

Which was probably why the ominous feeling that she'd been unable to shake all day slithered through her mind like black oil once again.

"What you thinking, Boo?" Rob asked her quietly, so quiet it was almost a whisper.

Fighting the tender feeling she got in her gut every time he talked to her that way, like she was the only person on earth that mattered; like her next words were so important that they would literally shape or shatter his whole world... like she just didn't mean something to him, she meant everything; Nina swallowed, forcing the feeling and those thoughts behind a locked door in her mind.

"I'm thinking its time for bed. Get rest. See you tomorrow. And don't get dead when we breach. That'll piss me off."

Having said that all in one breath and followed it with a click, Nina forced herself out of bed and headed toward the shower.

Praying the shower was powerful enough to wash the road grime away, she stripped and hopped in, anxiously knowing the truth; she could wash all she wanted. That black oil feeling was going to keep on flowing. Though, as long as it didn't touch her people, even the little liar? She'd be okay. And if it was finally coming for her, she was cool with that; would meet it head on, even. In fact, she'd be a little relieved.

Chapter 14

Ana

"I got it Max. Promise."

"I hope so Annie. I don't want you on this. Didn't want any of you on it; but especially you. What you know is too dangerous. If they get their hands on you...,"

"I know," Ana cut him off, "we're geniuses, remember? Plus, I know what's at stake. I wouldn't risk our families, let alone the whole world, over a whim. I need to be there Max. It's a trap. You know it. I know it. That's why you didn't call us from jump."

Silence hanging in the air on the other end all but confirmed her theory. Max had smelled trap, just as Ana had. She'd seen that video. She knew that guy. Her photographic memory had kicked in immediately as she watched the playback, having tapped into Amanda's feed as she eavesdropped.

Brody, the biker. That was his name today. She and Max had made a contest over the years out of him. He'd also been coined Brody the Bully, Brody the Butthead, Brody the Brute, Brody the Brick Wall and Brody the fatherless child (that was Max's, only he didn't say it so nice). Beside Cipher-Lewis and Zeke, he was the biggest baddie on their list. He was number one on Max's, for reasons she couldn't blame him.

Brody had a thing for Balboa. To the point of obsession, it seemed. Max had taken to hiding the little tokens Brody would ship via UPS, FedEx, DHL, courier or regular postal service. It seemed impossible to Ana how the toughest woman she ever knew could be experiencing such a difficult pregnancy. It was like life was trying to balance the scales somehow. Maybe Balboa had way too much good in her life. Maybe life felt like she needed a struggle; something to keep her on her toes.

Ana mentally shrugged, shaking the thoughts away. While she didn't think the gifts would bother Balboa, Max wasn't taking any chances. Nor would she if she were in his shoes.

"Keep me on standby for back up." Max finally grunted, apparently having given in to what he obviously couldn't prevent.

"No thanks, I've got that covered too."

"Annie," Max growled, a warning in his voice.

Chuckling her bye, Max as she disconnected, Ana rolled her chair back to her computer to begin working on phase two. They didn't have much time. But God had their back. Ana could feel it in her bones. Which meant, when the time came, they'd have everything they needed.

***

Cruz

"How about a bathroom break, Big Guy?" Cruz rasped.

His throat was so dry, he'd have thought his body would have fought its hardest to retain all the moisture it could. Of course, he'd be wrong.

"How about a catheter, instead?" Brody laughed it, his right eye twitching.

Cruz allowed his head to fall back to the chair with a frustrated sigh.

It was day two in that chair. And he was just on the other side of panic. Somehow they'd gotten word back to Max. And, while he couldn't possibly fathom how, something was telling him that Amanda was on her way. That he wasn't the "real" target for this mission. No. He was the bait.

It had taken everything in him not to rub his arms and body raw trying to escape that chair. He'd be no use to Amanda injured. It wasn't until three in the morning that he mentally worked out a semblance of a plan. All he had to do was get them to let him out of that chair. His training would take over the rest.

"Seriously, Man," he tried again, "this ain't cool. Its undignified. You'd really make a grown man crap his pants?"

"Let him loose," Benny growled, entering the room from the back, and laying his plastic bags of stuff on a workstation close to the sinks. "Because if he craps himself, I'm not cleaning that up."

The big dude blinked, mumbled something, then headed Cruz's way.

Right before he could hear the lock kick, Cruz felt a cold chill rush his spine. Looking up, his gaze was captured by the ice blue one of the giant.

"I don't have to tell you how put out I would be if I let you up and you tried to escape, right?"

Cruz tried not to roll his eyes, instead going for a mildly confused and disoriented expression.

The giant smiled a smile that, his gaze strangely didn't reflect. It wasn't until he heard the words that Cruz figured out why.

"So far as it stands, everyone has the potential to walk out of here alive. Mess with me boy, and I will make sure your girlfriend is the first to go down. And I will do it in a way that will make you shudder at the memory. One body part at a time. Capiche?"

"Got it," Cruz replied through gritted teeth, hearing the lock catch release.

He'd never taken down a giant before. There was a first time for everything. And this time, it really had to be. Because Amanda was on her way. Thus, this was one fight he couldn't afford to lose.

***

Amanda

I hated the airport. Too many smells, way too many people and a cesspool of germs from around the world. It symbolized to me everything that was wrong in society.

If one more person came within mere inches of knocking me over in their haste to make a flight, I swear I will scream bloody murder.

But then, it's not like it's the general public's fault I was in a bad mood and hadn't slept a wink.

No, that honor belonged solely to dear old Uncle Devin.

I checked the time on my watch again. Three oh six in the morning. Two hours until departure meant I had at least another hour to wait for the guys to join me.

Just enough time to catch a cat nap in my seat. Or not. I felt myself grinding my teeth again.

I couldn't get last night out of my head. Part of me was still trying to figure out what I'd done to deserve that little surprise, while the rest of me had settled on accepting the fact that I just might have to kill the man.

It hadn't been seeing him again or the thought of revenge that took me there. It had been the threats made against my sister.

Walking to my desk like my estranged uncle came to my office everyday for a visit, I stood behind it, crossed my arms, and waited. I was comfortable with the fact that

I was now only a hidden drawer pull away from my small Saturday night special.

My crossed arms and tapping foot didn't reflect that fact.

"What, no offer of refreshments or to take a seat? Surely you were taught better, niece."

"Don't worry, you won't be staying that long. In fact, state your business and be on your way. I said that much more nicely than I actually WANT to. So, let's not make me say it again, Kay?"

I felt my face lock up at his slick grin. It hadn't changed in all these years. Though he surely had. There was a time when he seemed so much taller than I, like he loomed over me from the highest of heights. Now, he was no more than an inch or two taller than me. Coupled with his pale, clammy appearance and middle-aged pot belly, the intimidating air he'd once used against me as a kid had quickly lost its luster.

"So much like your mother when she was your age. You should have been my daughter, you know."

I tried hard not to throw up in my mouth at that thought. Just being related to the man made me want to be sick. I didn't want to even think about what it would have been like to be this pervert's kid.

"Say what you came to say and get out Devin. I won't ask again."

"Fine," he shrugged, helping himself to the seat in front of my desk, "Your grandmothers on a ventilator. She doesn't have much time left. I need you to pack your things and come back with me to New York. It's time for you to claim your birthright."

"Hell. To the no. Now, if that's all, I've got stuff to do, you can see your way out." My calm denial seemed to bounce off his shield of apparent disbelief as he reiterated.

"What do you mean no? You must come back with me. It's your inheritance and your birthright; you can't turn that down."

"Sure, I can," I huffed, "You and your dying mother can stick all of that where it best suits you and leave me be. I hold no claim to anything that woman owns. Thank you for stopping by..."

"In that case," he said, grinning smugly, "I guess I'll be visiting with your sister, then. She's the next in line to receive it all."

I was halfway over that desk, my finger in his face before I or he had blinked.

"Stay away from my sister. I won't say that again either."

"It's fine. We'd rather not pass on the family jewels to the town idiot anyway. What would the neighbors think?"

It was the banging on the door that had saved me from prison in that moment.

Frowning, I rushed to open it thinking one of my girls was in trouble, only to watch with amazement as Dan blew past me, immediately taking a protective stance in front of me with Rob following close behind.

My head tilted in question; I didn't have long to wait for the answer I was looking for.

"Ana called. Your security camera's still on in here apparently. Is this really who she says it is?" Dan had said that part. Rob said the next.

"Because I can't believe a rapist would have the unmitigated gall to show his face anywhere near his victims, can you, Dan?

"I cannot," Dan continued moving from in front of me to sitting on the front of my desk, his knee now only a foot from my uncle's face.

"I cannot imagine that at all Rob. In fact, my mind is blown that said rapist would not only show up, but do so making threats? Inconceivable isn't it, Rob?"

"It really is," Rob responded, now standing behind my uncle's chair, his arms crossed while he stared down at the bald spot on the top of Devin's head.

"What," Devin stated, glancing from Dan to Rob then back to Dan, "am I supposed to be intimidated? Afraid? Of a couple of boys? Please." He finished, almost choking on his scoff as Dan moved as quick as lightening, snatching Devin out of the chair by the front of his shirt.

"No, Mr. Same. THIS is the intimidation part. We don't like you. My friend and I don't like your kind. This house is off limits. These women are off limits. You so much as think about Amanda or Ana, and I'll know. Trust me when I say, you don't want to see me on that day."

Devin's beady eyes shifted as he attempted to free himself from Dan's grip.

It took all of my strength to keep my humor behind my teeth as I watched Dan drag Devin to the door while

Rob whistled the "whistle while you work" song from Snow White.

The guys were a hoot. And honestly, had that been the end of that, I would have enjoyed at least three hours of sleep by the time that was all over.

Only the text message I got not even an hour after the guys left told me everything I needed to know.

"Make a decision. It's you or Annabella. I expect a response by the end of this week. Choose, or I will choose for you."

God was not a fan of murder. I knew that. But He'd forgive me. And He loved me. It was on that thought that I nodded off with a smile.

Chapter 15

Cruz

This time when he came to, the dank smell of mold and sewage flooded his senses.
The pain in his back and head screamed through his consciousness making him wish he was still out of it.

"Well. That was a colossal failure." Cruz sighed, frowning at the feel of a thin bench type object he'd been laid out on.

"I bet," a voice responded, then snorted from somewhere nearby. Fighting nausea, Cruz ab crunched up into a seated position, thankful that there was a wall situated behind the small bench mounted to the floor. It was a foul-smelling wall, but still. It was support.

Fighting the need to drop his torso to his thighs as another wave of nausea hit, Cruz focused to take in the dark dank environment around him.

Faint light from without showed him to be in some kind of underground cell. The floor was dirt packed and perfectly matched the hewn brick walls on two of the four sides in the room. Old iron bars covered the entire front entrance of what had to be an old school jail from God knows when. Those bars extended around to Cruz's left where he could see a shadowed figure standing there in a connecting cell, their arms resting through the bars.

Shifting their feet as the torso lifted Cruz could clearly see that Shayla had been the source of the voice. Her voice had been gravelly and unrecognizable. But her visage was unmistakable.

Swallowing the same response that almost choked him upon catching up to her outside of Sanctuary, Cruz couldn't ignore the thousand-dollar question sizzling like electricity between them.

"What have you gotten us into! Chara's message from you about Amanda and the blowback you hinted at coming her way, what the hell was that about? I want answers Shayla. Now is not the time to prevaricate so don't push me."

"Or what," the heifer laughed, "what will you do, exactly? Its not like you're a United States Marshall or anything."

Cruz felt his jaw lock. Calmly rising from the bench, he stretched to ease the tension out of his limbs.

He could feel Shayla's gaze heavy on him while he worked the tightness out of his muscles from his neck all the way down to his ankles. One thing that he appreciated about this new situation was the fact that he could move around at least.

Trying not to think about his foolish attempt to escape after using the bathroom via said bathroom window (a window way too high and small to fit his large frame through), then use misdirection when that failed to look like he'd gotten out while hiding in one of the most disgusting stalls he'd ever seen in life, Cruz blinked away the memory of the laughing Giant waiting for him outside the door while Ben ran out to try to waylay his escape.

That bear hug had been a monster. Even so, Cruz hadn't gone down easy. That didn't change the fact that he had gone down, but it still made him feel a little better.

"Still Jonesing for lil Miss Barbie I see," Shayla remarked out of nowhere.

Going still and silent, Cruz allowed himself no reaction other than his head to turn her way. Now she was gripping the bars with both hands, a sneer of disgust contorting her features.

Seeing that she had nothing else to add, he continued to focus on stretching, did some shadow boxing to get his blood circulating, and stretched again before dropping himself back down onto the thin bench.

"You think your ignoring me bothers me?"

Cruz pulled his legs into meditation pose on the bench and closed his eyes, resting his hands on his knee.

Focusing on his faith and on Christ who he placed his trust, he mentally recited Psalms 23 over and over.

"It doesn't. It's not like I haven't been stuck down here for days already. You don't matter. Nothing you do matters. Nothing you do bothers me."

You are with me, your rod and your staff, they comfort me...

"What's with you, man? Why rush down here at my message if you won't even try to help me!"

A table before me in the presence of my enemies...

"Oh, I see, you're here because of her. Amanda. They must have known you would come to protect her; this wasn't about me at all. That's why they..."

She wanted him to ask, "they what". Cruz knew she did. But he was done playing musical chairs with folks. If no one would bother telling him what he needed to know, he was done.

You anoint my head with oil...

"Did you know about her father's family? What they did to her?"

My cup runs over...

"Oh. Well. You must also know about the other rituals. Like, when the next female heir reaches twenty-four, she mates with the oldest male family member to bear the next child in their line. And people wonder why her sister was born autistic. They're a bunch of inbred lunatics."

Cruz's eyes shot open. Amanda had just turned twenty-four two days ago. And he ought to know. He tracked that day like it was a national holiday.

***

Dan

"I thought she was staying behind."

Amanda frowned before responding as she took her little sister's hand, "I don't know why. We clearly discussed the travel plans that included the four of us on a flight. You don't remember that?"

Dan's face tightened. He forced himself not to react. It was hard not to since Rob decided to snicker before covering his face and pretending to cough.

Fighting a teeth grind his gaze slid quickly to take Ana in again, almost as if he couldn't help it, before refocusing on Amanda.

He opened his mouth to argue that Ana could be of no real use in the field when Amanda cut him off...

"Okay, wait. I thought you two had, like a massive break through, yesterday. I thought you'd finally gotten over your little snit."

"Snit," Dan almost choked, "It took you a whole YEAR to get over it. But yeah, okay."

Amanda shook her head back at him pitifully as they moved forward to board the plane before throwing back over her shoulder, "She's my sister. My being angry at her doesn't count. It's a sister thing. Besides, we discussed this yesterday. And you were all in."

He was NOT all in. Point of fact, had he been less distracted by Ana's jasmine-vanilla scent and her profile that he couldn't help to take in through side glance after side glance, he would have told them that. She had no business being there. Nina could take care of herself. Amanda wasn't half bad either on the self defense front. But Ana had never had to defend herself before. He didn't want her in danger. He refused to allow it, in fact.

Opening his mouth to tell her she needed to get off the plane as they bustled toward their seat, Ana turned around, looked him right in the eye, winked and blew him a kiss before turning to take her seat.

Rob's coughing fit was all Dan needed to hear to know his friend hadn't missed one single second of that exchange.

Wondering why God hated him, Dan angrily packed away his carryon and flopped down into the window seat.

"So," Rob cleared his throat, "how about them Cardinals,"

Dan closed his eyes on a frustrated growl.

This was going to be a long trip.

***

Nina

She had two hours before her people's flight landed. Pulling her bike up to Sanctuary, Nina dismounted and jogged up the steps, having already checked her things into the hotel three miles up Interstate 75.

The old wooden door swung open. Lace, an ex-gang member that hated Balboa stood on the threshold.

"What?" She greeted, her voice a melodic contradiction to her attitude.

Nina's left eyebrow went up.

"You Lace?" She asked, putting to words the question they both knew the answer to.

"Is it your business?" Laciana sneered, stepping forward to tower over Nina.

Looking her up and down, Nina dropped her bike helmet to her left, slid her right hand into her pocket, dropped to one knee while slipping a set of connected rings onto her right hand and swung, hitting the towering Amazon right in the crotch with spiked brass knuckles.

Stumbling back in pain and surprise, Nina followed, swinging the wooden monster door closed.

Before the four women standing in the vestibule could respond Nina's leg swipe landed Lace on her back as she palmed her glock, pointing it directly at Lace's face.

"Denise sent me. She told me to give you a message. You ever mess with her family again, you won't have a face to breathe through. Now, I believe you have intel that you failed to pass on through Chara. You'll be giving me that info right about now." Nina finished, pulling back the slide to ready her first shot.

Chapter 16

Balboa

Putting her phone on silent, Denise "Balboa" Arpaio palmed it, expecting a text from Nina at any minute.

Quickly hiding the phone at her side, she smiled as Max glided through their bedroom door holding a tray laden with a breakfast she loved to hate. There was yogurt, granola, orange juice, an apple, a banana, oatmeal, some mystery gray crap that could have passed for a sausage or piece of meat, and a boiled egg.

Her husband was determined to push his chia seeds and hemp crap diet on her and the baby.

"My baby will be born healthy, woman. I refuse to let you bombard her with candy, ice cream and animal products!"

A vegan for as long as she'd known him, Balboa had accepted Max for his healthy eating and protein shake drinking habits long ago. But his diet choices were not her testimony.

She was lucky to have friends like CeeCee and Nina in her life. Both kept her supplied with hordes of junk. Junk she strategically hid throughout the loft so Max wouldn't lose his mind.

"How's my beautiful daughter doing this morning," Max asked, sitting the tray at her left side, while leaning forward to kiss her stomach.

"You keep calling my son a girl and you'll give him a complex. Don Juan is doing just fine." Balboa said, grabbing the teacup off the tray to take a sip and hide her grin.

The anticipated growl grated on her ears, causing her eyes to go wide in innocent alarm. Then she took another sip.

"Don't give me that look. My child would never bear such a pretentious name. I have spoken."

Balboa laughed into her cup, unable to hold it any longer.

"Really? That's all you've got? You have spoken?"

Max shrugged, his stern expression turning sheepish.

"Going to make my shake and hit the ladder. You need me to get anything else for you before I go?"

"A kiss is all I need," she grinned, putting her tea aside right before he dutifully swept her up to hold her tight.

After scorching her eyebrows off with a kiss that flustered and frustrated her at the same time, Balboa's smiling husband leaned down to kiss her belly once more before leaving the room to pursue his workout.

Dang but she loved that man. Shaking her head at how unbelievably amazing her life was, she reached for the banana on her tray right when her phone buzzed.

Nina's expected text said just what she thought it would.

Her babies were walking into a trap. Worse, they had no clue who they were dealing with. But Nina did. Throwing up another quick prayer, Balboa shot off a text with another contact and location that might be able to serve as back up. After doing this, she quickly deleted the evidence and took her phone off silent. Max would be so upset if he knew what she was up to. Luckily, she had ammunition of her own to use if he ever found out.

The silly man thought he could actually hide this from her. About her babies. She snorted before taking another sip of her tea and leaning back into her pillows. One day, he would learn. Today just wasn't that day.

***

Amanda

Landing in Miami just before 8:30 am was like landing in St. Louis at 2 p.m.

Miami International Airport (MIA – oxymoronic right?) was one of the largest airports I'd ever seen. But then, I hate them and generally avoided them as a practice so, there's that.

It didn't change the fact that MIA was huge. And busy. If I'd ever been a post-war veteran with an agent orange issue, it would be at defcon four right about now.

I couldn't breathe easy until Rob got us out of the rental car airport lot we'd been shuttled to.
Nina had already checked us all into our rooms according to Rob; all we had to do was meet her there to grab our key.

"Any leads on where Shae and Cruz were taken Ana?" I asked, saying without saying that my sister has a purpose on this little misadventure for Dan's sake. It was really starting to bug me how he kept looking her way, an introspective frown creasing his brow.

"Yep. I've tapped into at least three satellites that I was able to use to match up my facial recognition software with Brody the Bandwagon's handsome mug. Looks like we are going to the Miccosukee Caves near Northwest 18th Avenue..."

"On that," Dan spoke, keying it into the rental car's GPS as the next stop after the hotel.

"So, no Gangsta Nuns, then." I sighed.

"You sound disappointed," Rob said, eyeing me through the rearview mirror as he pulled onto the highway entrance ramp.

I shrugged and turned to stare out my window. I bit my lip subconsciously, letting go another piece of my plan to convince Chara and Bet to help us out. The guys would think I didn't trust them. That was far from the case. I just knew the truth and Balboa had taught us well. It never hurt to have as much back up as you could get.

Closing my eyes, I threw up one more silent prayer. For Cruz. For us. And for Shae.

***

Cruz

"I didn't want her hurt, you know that right?" Shayla's voice echoed in the darkness.

As was the case from the moment he'd regained consciousness, Cruz gave no response.

"I love that girl like a sister. I had a sister once. They Fried her brain. Turned her into a Barbie puppet. Totally changed her appearance and married her to some old gross guy that owns the largest IT company in the world.

Cruz grimaced but he didn't comment. His brother had given him details on top of details about their Brainwaiver missions. He'd made Cruz commit it all to memory just in case something happened to any of them. A pain in his chest overshadowed the cold numbness that inhabited it only moments before.

Cruz knew who Shayla was referring to. Exactly who she was referring to. And his heart broke for her. But she hadn't shared anything useful to him since he'd been stuck down here with her. Maybe her sharing something so intensely personal was a sign that she was ready.

On that thought, he sat up and rested his elbows on his thighs.

"What happened Shayla? Talk to me? You reach out to me through Chara, I come to Miami to find you and next thing I know, we're hemmed up here in some dank cave. What's going on? And what does this have to do with Amanda."

"I told you, already. I just didn't tell you everything. You know I left St. Louis to come here and find Sanctuary. What you don't know is that I'd been searching for my sister. Well, I didn't find her; but I found the next best thing. Our old friend Maria, the girl my sister had been hanging with when she was taken. Long story short, Maria told me to head to Miami, find Sanctuary. She said her cousin Lace could help me find Candicia. Finding and helping people was sort of their thing.

Only, I got lost. So, I called Amanda for help just outside of Georgia. Her phone number was the only one I knew by heart and I'd lost my cell phone at this bar. It was a back woods bar, one where a girl shouldn't be going by herself. I learned that the hard way when two of the ugliest men I'd ever seen followed me and this other lady out the door. I went one way, and she went another, toward her motorcycle. They looked between us and then followed her.

I doubled back to use the phone. I watched outside the window as the woman, like, she had to be five feet tall if that, beat the hell out of those guys, got on her bike and rolled out. I freaked when they got up to head back into the bar; knew they'd take that out on me for sure. I found the main road and hitchhiked my way to Miami. The driver, this nice old man, dropped me off at a shelter he said could help me. And they did. Things got weird after that."

Cruz didn't realize that he'd gotten up and was now resting with his arms in the bars to listen.

Catching sight of him there, Shayla shifted to a sitting position, her back against the wall before she continued.

"I'd found Sanctuary, was on the approach when a car pulled up. It was Maria. She told me to get in. That I was in danger. Someone called Shadow had been waiting for me to get there, had been tracking me the whole way."

"You believed her?" Cruz asked, noting the pause. Hearing the choking sound coming from the wall he gave her a moment to compose herself.

"I believed her. I thought she was helping me."

"So, what happened?" Cruz asked, trying not to sound impatient but desperate to hurry this along.

"I met Shadow." Shayla mumbled, her arms gripping her torso tightly.

"And?" Cruz prodded, he needed something he could use.

"And... she changed my life."

Chapter 17

Amanda

We pulled up into a Red Roof Inn parking circle (not even a mile away from the airport) to Nina lounging on her Black Yamaha R6. The bike was sweet. Just not as sweet as my rebuilt 2011 Indian Chief Classic. I'd been sorry to leave my baby at home but taking the flight had been the most expedient course of travel for us. Still... I missed my cycle almost as much as I was missing my morning Starbucks right about now.

We'd barely come to a stop before Rob was out of the driver's side door, pulling Nina off her bike and into his bear hug.

Ana and I side glanced each other as Nina wrapped her arms around his waist without hesitation, hugging him back.

"Um…" Ana started throwing a side glance at Dan.

"Don't ask." He mumbled, exiting out the passenger side door after popping the trunk.

Raised blond eyebrows turned my way.

I shrugged and grinned, "Not my circus, not my monkeys." I joked before getting out of my own side of the car.

Grabbing my bag from Dan I quickly approach the two, who incidentally had separated, yet somehow seemed… closer.

Nina's face had its usual closed down expression, her brown eyes flat and seemingly vacant, though I knew they missed no detail; nothing escaped Nina's notice. I knew that for a fact.

And Rob, looking extremely relieved like he'd just been granted a new organ or something, as always, wore his heart on his sleeve. Logging this data for later scrutiny, I communicated with Nina the best way one could these days without getting attitude.

I held my hand out. Two card keys landed smartly in my palm. I chin upped my thanks turned toward Ana and with a head point toward the entrance, I got a move on.

It wasn't until we got to the elevator that my little sister bust out laughing.

My eyebrows went up. I still couldn't get the one eyebrow thing down like Balboa, but I'm sure I'd made my point. Only Ana laughed harder, clutching her stomach like we had time for any of this nonsense.

"What?" I asked in exasperation. Because thumping her would only make her laugh harder. And I had to use the bathroom, so I really had no time for that.

"You! You are what! You're becoming a Max clone." She giggled.

I frowned. "I am not." I protested, happy to hear the ding that signaled we'd reached our floor.

"Like, you haven't spoken a single word since we left the car. I swear, if you start grunting like him when you agree with what I say, I'm legally filing the paperwork to change your name to Max, Junior."

"Har Har," I snorted, moving quickly toward our designated room. "Just hurry up and get set up, we are rolling out in 10 minutes."

"Righto, Captain Max, the second."

"Heifer." I snorted, unlocking the door and running for the bathroom. Enjoying her tinkling laugh as I did so, I prayed that this wouldn't be the last time I heard it.

***

"What do you mean, were going back? I thought we decided it wasn't necessary to stop by Sanctuary?"

A part of me was relieved that we were, like I said, back up was always a good idea; and you could never have too much of that.

But that impatient part of me that wanted to get this done and get Cruz safe, that part was hijacking my mouth at the moment.

Nina shrugged, "Meeting another contact there. It's not like we're far from Cruz. It's only five miles away according to google maps."

My lips grew tight. She knew just as I did that five miles could mean the difference between life or death when dealing with Brainwaiver fallout (which I had no doubt was exactly what we were dealing with).

"You can always stay back or ride ahead." Nina shrugged, her nonchalance grating on my nerves.

"No no," Rob chided, "we're not doing that. At all. No one's separating, ya'll got that? I need eyes on all three of you at all times."

Nina and I snorted at the same time. It was Nina that responded, however.

"Going to be hard to do Action Jackson, considering everyone of us will be in open combat."

Dan looked at me, his head tilted in question, "Did she just call him Action Jackson."

I bit my cheek hard to keep from laughing out loud before responding, "Yes. I believe she did."

Dan nodded, his face dead pan. "Okay, I just needed to make sure I heard what I heard, " looking back to Nina and Rob who were both frowning at us like we'd just drowned their dog, Dan nodded again, this time toward them and said, "As you were Action, please continue."

I had to turn my back to hide my grin at Rob's expression, now smeared with attitude.

"First off..."

"Here we go with the first off," Nina interrupted, though Rob spoke over that.

"Ana is not going to be in combat, she'll be in the car keeping tabs..."

"Uh hmmm," Ana cleared her throat, "that is inaccurate. I would be a sitting duck and easy target to acquire were I to wait in the car. I will be outside the caves monitoring the situation, but not outside of range."

Almost comically, Rob and Dan both said it the same time, "Excuse me?"

And at that point I was done. Ana knew her job. The guys were being overprotective and stupid, none of which we had time for.

"If we are rolling let's roll. We got a job to do. Nina, I'm on your bike with you. Guys you got Ana. No bullying her on the way. The plan's already been discussed. Let's go."

Moving toward Nina's room door I caught the motorcycle helmet she threw at me.

And walked out without another word, surprised but pleased with the silent shuffling of feet behind me. Sighing in relief, I allowed myself a small smidgeon of hope. We might all just make it out of this unharmed after all.

But I should have known better than to think that. Murphy's law was always in effect. And today, it would come after us all with a vengeance.

***

Outside of Sanctuary...

Randy Perez

Reading the text from the unfamiliar number again on his cell, Randy wondered if he'd finally lost it. He didn't want to think that he was nuts, but life had a funny way of making sure that people reaped what they sowed. Some called it Karma. Some called it justice. He didn't really care what it was called.

All he knew is that it had a right to come for him.

He should have been the one sold. He should have been the one taken that night. He should have made his older sister Tandy and Michelle, the youngest, get on that bus.

She might have been one year older than him, but he was the man. Instead, he'd been afraid. He'd let her do it; sell herself to save him and Michelle.

For as long as he'd live, he would never forget the look on his sister's face. So strong, so proud... so good. And smart. Man, Tandy had been the smartest of all of them.

Too smart for her own good. She'd been the one to discover their mother's boyfriends plan to sell the kids. Their mother had been so drugged out, she wouldn't even hear Tandy asking her for help; crying and pleading to get us out of there before it was too late.

Her measly part time job at a burger joint was no help for the funds they needed. His mother's boyfriend would threaten to hurt him if Tandy didn't give him all her money every time she got paid. Apparently that hadn't been enough.

Shaking his head at the memory of his sister's bravery, trying hard not to remember but unable to forget, Randy felt his eyes grow wet. She'd hugged him fiercely when she put him and Michelle on that bus.

"You can keep her safe better than I can, so it's gotta be you." She lied. They both knew who really was the strongest. But she allowed him that. Allowed him to save face.

He'd never forget her, just because of that. Or forgive her. Because it should have been him. And now he was tormented with regret.

Another text. This one from a different strange number. Randy had no idea what was going on; but he felt like, for some reason, he had to be here.

While Little Havana wasn't the safest place to be hanging out, it wasn't the worst. The people took care of their own around here. It has been, as long as he'd known it, a place where street justice prevailed over the legal system. And that generated more fear, more respect than anything. Because money could buy you just about anything in the legal system these days. But street justice was swift, unerring, and not negotiable.

The fact that he was standing across the street from some old church, waiting for not one, but two strangers to meet him there, should have been his first clue that this would be an unusual night.

Michelle was constantly badgering him about church; about having a relationship with God and Jesus, or whatever. But Randy had been emphatic about shaking off her concern. There was nothing in existence that could save his soul. No God strong enough to erase his guilt.

Pulling out the cigarette from behind his ear, he settled down to wait, responding to both texts with a simple, "yep".

It was going to be a long night. But, he had a feeling (and his "feelings" were never wrong) that it was going to be far from boring.

Chapter 18

Ariela

Ariela Killian smiled into the phone as her two-year-old son babbled nonsensically in a way that, she was sure, was exposing the shenanigans his dad had been up to.

Giggling as she heard Matthew "K.C." Killian fuss at their son to give him his wife back, she couldn't keep back her grin despite the heavy feeling in her heart.

"Babe, this kid you made. I'm telling you. I blame you for his attitude."

Rolling her eyes at that, Ariela laughed into the receiver of her cell phone.

"Oh no sir, I'm afraid your son's hot-messness comes directly from his paternal line."

"No," he argued, "you're the one that insisted on naming our son Sampson. I told you that was the name of a stubborn, obstinate man. But did you listen to me?"

Ariela giggled some more. It had become a running joke between them, yet the roots were strong and very serious. Because Ariela, seemingly in a whole other life, used to be known as Delilah. Delilah Robinson.

And that life, with that name, had been horrible. A life full of bondage, sorrow and strife, Delilah had been a broken and defeated woman. Enter Celine Baltimore-Sampson.

A woman of faith, Celine became the inspiration that Ariela had needed to believe that there could be something different. Something more for her, despite how horrid a person she'd been. Despite what she'd deserved.

And just like that, her enemy became her friend. Her life had been turned on its head. And Christ had burst into her life, right when her old captors had tried to take it from her; and had given it back.

When he did, he gave it back to her with a new name. Ariela. The name meant Lioness of God. And after giving birth to her Sampson (the namesake of the woman that showed her a better way; the name of one chosen by God), she'd understood her new name perfectly. However, there was to be more to her story than she'd thought.

"How's the opening going?"

K.C. asked, making sounds with his mouth that she was sure indicated his blowing raspberries onto their baby boy's stomach. The answering baby giggles all but confirmed her suspicions.

"It's going well. I would have never thought we would have expand this far south but, you were right. The market down here is fabulous. Tourism is heavily established between Little Havana and the Miccosukee Caves here. It seems God directed us to the perfect spot for another gas station and store."

"What's wrong."

Ariela sighed. She knew she'd sounded distracted. It was because of the text message she'd just sent. A message she hadn't told her husband about. And wouldn't. God had her on another mission it seemed. One she prayed that would have a happy ending like the one she'd been blessed with.

"I was just answering a text. You know how we do, Love. We can't stop talking; even while we're talking."

His answering chuckle was all Ariela needed to slowly exhale in relief.

"Alright. Well, I have to go change your son, then I'm taking him to Mother Jenkins while I head to the store. Don't worry, Destiny is hanging around tonight. She won't let her do too much."

Sighing again in relief, this time louder, Ariela responded, "Alright Love, I'll let you go. Miss you. Miss both my boys. I'll be seeing you soon."

"Ditto Ari. Love you baby. Be safe. Okay?"

"Okay," she promised, soberly before disconnecting.

And she would do everything in her power to keep that promise. On that thought, she grabbed her jacket and keys, locked up her room at the Holiday Inn and mapped the address Randy had sent to her phone.

Heart beating wildly, she marveled at the power of God. Randy had been led right to her as her first applicant for the night manager position at the store. Taking one look at him would have been all she needed, even if the Holy Spirit hadn't slammed her with awareness.

She'd been staring, for the first time in forever at the impossible. Those eyes, hooded and blue with specks of silver had been unmistakable. They were the eyes of someone lost to her so long ago, it felt like a dream. Tandy's eyes. From that moment on, God had been speaking. She'd been listening. And now it was time.

***

Amanda

Nina and I pulled up to an old rusted corvette sitting across the street from Sanctuary. A cloud of smoke exited the front window just as the driver side door opened, letting the man who was obviously the driver of the decrepit old car, out.

Our helmets coming off at almost the same time, Nina chin-upped her greeting. Never one to beat around the bush she asked in her no-nonsense way, "You Randy?"

The long puff on an almost puffed out cigarette was drawn out before the man in question responded with a gravelly voice, "Yep".

He looked like a Randy. And at the same time, he didn't.

Slightly taller than me at about 5 feet 11', Randy was an enigma. It was clear that his heritage was Latin. But his eyes. They were the strangest, most beautiful pair of eyes I'd ever seen. Not blue. But not gray either. With silver flecks of light racing within, they were the perfect contrast for his dark hair and long black lashes.

If the man whose life we were right now trying to save didn't practically own my heart, I would have gladly cut it out and given it to this guy. Not because he was handsome. Handsome wasn't really the right word. In truth, his square jaw and hawk nose was on the average side.

It was those eyes. I couldn't explain it if I wanted to. And I was glad I didn't have to. Instead of wondering about it further, I watched, my mouth hanging open, as he flicked the butt of his cigarette into the street, grabbed his keys out his car and started walking. Right across the street to Sanctuary.

"I guess we're following," I mumbled, as Nina moved us into the space in front of his car before kicking down the stand and dismounting.

"Let's go." Was her response as she palmed the strap of her helmet and followed.

"Okay then." I shrugged, watching our rental car pull up and park in front of where Nina had situated us.

Waiting for the rest of the crew, we followed in single file fashion, with Rob at the front and Dan picking up the rear behind Ana.

Whatever it was that was waiting for us inside of Sanctuary this time, I knew one thing for sure.

This time, we were ready.

Choking on that thought as the front door swung open to reveal the vestibule, I stood corrected.

Four Gangsta Nuns; Coco, Bet, Rho and a redhead I didn't recognize from my first visit, had positioned themselves in a half circle spaced evenly around the center of the room with guns, all pointed right at us.

Coco had a sawed off shot gun. Bet was holding what looked like a silver Sig P238. Rho, as only Rho would, held a Glock 19 in one hand and a Kimber Micro 9 in the other. Last, the redhead held a beautiful carbon colored 9 mm Luger.

Nina just stood there with her hands on her hips and a twinkle in her eye. A stance that all but screamed that, while we had no clue what was going on, she definitely did.

Randy was holding both hands up with a confused look on his face and a folded piece of what looked like photo paper hanging from his right fist.

"Um. Hello." Ana spoke into the tension, "Did we come at a bad time?"

Dan and Rob both broke out in poorly faked coughing fits, forcing me to grit my teeth and roll my eyes instead of popping them both upside the head.

Because really, we had time for a shootout akin to pissing on territory with folks that were supposed to be our allies?

"I'd ask your friend here exactly what you have time for, considering she started it."

Bet said, looking right at me, along with everyone else in the room.

Oy Vey. I felt my eyes get big. When was I going to stop saying crap out loud?

***

Cruz

About to ask exactly what this Shadow person had done to Shayla, Cruz blinked as she shushed him.

She'd heard what he hadn't, with him being so engrossed while listening to her story, footsteps. Footsteps that grew louder and louder with their added echo off cavern walls. He mentally cursed, departed the bars where he'd been resting and in two strides, crossed back to his bench to sit.

Light flooded the passageway and nearly blinded him. Feeling a sting on his shoulder near his throat, Cruz swatted at the bug that must have just bitten him, only to feel a small tube sticking out.

Snatching it out he heard the big guy's humorless chuckle. Throwing it to the ground Cruz leapt to his feet, only to lilt to his right until he hit the wall.

"I know right? That stuff is potent, man."

Cruz blinked as the shadows he saw started to blend and grow fuzzy.

"It's time to get your first tattoo my friend. Don't worry, though, my friends have the perfect design to ink you up with. Your girlfriend will love it," Cruz heard, the voice speaking growing deeper as he dropped to his knees, shaking his head. "We'll make sure of it," the voice, now slow and deep like a record played backward pronounced.

The clanging click of the cell key and the cage door swinging open was the last sound he heard before his face landed in the dirt.

Chapter 19

Amanda

This time when we shuffled up to the conference room, the tentative welcome and invite to grab refreshments was conspicuously absent.

As on guard as everyone was, it was becoming extremely difficult not to roll my eyes or kick Rob or Nina; both of which were ensconced in the whisper fight battle of the century.

For the entire trek up to the conference room the back and forth became outright comical because, even though they were whispering, everyone heard exactly what they were saying. It had started downstairs when Rob, frowning at Nina, completely disregarded the arsenal of weapons pointed at our bellies. Storming over to her, he snatched her by the arm and pulled her to the side of the vestibule near the stairs.

"What did you do!" He whispered loudly, his hands on his hips as he leaned threateningly over her.

"Who, me?" Nina asked, whispering also.

I elbowed Ana who was the first to giggle at the foolishness.

"No, the owl in the rafters. Yes you! What did you do that had us walking blindly into a firefight!"

"Not a firefight, Action Ja..."

"Don't call me frikken Action Jackson! Not one more time. Answer the question!"

"Dude. You need to back off."

"Nina!"

"Action Jackson?"

"Grrrr. You.... I... You did this! I know you did."

It was at this point in their conversation that Coco, grinning, had let the shotgun rest at her side.
With a nod to the rest of the crew, all guns lowered and pointed at the floor. Everyone except for me and the red head who was staring at Randy with a strange look on her face, seemed enraptured by the clowns arguing in the corner.

"...so, you're just going to lie to me then," Rob announced, his whispered voice going up an octave, something I would have said was impossible by the way.

"I'm not lying. I'm just not telling you. Big difference."

"Woman!"

"Hey! Look! I took care of business, alright? That's all you need to know!"

"Oh really?" Rob asked taking a step back as he leaned back, the wounded expression on his face a clear indication of how that little pronouncement made him feel.

I didn't realize I'd started growling under my breath until Ana turned to me, one eyebrow raised. Getting myself under control, I cleared my throat to end this little tete' a tete'. I didn't like where it was going. And, Badmammajamma or no, if Nina hurt my friend's feelings again, it was going to be on and popping off with me swinging for the fences.

"Coco," I called, "as you can see, we're in the dark about what went down before we got here. Do you mind if we relocate to a space better suited for collaboration so we can talk this out?"

Bet, turning to Rho grinned, "I do like the way this one talks. Can we keep her?"

Rho snorted and made both of her guns mysteriously disappear. Glancing askance at the redhead and Randy, she sucked air through her teeth before marching over to the steps that led up to the second floor.

"After you," Coco nodded at me and Ana in invitation to follow.

Which brought us to now. The entire time of which, the whisper battle was still going on.

"I didn't ask you about your mission up north to Baltimore years ago, nor did I ask you about Iowa. I didn't even get in your grill about Florida that time. So, don't act like I don't give you space!"

At this Nina rolled her eyes, "stop fussing, already will you? You're starting to sound like CeeCee."

Ana choked at that. Dan faked a coughing fit. And I growled again. And prayed for at least a lukewarm cup of Starbucks as we filed through the door to find a seat around the table.

***

Cruz

Coming to consciousness this time included a dry sore throat that felt like Cruz had tried to swallow a brick, and a migraine that would probably last for days. One the neon lights flashing in the room wasn't helping.

It was when he went to grab his head that he realized where he was. Back in the tatoo parlor, strapped in a chair, with his old friend Benito hovering over him.

"Yo, he's up." Ben stated, reaching behind himself to the wall where a leather apron hung.

"Your girl will be here soon, man. I hear she's a fighter. I can't wait to meet her."

Cruz ground his teeth, relief and rage warring for the primary position in his mind. At least he'd figured out that the "girlfriend" they kept referring to must have been Shayla. The relief flooding his system only intensified his shame. Amanda was safe. Hence the rage following quickly on its heels. Because Shayla was not. This is what he couldn't piece together to get the complete picture.

They'd had him and Shayla from the beginning. Why confine them in separate places? Why wait until she was brought to him? And if they were waiting for her, why take him to the caves instead of bringing her here, to the shop? That was the part that didn't add up.

"You know Shayla's not my girlfriend, man. Why do you all keep referring to her as such?"

Cruz moved from one side to the next to test the tightness of the straps while waiting for Benito to respond.

It was when Benny turned to grin at him before tipping his head back to take a sip out of his water bottle that Cruz saw the shimmering gold and silver tatoo under his chin. Similar to wires in a circuit pattern, the tat had a slightly raised appearance like a 3-D circuit board. As he swallowed, the lines seemed to shimmer and shift, like the tattoo was moving- responding somehow to Ben's actions.

After he was done Benito swiped at his mouth with his wrist and chuckled.

Cruz tried again.

"I barely know the girl, man. I don't know what you and the giant there think is going on here but, really, you need to let me out of here Ben."

"Nah," Ben smiled before tossing the now empty water bottle "basketball shooting" style into the trash can near Cruz.

"I'm having too much fun watching you sweat. Oh, lookee here, speak of the devil, and she does appear."

Enter the giant, dragging a wide eyed, wild haired Shayla to a chair not far from Cruz. A goon wearing a blank expression followed them in, dragging some random guy whom he'd also thrown into a chair. It wasn't Shayla or the goon however that caught Cruz's attention as they filed past, but the wizened old man that brought up the rear of the group.

"Well hello there, young man. I don't believe we've met before today, though I must be honest, I've read an awful lot about you Mr. Arpaio."

Cruz felt his eyes narrow. This couldn't possibly be who he thought it was.

"Mistuh Cipher at your service," the old man nodded to Cruz, his smart canvas hat held in his hands.

Cruz's jaw dropped. You could have knocked him over with a pinecone. One of the old geezer's himself had just made an appearance.

"Old Geezuh, huh? I like that" The old man chuckled, "That must be what they called me, "he remarked to the Giant, amusement heavy in his voice.

Cruz's head dropped back to his chair, a hard sigh escaping on impact. It seemed he was picking up Amanda's habits. He'd just said that out loud. But he refused to say Oy vey. Crap was way better.

***

Amanda

It was like they had all conspired as one to not let me even get a sip of my piping hot Starbucks in.

Bet's summary of Lace's condition after Nina landed what she called a "crotch shot" with spiked brass knuckles started us off hot (a story that forced Dan to leave the room suddenly, coughing his "excuse me", as he went)

She'd paused after the telling, my guess? She was waiting for Nina to apologize. I laughed to myself at that thought. She'd be waiting until the cows came home for Nina to say she was sorry. If Nina had actually done that (in truth I didn't doubt it) she'd done it for a reason. Having met Lace, I didn't even question the why of it. She'd rubbed me the wrong way when I met her too. I mentally shrugged, Nina being Nina, that was that.

Then there was the mystery guy Randy. Apparently he and Rho were far from "strangers". This became clear to all of us when Chara asked him who he was and why he was there.

Nodding his head to Rho seated on the other side of the table, he shared, "Know Rho from way back. Figured she had resources, intel that I would need. Helping these ladies out since I owe a debt."

Rho had rolled her eyes and slouched back in her chair; arms crossed. It was the first time I'd ever seen her in a full-blown attitude snit. However, Randy had "known" her, from her reaction I'd bet gold it wasn't platonically.

It was when the red head I didn't know but had been introduced to as Madd or "MAD-D" (as it was spelled out on her black tee) suddenly asked Randy, her voice strangled, "you got sisters, Randy?"

"Just one," he'd responded, head tilting to the right. His gaze shifted from Madd then back to Rho, like it couldn't help itself. Rho suspiciously scratched her chin with a middle finger before crossing her arms again.

Madd had slumped back in her chair. Her expression was blank, but I had the strangest feeling that she was disappointed. Briefly I wondered if she "batted for the other team".

That was when Dan had decided to rejoin us, bringing us up to now when Chara calmly asked, "Nina, when you were here before, you mentioned Niecy sent you. I'm assuming you meant Denise or," with a nod to me, she finished, "Balboa. Yes?"

At that, both of Robs hands moved to cover his face. Ana's eyes got big. And I found a spot on the ceiling that silently accused me of being the dumbest person on the planet.

It was Dan who voiced what all of us were thinking. "I should have known."

In unison we groaned. Balboa had known the whole time. She probably knew everything, even the fact that we were trying to keep her free and clear of the blowback.

Nina shrugged.

"Yes, you really should have." Was all she said, her face blank, but her eyes twinkled.

And Ana, my beautiful sister and blessed soul was the next to say what the rest of us wanted to.

"Evil heifer."

I concurred. Nina's cheek twitched. And Coco laughed.

Chapter 20

Cruz

Benny stood over the unconscious guy, waiting for something. With his chair behind him and the desk with ink and drawings to his left, Ben had switched on the overhead light and was all set to do his job.

But still he waited.

Cruz's discomfort increased. For some reason, everything seemed suspiciously drawn out. Like they were waiting on something. *Or someone*, his brain silently assented. If he knew his clan, they'd be showing any minute. While he hoped avidly that it would be Nina with Max and Sam as back up, he knew better.

Sam was adamant that they begin the process of passing the torch to the next generation. A strategy that Balboa was passionately against. She insisted on calling them (all except for Cruz) her "babies" and maintained that they weren't ready mentally for the challenges.

The men didn't agree. Balboa felt that it was their way of conspiring to get her and CeeCee out of the field once and for all. She was not wrong.

Like his brother, Cruz admired the strong and independent woman with her own mind and power. But, also like his brother, he was part Italian; a heritage that reared its ugly, misogynistic head on occasion. One of those occasions included doing what it took to keep a man's woman safe.

For Cruz, specifically, keeping Amanda safe. Even if it meant moving halfway across country to do so.

A small packet was handed to Benny from one of the goons. Putting it under the unconscious man's nose, Ben smiled creepily as the man started awake.

"Welcome back Antonio," he pronounced to the room as if he were a stage performer reciting lines.

"Man, let me outta here, *Puto*!" Antonio shouted. His dark ebony skin already beginning to glisten with sweat. Eyes wild, Antonio cursed and shouted while Ben talked nonsensically and situated himself to go to work.

Turning to me with a wink, Ben leaned over Antonio's right wrist, singing Selena's "Bidi Bidi Bom Bom," all while Antonio cursed.

The silver swirling ink bubbled as the electric drill-pen buzzed, stitching into Antonio's skin along a pre-drawn marker pattern Ben had made.

Cruz realized that, just in a matter of moments, Antonio had gone silent.

Unease tightened his chest as his gaze flew to the once cursing and spitting Antonio.

A placid, unfocused glaze was all that remained of a man that had been furious moments before.

Ben stopped singing to ask, "How you feeling there Tony?"

Antonio looked to Ben and smiled blankly before saying the words that turned the unease in Cruz's chest to gut wrenching fear.

"However you wish me to feel, Benito."

***

Amanda

Urgency grabbed me like vise grips, filling me with dread.

I knew that feeling. I'd had it when Max was taken on his wedding day. I'd had it the day Cruz disappeared. I'd had it on my thirteenth birthday when my uncle took us to the Hamptons.

Cruz was in danger. We no longer had the luxury of time. I cut right through the chatter to get to the heart of our discussion. We needed to move, and we needed to move now!

"Randy, the photo," I nodded toward the photo paper sitting folded in front of him, "you said you came here for intel on it, can you elaborate."

With a half shrug, Randy slid the photo across the table to Rho. Grudgingly picking it up and holding it with two fingers, she unfolded the photo before passing it to Bet.

"Okay," Bet announced, before passing the photo to Coco.

Coco checked it, shrugged, and passed it to me.

It was a grainy pic of Shae wearing a pair of sunglasses and talking to some girl. The girl, while older, appeared to cower in front of her; shrinking in fear, almost as if she were trying to fold into herself.

It wasn't a close up shot, but I could feel the woman's terror. My heartbeat increased as I passed the paper to Ana.

"That's Shae, right?" Ana confirmed, her head tilting first left, then right, most likely taking in every little detail.

"Looks like it." I answered on automatic. What did it mean? The Shae I knew? She wasn't the kind of person that would strike fear into the heart of people, let alone someone helpless. I'd seen her with those women in that warehouse. She'd been compassionate, kind. I felt my brow tighten in confusion.

Ana, apparently done, passed the photo around the table to Dan, then Rob, who, after shrugging, passed it to Madd.

Madd's glance was almost nonchalant as she looked down and back up at us. It was her double take, then her snatching the photo off the table that caught my, and Nina's attention.

"What?" Nina asked sharply, a split second ahead of me, both of us sitting on the edge of our chairs.

It was when Madd's mouth opened to speak that the conference room door swung inward.

Aim (a caramel skinned Gangsta Nun-in-training we'd been introduced to on the way up) stood on the threshold with a woman behind her.

"Excuse me Coco, I think this lady is supposed to be in your meeting? She said she's here to meet Randy?"

"Ari?" Nina asked, shocked, as was I to see K.C.'s wife breeze into the room. The sweet, welcoming smile she wore froze as her shifting gaze stopped on Madd.

The same Madd that had dropped the photo as if it were no consequence.

"Delilah?" Madd choked, her hands clutching the table, her eyes wet.

"Oh my... Maddie?" Ari responded.

Feeling a breeze that couldn't have possibly been in the room as all windows and the door had been shut, I watched dumbfounded as the two women rushed each other. Hugging, clutching, and crying, the women babbled back and forth. Ari was holding Madd's face in her hands and kissing it all over as she did so.

Not speaking for everyone else, my mouth was definitely hanging open. Madd, possessing the calm exterior of a hardcase just seconds ago had transformed. Petite and appearing younger than she probably was, she now seemed more like a lost little girl who'd finally found her mom.

"I take it you two know each other?" Ana remarked into an atmosphere thick with silence from the rest of us.

My forehead hit the table. An act quickly followed by the entire room cracking up. Including me.

***

Ana

As inconspicuously as she could, Ana took the opportunity to check her phone while everyone laughed.

Stating the obvious never failed to break tension. While she couldn't remember where she'd learned that little tidbit of human nature, Ana was quick to try anything once that would get her to a goal.

It was an effective tool, she had to admit. One that tended to give her exactly what she needed when she needed it: anonymity in a room full of people. Even those who know you're a genius tend to forget that fact when you said or did something foolish.

Which was why she'd used the opportunity presented to do so.

And she was glad she did. Cruz had been moved. She felt bad for lying to the team about how she knew his whereabouts, but she wasn't about to tell them what she and Max had done.

That didn't mean she was sorry they'd done it. It just meant that she was sorry it would piss everyone off. Especially Nina.

Everyone, and that meant every single one of them, had some item that they never parted with. Amanda never took off the locket her mother had given her on her tenth birthday. Ana couldn't fathom why it was more important than any other gift their mother had given her, but for some reason it was.

Rob never left his wallet behind. It was always the same wallet. He never bought a new one. Just refurbished, polished and took care to preserve the old leather one he possessed.

Wherever Nina was, her bike was. Case in point, she didn't fly down like the rest of them did. She'd ridden her motorcycle. Like a trusty steed, Nina's bike was like an extension of her very self.

For Dan, it was his father's wedding ring, the one that had belonged to Sam when he'd married Dan's mom. And for Cruz it had been a silver crown in his left rear molar. A crown that his brother convinced him to take care of before his tooth ache became an abscessed tooth.

In fact, Ana was the only person that didn't have such an item. But then, she didn't need it. She was the tracker, not the trackee. She made sure that everyone knew her whereabouts, her schedule, and her habits. She purposefully surrendered her own privacy on the regular to give Max peace of mind. Besides that, she and Max had a unique way of communicating that no one, as of yet, could hinder or trace. They were two of a kind it seemed.

A thought that brought her back to the information at hand. Cruz was now located near SW 8th street. In Little Havana. Not far from them. Ana swallowed.

Glancing up from her phone her gaze collided with Bet's. A knowing stare robbed Ana of her breath before Bet looked to Chara who'd called her name.

While Ana exhaled. She began to recalculate their next move. Firing off two quick texts, she escalated the plan straight from stage two to four. It was now or never. One wrong move, and the mistake could be fatal. For all of them.

Chapter 21

Amanda

I hated breaking up reunions. Despite the urgency burning in me, I had to hear the story. So, I did. Coco had insisted upon the telling and we'd all paid rapt attention. Trafficked victims when they were young, Madd had been Ari's responsibility. In trying to help her girls escape one day, Madd disappeared. Ari had always hoped that she'd somehow gotten away and was relieved knowing she had. The other girls hadn't been so lucky. Especially Ari.

And, besides the guys that suspiciously cleared their throats on occasion, there was not a dry eye in the room.

As such, I thought we'd had all we could take with the reunion causing bitter-sweet tears. Again, I was wrong. I learned this when Ari turned to Randy and said, "This cannot be a coincidence. That my Maddie and my Tandy's brother happen to be in the same room, on the same day; God has truly given me my heart's desire."

Randy hopped up and backed away from the table, his eyes wide and hand out, like he was trying to ward off an attack.

Madd interrupted, "It's the eyes, right? I thought so too. But he can't be Tandy's. I asked him if he had sisters, he said he only had one so..."

"Not always," Randy croaked. His head was swiveling back and forth between Madd and Ari. Slowly at first, then picking up speed.

"I...," he cleared his throat before continuing, "Tandy... she was my... she is my older sister. By a year. My aunt drilled a story into me and Michelle when we were young. Telling it is a habit. I..."

Movement in the corner caught my eye. Rho had also stood. As her head turned from watching Randy, clearly in pain and distress now, her hand had gone to her back where one of her guns probably rested. Eyes narrowed at Ari and Madd, it was clearer than crystal that things were about to escalate.

"Tandy," Randy croaked again, his hollow voice completely belying the speed by which he crossed the room to clutch at Ari, a move that had Dan and Rob flying out of their seats.

"You know her? You know where she is? Tell me. Tell me how to find my sister!"

At that he shook Ari, his eyes wild.

"Aye man," Rob gritted, having reached Ari's side and pushed Randy back, his hand tight in the front of his shirt. "Hands off."

"And keep 'em off," Dan added, moving to stand so that he blocked Rob's view of Ari.

"Aye yourself there, Black Beauty," Rho nodded, her 9mm Luger now pointed right at Rob. "Let him go." Stunned at Rho's offbeat way of acknowledging my bestie's handsome visage (it was a fact, Rob would give Morris Chestnut a run for his money easy) I almost missed how Nina was on the move.

In the blink of an eye there was a switchblade touching Rho's carotid artery just at the base of her chin on the left side of her throat.

"Even think about pulling that trigger, sister, and I'll bleed you like an atoning sacrifice."

Rho's side eye to Nina said it all when she didn't even move to drop her weapon, though Rob had already released Randy.

"Stop it!" Ari shouted as crazy number one and crazy number two stalemated.

"Randy," she began, pushing past Dan who tried to catch her arm to hold her back. Shaking him off with a quiet, "I'll be fine," Ari crossed the five or six feet that separated her from Randy.

Watching her take both of his hands into hers coupled by the fresh wet sheen of her gaze, I knew. A hollow feeling grew in my gut.

"Your sister had to be the bravest, sweetest, most thoughtful person I knew."

Madd was choking in the background, her face wet as new tears raced to join the former tears of joy.

I wanted to leave the room. This moment was intensely personal. The pain I felt coming was almost unbearable for me. For Randy it would be shattering.

It was like watching a movie at half speed. I watched Rho slowly lay her gun on the table. The switchblade retracted, with Nina taking a step back.

"Go to him," I heard Nina say to Rho. She didn't have to say it twice. Rho moved and got there moments before I heard what Ari said next.

"When the escape plan went bad, the enforcer on us, Frank... he..."

"Aimed his gun at me, "Madd finished when Ari swallowed, "he aimed it right at me. I was the smallest. The baby. The favorite. He wanted to punish us for trying to leave so I became his target. That's when your sister... then MY sister too, dove in front of me, taking three bullets center mast. She saved my life. Saved me"

The choke-growl sound emanating from Randy was hard to take. I'd never heard a wail of pain behind gritted teeth and a closed mouth until that very moment.

And had Rho not grabbed hold of him and pulled him through a door situated behind the refreshment table into another room, shutting them off from us. I would have drowned in the atmosphere of grief that exploded from him.

The emotional highs and lows of this day was ripping me to shreds. All of them making more poignant than before how important it was that we get to Cruz.

Tomorrow wasn't promised. Today could go so many different ways. We really needed to get a move on.

Opening my mouth to say just that, I groaned as Madd continued in an aside to the group, "I'm not a big believer in God, even when I have seen so many miracles. But today just might make me a believer." When she moved to pick up the photo, I sighed in relief. FINALLY!

"Because apparently God ain't done." Walking over to Ari, she handed her the photo.

"Good Lord! Is that? Is that Maria?"

"One and the same," Madd answered somberly.

And I kid you not, the entire room said with me in perfect synchronicity, "Oy VEY!"

***

Max

Casually moving to put his phone in his back pocket, Max situated himself next to Balboa on their sofa while she pulled up Netflix.

"Who was the text from?" She asked, nonchalantly, biting off one of the strawberries from the fruit tray he'd laid out for her.

"What text?" he mumbled, hoping he appeared engrossed in the arduous task of paging through movie listings.

"The text you just got, glanced at when you thought I wasn't looking, then pretended you didn't get as you sat down next to me. That text."

Max ground his teeth. The woman missed nothing. Eight months pregnant, she could have the baby at any moment. Still, she never let one single detail of life slip her notice. Truly, just trying to surprise her with a gift was exhausting, let alone keeping secrets. Max exhaled, reached behind himself for the phone then handed it to her.

"Thaaank you." She responded, biting off another strawberry. With just her thumb while holding his phone in one hand, she swiftly keyed in his code. Max grumbled. He changed his code regularly, not because he wanted to keep stuff from her, but to keep her on her toes. Balboa decoded his encryptions, every time. He pretended it frustrated him to no end, like now, with growling and protests. Secretly, he was proud. His woman was one of a kind. He wouldn't have her any other way, even when she bombarded their future genius with the crap food and junk she thought she was hiding from him.

Watching her sit up straight, he knew she'd read the text. And knew right then that he was going to have to hurt her feelings.

"Ana's got this. Let her do her job."

Balboa's narrowed side eye silently shouted at him that she didn't think so.

Her phone magically appeared in her other hand, a hand that she used one thumb (much like with his phone) to key in her code and text a message.

"That to Nina?" He asked, exasperated that he'd believed for one moment he could pull this off without Balboa getting involved.

"Am I the baddest Mamma Jamma you know?" She snorted

Max sighed. Since they both knew the answer to that would be yes, he moved to create a space for her with him at his command center. It was time for them to go to work.

***

Cruz

"Lance my boy," The old geezer announced into the Sat phone he was holding in one hand, a Hostess snoball cake he'd been chewing on in his right, "get here pronto. Got a new bodyguard for you. This one's a strapping young one. Looks like that one in that Get Out movie you had me watching the other day. Wheels will be up in twenty or so. I can't wait to get the fresh batch to the compound."

Gobbling the rest of the snoball up in one bite, the old geezer pointedly glanced at Cruz with a sick, cake filled grin on his face.

"Brody, son. Show Mr. Arpaio here your ink, why don'tcha?"

Smiling a half smile that made Cruz uneasy, Brody approached his chair, pulling up his tee's sleeve to bare his left wrist.

At first glance it was a tat of the American flag slightly below a pole clutched in an eagle's wings. It was upon closer inspection that he could see the shimmering moving lines of red and blue, making the tat bunch and swirl like it was a flag waving in a breeze.

"Nice right? You can thank your little miss Shayla for this new technology. You think this girl is a goody goody, like the rest of you don'tcha? Well she ain't! At least, she wasn't when she offered to create for us a better way in exchange for the life of her sister and my wife.

But why bother making a deal with her, when I could find her boss, the Shadow, and make a better deal with him?"

The old geezer cackled, moving to the chair holding a cowering Shayla.

"Benny, boy; I want her to have a special one. Give her the eye of the tiger on that pretty left wrist. I think I might just retire Candy soon. There's no fight left in her. Shayla will do nicely to take her place. Right after she arranges that meet with the Shadow."

Cruz watched Ben take his seat over to Shayla's area and move to situate himself to go to work.

And as quickly as it took Cruz to blink and look again, Ben had been lifted out of the chair, punched twice in the face until he was out cold, and dropped to the ground in a heap.

The Giant, with speed that was unbelievable, snapped the leather bonds holding Shayla and pulled her out of the chair.

Turning at the old geezer's shout, Brody moved; crossing to him he grabbed the little man by his throat and held him dangling in the air.

"Well now, that's better. Thank you Brody," Shayla said with a shiver.

"I don't know what grossed me out more. A tacky eye of the tiger tatoo or being sexually harassed by Mr. Magoo."

Chapter 22

Amanda

Instead of passing the photo around this time, all of us hovered around a now sitting Madd, whose finger was positioned near the cowering girl in the photo.

"So, to be clear," Ana summarized, "that girl in the picture, the scared one, she's one of Ari's girls. But the other one is still Shae, right? There's no like, secret identity for her about to be revealed? She's not Ari's long-lost sister or anything?"

Elbowing my sister I told her to chill. Today had been full of surprises for everyone. None of this was Ari's fault.

"I'm just saying," she mumbled and shrugged. Rob and Dan both studied their feet suspiciously while Nina's eyes shone with a strange light.

I really needed to get a new crew. These clowns would laugh at a funeral.

Deep sighing, I turned to Coco.

"I'd hate to ask this of you, tonight being a big night for Madd and Ari." And Randy who, coincidentally was still conspicuously absent along with Rho.

"But if you can spare some back up, we could sure use it."

"Sister," Coco grinned, a glance passing between her and Bet that had Bet's dimples showing, "you couldn't keep us out of this if you wanted to."

"Good," Madd interjected, "Because, I'd hate to say your sister was right, but when she's right..." Madd shrugged.

"What do you mean?" The ominous feeling in the pit of my stomach grew and spread throughout my entire body.

"The woman in that pic? The one you know as Shae? We call her something else in the underground."

"NO!" Coco shouted, disbelief making her voice carry.

"Yes ma'am," Madd shrugged, "Ghosts (folks that work the black market and underground transport of illegal property and people are called ghosts) from Louisiana to Miami know her well. Is Randy coming back soon?"

"Why, and who is she?" I asked hurriedly, impatient to get this done.

Madd shrugged yet again; I tried not to let it bug me, "Because it's been known to be impossible to photograph the Shadow. Somehow he pulled it off. I wanna know how."

***

Cruz

"What do you mean, you're The Shadow?" Cruz shouted. Fighting against his bonds, he cursed and strained, all the while watching amused glances pass between Shayla and the Giant.

"Don't make me say it twice Bro," she sighed, flexing and stretching her neck and arms.

"You men. Always so quick to believe that a man has to be the big boss. Always underestimating the power of women despite powerful women being a constant in your lives. Its sad how pathetic you all are when confronted with the truth."

"What truth?" Cruz asked warily as Shayla made her way over to his chair.

Her fingers danced up and down his exposed arm; one that he didn't fear for now quite as much considering Ben was out cold.

Not having the first clue what their plan was since Brody still held the old geezer dangling in one hand; Cruz had one move left; he had to keep her talking. Strong, weak, indifferent; there was one universal truth about women that he knew he could use to his advantage. Women loved to talk.

"Oh, look at you, boyfriend, so clever aren't you," Shayla said, reaching forward to pinch both of his cheeks and shake his head like an old lady with a toddler.

"You think this is the movies honey? That the big baddy is going to spill all about their master plan right before the calvary arrives to save the day? How cute!"

Reaching into one of Benito's drawers, Shayla grabbed two sticks of gum, unwrapped them and popped them in her mouth.

Turning with the packet to Cruz she offered, "Gum?"

"No," Cruz gritted.

Brody chuckled. The old geezer wheezed.

"The thing is, " Shayla sighed, moving toward a different work station where a drawer stored hair tie holders and other miscellaneous junk, "I do want to have a chat with you before company arrives. Because the truth is, I'm not your enemy." Nodding her head toward Brody and the old geezer, Shayla blew a huge bubble while pulling her hair into a ponytail on top of her head.

"I'm his." This she said with such finality that Cruz didn't know what to expect. Which was partly why he shouted in surprised when she turned to Brody, hands on her hips, her face openly malicious and said in her next breath, "Kill him."

The groan just before a crunching snap filled Cruz with dark fury. Not because they'd just killed the old geezer. The man and his brother were pure evil. And, while he wasn't a supporter of outright murder, the world was a better place without such undiluted wickedness.

No, rage burned in him because, the Shayla that had just callously ordered an execution right in front of him like she was ordering breakfast had proven her point. She was and had been the Shadow all along. She'd been playing him. And there was only one reason why she would. A reason that was probably on her way to rescue him. Right into an obvious trap. Amanda had been the target all along. And it would be his fault if Shayla got what she wanted.

***

Amanda

Watching Nina palm her cell to check it, then put it to her ear and move out of the conference room, something told me we'd just run out of time.

Randy had composed himself and made no bones about wanting to be in on the breach.

He briefly explained his less than exemplary life in making underground runs for the black market. A friend of his aunts (that would be Balboa) had provided connections that could get him out of the life if he promised to go straight the moment they did. Thus, his applying for a job at Ari's new store.

That said, his primary cargo had been arms and guns. His original intent in getting involved in the black market had always been targeted to finding his sister. Until a shipment of guns he'd been responsible for came up missing, he'd pretty much become a regular part of the underground.

Following as many leads as he could in hopes of recovering the missing shipment, he'd lucked upon the exchange with the woman known as the Shadow. Quickly snapping the pic while the two women were talking, he'd hoped that having a picture of the Shadow to trade for information or assistance could save his life one day.

He'd never expected to have to use his trump card this way. But they'd made him an offer he couldn't refuse. An offer he wanted to follow up on for a whole other reason as well, one he didn't have to verbalize since his body language exposed him (as in he couldn't keep his eyes off her). Rho.

Despite all that, Randy offered his help. Figuring we could always use another body, I asked if he'd mind standing guard over Ana.

This brought us to now. We were all gathered in the vestibule getting new schematics from Ana about the change in location.

We'd decided to continue the plan as intended; splitting in three groups now instead of two since both Ari and Madd refused to stay behind.

As Nina walked into the room, Bet called out, "Forgot to ask you Irwin, what happened with Lace for you to punch her in her lady balls?"

My mouth dropped open.

"Oh, my Lord," Ari breathed.

"Good gravy," Ana snorted.

Dan and Rob silently studied the ceiling.

"She knew the Shadow; knew she'd be our best bet in finding Cruz or Shae. Shadow is the biggest name in trafficking around here. Lace tried to hide her connections. She failed. Balboa found a link and thought it suspicious that Lace never shared."

"Yeah," Bet asked belligerently, "How so? What link?"

"Oy," Nina sighed, "That girl in the pic, Maria? That's Lace's cousin."

I felt my eyes roll.

"Of course," Ana nodded, throwing her hands up then dropping them to her thighs with a slap.

I gritted my teeth at God. Because really, Father? You're making the coincidental connections a bit obvious aren't you?

Rho, grinning at me, announced, "Maybe He figures you're too dumb to follow breadcrumbs. And yeah, before you ask, you said that out loud."

Chapter 23

We'd piled into the Sanctuary passenger van that normally picked up seniors on bingo night. This was right after the center's chaplain mysteriously appeared to say a brief prayer over us. An actual chaplain! One thing you had to say about these Gangsta Nuns; they owned that title despite Coco's insistence that they weren't really nuns.

I didn't know what to expect when we rolled up SW 8th street, but what I saw was consistent with everything I knew of Calle Ocho. Sort of the main street (what us Midwesterners would call it anyway) it was home to the Little Havana Visitors Center, shops, restaurants, and tourist catchalls.

While there were some places I recognized from the Midwest such as a Walgreens Store, Dollar Tree and Motomart gas station; there were unique calling cards of the area that stood out; like palm trees, mounted police, cigar shops and double decker buses. The traffic was semi-light, even at this time of near twilight, still the festive atmosphere of Cuban culture was a notable influence. Always present, the culturally rich sites, aromas and attractions continually grabbed the attention of unsuspecting tourists like me.

One thing I knew for certain; there was no way to approach unseen. Unlike the prior locations the Mu-whatever caves Ana had mapped; there was no terrain to mount an attack. We were out in the open, from the front and (according to Nina who had scouted ahead) semi open via a parking lot in the back. Located on the second level of a multi-shop building, there was only one way up and out from the front. We weren't going to be taking anyone by surprise.

The plan had to change. Dan and Rob were opposed to the new approach. One that I was wholeheartedly down with.

Because I was beyond angry. One could say, I was downright furious. Shae was the Shadow. And, despite Balboa's warnings, I'd trusted her. Even when she came under suspicion for getting into that car, there was a part of me that refused to believe what I saw.

I felt more than hurt, I felt betrayed. Balboa once told me that every person, at one time or another, had to experience a Judas. Shae was mine. And unlike Jesus, a kiss on my cheek was the last thing I wanted to accept; rather, I'd like to punch her in hers.

Thus, the new plan took a more brazen approach. Me walking in the front door like I owned the place. Alone.

Nina surmised that Shae had gone through all this trouble just to get to me for some reason. I did know this: if she wanted me so bad? She was going to have me. Settling back to pray with only an eta of 4 minutes to go, I focused on the One that was my center. It was time for the Shadow to meet up with the Light. Even as I felt my stomach pitch and turn in anticipation; I held fast to the truth. The light would win. In fact, He already had.

***

I snorted at the name of the tatoo parlor, "The Shady Eight". The play on both Shae's name and "the Shadow" was not lost on me. I would have actually been proud of the cleverness of it if I didn't want to really hurt the woman.

Giving a nod to Nina who peered at me from the roof a brief second before she disappeared, I pushed through the front door into the smoky, neon lit atmosphere.

Having changed into my battle gear of a light leather bomber jacket (loose enough to allow flexibility and thick enough to fend off weapons), I grimaced at the snug fit of Nina's bullet proof vest. She'd forced it on me the minute we decided the plan had to change.

A good idea, despite the snug fit since, as mad as I was, I still wasn't bullet proof.

My eyes had finally adjusted to the low light of the room with neon accents just in time for me to duck the swing at me coming from my left.

Without thought, my self-defense and Krav Maga training kicked in. Coming out of my dodge, with a reverse spin hammer strike, my right slammed into the ear of the attacker:

The burly barrel-chested black man stumbled to his left. Advancing before I lost my advantage, I pressed in with a right cross, a hook, then another spinning hammer strike to increase the force of the blow. Going down, my attacker took out an equipment table and lamp on his way to the floor.

Before the clatter of falling objects stilled, I heard clapping coming from the back of the room. Unsurprised to see Brody and Shae standing there together with disturbing grins on their faces, I cracked my neck, sliding both hands into my pockets to grab the Kubatons there.

"She's good isn't she? I told you she was good. Almost as good as that Nina chick you told me about Bro."

"Yeah, "Brody grunted, "Balboa's better."

Nodding, solemnly before adding, "We'll see," Shae looked back to me and bared her teeth.

"So, Mandy... How's things?"

***

Ana

Biting her lip in frustration, Ana wanted to hate Nina. She'd made climbing onto that roof look hecka easy.

Then, being yanked up by her in frustration when Ana finally managed to get one leg and arm up over the edge (with Randy's help), didn't add any positive vibes to already turbulent emotions.

Her sister was about to be in the fight of her life and here Ana was, struggling to climb an 8-foot wall. Forcing feelings of shame and inadequacy down in her gut so that she could focus, Ana immediately found and settled into the southern corner of the roof. Opening her laptop and connecting it to the hotspot on her phone, she went to work without a word.

Having seen the slew of motorcycles parked in the small open spot between the buildings, it was obvious that both rounds of reinforcements she'd calculated would be needed.

Looking up as Nina blew past her, "Where do you think you're going?" flew out of her mouth before she could catch the words.

Nina halted for two seconds, then with a swift about face and three steps, dropped to one knee right in front of her.

Ana reared back, her eyes growing wide.

Nina smirked.

Opening her mouth to apologize, Ana squeaked as Nina's hand flew forward, her finger jabbing right into her nose.

"Listen up little Liar. When this is over. You and me? We're having words. Whatever the plan you might have concocted, it better be good. It's not lost on me that you've been playing all of us, moving us around like pieces on a chess board. So, all this? It's on you. Anyone get's hurt? I hold you responsible. And if anyone dies? You and me gonna have more than words. Understand?"

Nodding quickly with a hard swallow, Ana deep breathed as Nina got back to her feet and, in two seconds slipped over the side of the building by the clearing where all the bikes were.

With a quick shake of her head, she focused again on her keystrokes. If keeping her sister safe wasn't already a hefty incentive; she had more reason not to fail than ever. In reality, Ana knew that she could strategize and think circles around the best of the best. However, she wasn't so smart that she was stupid. If Nina ever decided to come for her, no matter how intelligent Ana was, there was no place she would be able to hide.

Cracking her neck on both sides, a bad habit she'd picked up from her sister, Ana whispered a silent prayer. Her plans might be many. But God's always prevailed. Deciding to trust His plans over hers? That was the challenge. One that Ana strangely felt she was about to meet head on.

***

Dan

Slapping hands and fist bumping Rob before he headed toward the back of the building, Dan looked up to see Randy slip over the top of the roof after boosting Ana up. With his hand right on her behind.

Fighting the growl in his throat and forcing himself to focus, Dan peeked around the corner into the back-parking lot before flattening himself against the wall.

There were at least six bikers back there, two leaning through the windows of a Ratrod classic truck, checking out the inside; there were two looking at the same car from the back with the last set of two standing with their backs to a cherry red mustang.

Closing his eyes, Dan did what he hated that he knew how to do. Being a BW had some advantages. Having had the bypass for controls on the chip in his brain removed by Cheryl, he'd had to learn how to mentally harness the power of the chip.

While his physical body had adapted to the implant, growing stronger and more muscular in a way that aged him almost five years overnight in development; the rest of the chips abilities that could be used to manipulate synapses, neural activity and cellular responses had been cut off when Cheryl severed the chips Wi-Fi capability.

Over time, Dan had learned through prayer and meditation, to mentally access the chip as if it were a body part, like an arm and a leg, and trigger synapse and neural manipulation by accessing the bios and tiny hard drive of stored knowledge. Without a continued WiFi connection, new information couldn't be added to the chip, but it had no problem accessing the data already stored there.

However, Dan had learned something else. Once deciding to become a law student, he'd studied for his courses heavily before realizing after one night of horrible sleep and barely glancing at his book, that he didn't have to.

He now possessed and eidetic, tonal memory as well as photographic one. All he had to do was look through, hear or see something once. His brain would store the information in short term memory like usual. But the chip having access to both short term and long term, would use both like a computer would access data on a hard drive. Data that, like with the click of a mouse on an icon, could be accessed, harnessed and recalled.

Thus, a sweeping glance of the men, cars and positioning of possible exits in the back had been taken in and recorded with just a glance. Pumping himself with adrenaline, Dan moved forward into the open.

"Hey guys, you happen to see a lost puppy around here?"

Cuban, Spanish and English cursing littered the air as the six he knew about (and three he didn't from out of a back door of the store behind him) moved toward him.

Dan grinned and pulled his collapsible fighting baton from his sleeve. Hearing Rob behind him going to work inside the store that the three had just come out of. He twirled his stick and slammed the base into the ground, assuming his fighting stance.

With a Bruce Lee "come with it" gesture from his right hand, Dan's grin morphed into something dangerous.

It had to have been so unnerving that, with one glance at each other, his attackers came at him en masse.

Which was good. More than good, it was exactly how he liked it.

Chapter 24

Cruz

"Amanda, get out of here! It's a trap, she's the..."

"The Shadow, "Amanda finished before he could. "Right? The Shadow? Shae? Shady Eight. All in Calle Ocho?" Shaking her head, she crossed her arms, freaking Cruz out by the fact that she hadn't moved to escape like he hoped.

"One thing I can say about you Shayla, you've always had style."

Cruz cursed. But he didn't try again. He knew the look on Amanda's face. Had committed it to memory like so many others. She was pissed. At the same time, she was eerily calm. Calculating. It was impressive. And even more frightening.

His Amanda had grown up and come into herself in a way he'd hoped she never had to. So much like CeeCee when he'd met her, he felt something like sorrow at the absence of that unique vein of innocent expectation that had defined her.

The woman before him was hard as nails, smart as a whip and as dangerous as a striking Cobra. She'd taken out Antonio with a combination that smacked of Balboa's training. With a little something new thrown in. An edge that made it her own.

"I have haven't I?" Shayla shrugged, moving casually in front of Brody and around Cruz's chair.

Stepping over the body of the old geezer they'd just left there in the floor, she approached Amanda, then walked a circle around her, like she was surveying a thoroughbred.

"But then, sis," She said softly from behind Amanda into her left ear.

"So have you."

Amanda hadn't moved or even started at the wind of breath that blew at her hair. In fact, her eyes were completely focused on him. They were assessing, looking for clues or signs of injury was his guess.

"I'm okay, Baby." He said it softly, watching her exhale as if in relief before she tensed when Shayla came around the front of her in a face off that blocked his view.

"He is. Okay, I mean... at the moment. But he is not what I want to discuss right now. You, however? Look at you girlfriend! Looking like Mulan, you're all grown up and saving China."

Amanda's head tilt and narrowed gaze shifting from around Shayla to right at her spoke volumes.

Realizing what Shayla said somehow struck a chord, Cruz cursed.

"And just like always," Shayla continued, apparently unfazed by the burning in Amanda's eyes, "China revolves around a man who threw you away like molded cheese. Something a sister would never have done. I'm not your enemy, Amanda. I'm here to right some wrongs done to me, and several done to you."

"What? You disappear without a word, call me to draw me down here to look for you, then become the Queen of Trafficking, and suddenly you have my best interest at heart?" Amanda snorted. "Do tell," she ended sarcastically her arms crossing with a Kubaton grasped in each hand.

Good girl, Cruz thought. She couldn't afford to be caught off guard. A thought that was better reserved for himself after Shayla's next words.

"I will. I started with one of them, aka, the old pile of crap there on the floor. That was one of mine. Now, we get to do one of yours. Isn't that right, Cruz?" She said, just as Brody pulled a stool up beside his chair and grabbed a tatoo pen with swirling silver ink attached.

"He's my gift to you Mandy," Shayla shrugged, "that human stain on the floor stole my sister from me, he turned her into a brainless, spineless, walking puppet." Having walked over to the body of the old geezer, she kicked it hard in the side twice before turning back to Amanda with a smile.

"See, he's a goner. I did that. I may have lost that sister, but I never lost you. You became the sister I needed when I thought all was lost to me. I'd found her, you know. I'm surprised your Max didn't tell you about feeding me that intel. I'd found her, followed her, and watched her shop at Niemann Marcus in Frontenac. I whispered her name from one of the rounds. She didn't even move. Didn't even look my way. Seeing her bodyguard step out to use the phone, I ran to her, grabbed her, hugged her, and cried. Do you know what she did? She snatched away from me in disgust and pushed me. I told her it was me, her sister. Didn't she recognize me?" Shayla laughed; it was an unsettling sound.

Hearing the buzzing of the pen kick in, Cruz allowed his gaze to drop to Antonio on the floor then burn a trail through Amanda's who'd been watching Brody near him the whole time.

"Run baby, get outta here." He mouthed, hoping to God that she would listen before it was too late.

"She called her security guard on me," Shayla finished, her laugh hollow.

"So, she was a lost cause," Shayla shrugged before turning to me with a malicious stare.

"One that gave me a purpose. I would find out what they did to her. How they did it. And when it was time, I would even the score. I lost a sister. One of these evil bastards just lost a brother."

"But hey!," Shayla shouted and clapped with false cheer, "Enough about me, lets talk about you! This one right here, he left you didn't he?" Moving around behind

Cruz's chair, Shayla pulled his head back so that he could only stare at the ceiling versus urge Amanda to leave with his eyes.

"He left you. Left you behind like you were a used maxi pad. Gross right? I had eyes for him myself until I saw how he looked at you. You were my new sister though. I didn't begrudge you happiness. In fact, the only reason I left is because I felt like he would take care of you. But did he? Did he take care of you?"

"Shae..." Amanda said cautiously, right before Cruz felt his head lifted and slammed hard back into the chair.

"No! No, he did not! He left you! I trusted him to stay there and take... care ... of... YOU!" She gritted, pounding Cruz's head back into the chair four times, punctuating each word.

"So, I've decided to make him your first."

"My first what?" Amanda asked, her eyes growing wide with the same horror that Cruz felt consume him.

"Your first slave, girlfriend. You can use him however you want; sex slave, bodyguard, butt wiper... whatever you need, he'll be. And he'll do it with joy. Like I said, my gift to you."

"What the hell," came from the front door as the bell above it rang simultaneously, "do I have to do to get a little service around here."

It was Nina, with Bet and Rho coming in behind her, the latter two holding guns; at which Cruz exhaled quietly in relief.

"Welcome to the party ladies," Shayla grinned, before making a 9 mm appear out of nowhere with lightening reflexes and firing two rounds, right into Nina's chest.

***

Ana

Hearing the gun shots, Ana palmed her cell. They were out of time. Texting one word, "NOW," she was back at her keyboard, pulling up a chat window that gave her direct access to Max.

"Status?" Max grunted as soon as the video chat focused to show his face clearly.

Balboa's face appeared briefly beside his. Ana rolled her eyes.

"Not good. Unknown. I've got two drones watching the back lot, the guys have neutralized approximately twelve. I've got heat signatures in the other two lower level stores, so many that I can't get a lock on a number. They are on the move."

"What happened?" Max asked, pen now to his mouth between his teeth as both of his hands went to his keyboard, typing as fast as, if not faster than Ana.

"Gunshots, two. Show two heat signatures on the floor, one cooling rapidly, the other still bright orange. Four other signatures are standing, and another is sitting. There are three more in a room the main one, also on the move."

"What's the play?" Max asked around the pen, a pacing Balboa moving back and forth behind him.

"Old friends that just happen to be in the area are en route."

Max paused.

Balboa didn't. Pushing his chair aside, her face bent into the webcam, her expression stern,

"Anabella Same! What did you do?"

Ana grinned. "Who me?" She joked, despite the hollow feeling growing in her belly at the thought that her sister could be on the floor bleeding out below her.

Balboa didn't bother to ask again. Which was fine because Ana wasn't listening. More was going to be needed. And she was just getting started.

***

Dan

Two gun shots. Dan and Rob's gazes collided before sprinting to the front of the building. Only to meet up with a crowd of bikers heading toward the same set of stairs that they were. Ari and Madd were already up there, holding their own surprisingly well against a crowd of hairy testosterone.

There were no shouts, or yells as the women crushed knees with well-placed kicks and executed hip tosses, sending bikers over the second story handrail. It was downright creepy when Dan thought about it. Moving quickly, he and Rob began to take on the crowd from the back.

The stairs created a bottleneck effect that was perfect for them as well as the ladies above. Only two bikers could attack at a time. It was why the guys were able to do so much damage before reinforcements started piling in from behind.

Confident that the women were going to be okay because of the bottleneck, Dan and Rob turned to confront those behind them, moving faster than the eye could track.

But it was like fighting a hydra. One went down, another took its place.

Even when Randy had appeared out of nowhere to join the fray, it just wasn't enough.

Dan was starting to take hits from all directions. As fast as he was, he couldn't block them all. There was just too many. But he couldn't stop, they had to keep fighting. If they went down, there was no other line of defense besides Ari and Madd. Once the goons realized that they could approach another way from the back and use the roof, it would be all over.

That realization alone had Dan pushing through the pain, swinging wildly, desperate to take them down before he, Rob or Randy faltered.

Hearing crunching somewhere in the distance, Dan peaked through the arms he was using to block kicks and blows flying his way.

Groaning in relief, he'd never been so glad to see Coco and her sawed off shot gun. Butt end up, she was using the rifle to bludgeon goons left and right, swinging like she was an all-star ball player. Soon, however, she wouldn't be enough. The crowd around them was increasing.

Having no idea where more reinforcements were coming from, Dan was about to snatch Rob and Coco out of there (Randy had already gone down and rolled several feet away to avoid being trampled) until he saw chains appear.

Wrapping around the necks of their attackers, he watched many of them be yanked back as loud banshee yelling rent the air.

Dan dropped his guard, his mouth falling open.

An ebony Amazon with a nose ring and lip hoop, two long thick braids down her back Indian style, and a tat across her throat ACDC style that read, "SLICK CHICKS," yelled out with a voice full of gravel and base; "YO! SAME!"

Ana appeared at the edge of the roof frantically waving her right arm.

"Up here," she yelled down.

With a chin nod, as the rest of the women dressed in black leather like the Amazon continued taking out the rabble, she moved.

"Where's my girl?" She gritted out, the gravel sound hurting Dan's ears.

"Inside the tattoo joint. She might be down." Ana shouted back.

"The hell you say!," The Amazon bellowed, incredulous.

Though he knew he wasn't the target of the wrath that emanated from her, Dan took a step back.

And watched in awe as every goon between them and the front door of where Amanda had entered became the Amazon's focus. Her gravel war cry was like nails to a chalk board as she took them on.

Dan and Rob along with Chara and Randy rushed to help, Ana's assessment that Amanda might be down, echoing in the night.

Chapter 25

Amanda

The sound of rushing wind beat at me as cold fury blurred my vision. Life suddenly transitioned into slow motion mode while I watched Nina take two hits to the chest, falling backward to the floor, her eyes closed. Strangely, the serenity prayer came to mind. Because that was the perfect way to describe her expression as she went down. Serene.

I breathed a sigh of relief after seeing no blood spatter. Nina always wore a bullet proof vest. Balboa insisted on it. Bounty hunters didn't walk into nice, hospitable situations. It was the one thing Nina budged on when it came to Balboa and CeeCee's nagging.

Ready to turn and deal with Shae who was on the move toward me and Bet, a hint of wet shine caught my eye. The holes on Nina's chest, one was leaking through the black leather of her jacket. And that's when I remembered.

I was wearing her vest.

Shae and Bet were into some heavy hand to hand combat when I ducked out of range, hit the floor and slid to Nina on my knees.

For some reason, only one of the wounds was leaking. From what I could tell, the bullet should have hit and shattered the breastbone, ruptured an artery and lodged in her spine. Nina exhaled.

"Hold on, Neen, I gotcha." I choked, fighting back nausea.

My mind moved a mile a minute as I tore fabric from my shirt to pack the leak that, for the kind of injury it was, was surprisingly light. I tried to apply pressure without pressing too hard. If her breastbone was shattered, a piece of it could penetrate the heart and lungs underneath.

Another breath had me praying harder than I'd ever prayed before.

I was so focused on Nina; I almost missed that Bet and Rho had been thrown into the work area near Brody where three enforcers spilled out of the back room, obviously to contain them.

Shae sauntered toward me, shouting over her shoulder, "Let's go Bro, and make it something nice, yeah? Like a badge or a cross. Oh oh! A motorcycle! Amanda likes motorcycles! Right sis?"

Ignoring her, I focused on keeping Nina breathing. I should have known better than to take the vest! I should have known that she would need it more than I did.

Stooping beside me, Shae announced, "hmmm. That must be bad. Tough break, Right? She usually wears a vest, or something doesn't she?"

I felt my teeth grind, continuing to pray under my breath. Shae had done her homework.

"I saw her you know. Just outside of Georgia on my way down here. Watched her take out two goons," she snapped her fingers and finished, "just like that."

My vision, before blurry with rage, cleared as I felt Nina's heartbeat steady. Eyes narrowed, my focus centered on her serene, Mona Lisa expression.

"That day was the day I decided not to be anyone's victim, thanks to her. It would be a shame if she died." Shae shrugged.

My focus so intent on Nina's face, I couldn't help but start in surprise when her eyes popped open, I saw her wink, then she exploded. And that's when I realized, what I really should have known. That Nina was too stubborn to die.

Rising fast with an ab crunch, Nina throat punched a shocked Shae before raising a knee to kick her backward, only to follow; announcing with glee, "It would be a shame, wouldn't it? Lucky for you, it's not my time just yet." Swirling her switchblade and palming another, Nina grinned. "Too bad I can't say the same about you. It wouldn't be a shame if you died. At all."

A cacophony of sounds seemed to erupt into my ears all at once. The sound of Brody and the drill pin that was inches from Cruz's skin, shouts from outside and inside as Bet and Rho finished disarming their attackers.

All of which faded just as quickly when I took in Cruz's face. His sad smile. *Always you*. He mouthed. *Always*, as the pen touched his skin.

I screamed and moved. Just not fast enough. I heard the door crash open behind me but what I didn't hear was the drone that had entered. One of my sister's technical pets, the drone rotated once in the room, seeming to take everything in.

Then, zipping past me, three projectiles flew from the thing. One shattering the pen Brody was holding, one landing in Cruz's arm where the first bit of ink had been sinking in, and one directly into Brody's throat.

I don't know what I expected. But I can tell you what I didn't.

I didn't expect Dee to come busting through the store entrance, screaming bloody murder; her gravel laced voice music to my ears.

I also didn't expect to see Brody pull the projectile out and toss it to the floor. Whatever Ana's plan had been, whatever cocktail of geniusness she'd put in that dart; it had failed miserably. Last, I didn't expect my sister's voice to greet me from her flying watchdog, "Thank God you're okay! I was up here losing my mind." Rolling my eyes, I refocused to confirm that Cruz was okay.

Black smoke rose heavily from Cruz's arm, making my breath hitch. Looking to his right, I watched in horror as Brody's left wrist also began to smoke and catch fire while, strangely, his right eye twitched systematically. Since Dee was moving quickly in Brody's direction, I was less concerned about him and much more concerned about Shayla.

Breathing another prayer before turning to help Nina, I reminded myself to hug my little sister's big genius head if we made it out of here alive.

***

Ana

"Talk to me," Max grunted, his fingers flying over his keyboard.

"Cruz is stable. Looks like nanotechnology combined with enhanced skin-grafting tech and some seriously advanced bioengineering goes into this "tattoo". Our best guess, we're looking at the newest version of Brainwaiver."

"Dios mio." Max mumbled, pulling up the schematics the drone had recorded onto his screen.

"You realize what this means," Ana conversed casually as her typing speed increased.

"No surgery. No muss. No fuss." Max stated matter-of-factly, quickly mapping the data to his software for a closer look at the nanotech used.

"More than that. Think less logic, more myth. By the way, the EMP dart worked perfectly. In Cruz's forearm, the charged serum burned out the nano's there upon contact. His injection was small and localized to that region of his arm. It didn't take long to rid him of any trace of the bots."

"Good," Max grunted, sitting back for his wife, the weapons engineer scooting in for a closer view.

"The test will be to see how Brody reacts, however," Ana continued, "Not only has he been chipped with the traditional Brainwaiver, he also has the nanos. The nano protocols and tech had no problem overriding the initial Brainwaiver chip. Do you think his old BW programming will kick in once the nanos are burned away?"

"Let's hope not, "Max grunted, "Cruz will have his hands full either way."

"I concur," Ana grinned, "I can't wait to see it."

Max snorted. He knew that Ana was recording the whole thing with her drone hovering on watch.

More than entertained at the thought of Cruz getting his butt kicked after what he did to her sister, she set her sights on activating the next wave of back up protocols.

Typing some more before entering the final three keystrokes she asked, "Did you guess what the tattoo means, yet?"

Max grunted. Translation: don't know, really don't care.

"Really, babe?" Balboa fussed in exasperation.

"What?" Max shrugged, leaning closer to his screen.

"It means we are looking at prototype numero uno of the mark of the Beast."

"What beast?," Max returned, obviously distracted.

"Oy Veh," Balboa sighed before rising to waddle off.

Ana laughed, unnerved at what she knew to be true. Oy Vey indeed.

***

Amanda

Nina flew sideways, giving me pause. It was clear to me that Shae would require a more strategic, less forceful approach. Not only had she learned how to fight, she was enhanced. Plus, the grin on her face indicated the truth: she was just playing with us.

A quick glance to my right told me Bet and Rho had gotten Cruz free.

Dee and Brody were locked together, combatants in a wrestler's clutch.

"Explain to me again why we're fighting exactly?" Shae asked, dodging Nina's right cross to dance backward.

"What do I have to do to prove that I'm doing this for us?" she fainted left then right, dodging two more punches before executing a perfect roundhouse that sent Nina backward six feet.

Nina growled.

I'd seen enough; attacking Shae from her left (her weak side), with a well-placed knee kick, I caved in her left leg. Stumbling, she quickly righted herself then stopped, hands on her hips.

"Don't you get it yet? We're both victims of a sick, misogynistic society! They stole me and my sister and SOLD us for sex, Mandy? You get that right? This world is evil sis, and that evil begins and ends with men. Somebody must make it right Amanda. By somebody, I mean us."

Dan and Rob followed by Chara and Madd burst through the door.

"I see," Shae sighed shaking her head. "Your calvary has arrived before we could even finish our chat. Lucky for me though, you're not the only one with a calvary.

A loud whooshing noise over our heads indicated a helicopter was directly above us.

"Ana!" I shouted toward the drone, only to watch it list to the left, then right, then fall to the ground unresponsive.

"This isn't over, sis." Shae grinned as the drone clattered, "I have so many plans to take back what's ours. Starting with your uncle." Laughing at the shocked look on my face, Shae ran to then dove out of the north window, shattering it completely as she went.

I didn't think twice. Running for the back, I prayed one last prayer for Ana. And myself. I couldn't imagine what I'd become if Ana had been hurt. I just knew that, whatever it was, it wouldn't be good.

Chapter 26

Ariela

Urged by a force greater than herself, Ari didn't follow the guys into the tattoo shop with Coco and Maddie.

She needed to get to the roof. She didn't know why, she just did. And when an urge like that took hold, she never bothered to question it.

Racing to the back of the second-floor landing, she found the ladder that led up to the flat roof where she knew Ana and Randy had gone earlier. A quick glance to the ground beneath showed Randy still taking on random soldiers intent on getting to the second floor.

Climb.

Hearing that voice crystal clear, one that had grown more familiar than her own, Ari didn't hesitate.

Her feet hit the roof just as a helicopter came into view from the south, reaching their location in just minutes.

Racing toward Ana who was desperately packing up her gear (why it was a greater priority than Ana's safety she couldn't possibly guess), Ari jumped backward as a large body, having launched itself from the helicopter apparently, landed right in front of her.

The face of the man grinning scarily at her was an unknown. Taking her battle stance, pulling a stiletto from her boot as she did, she was ready to attack. Two more bodies had hit the roof and were heading straight for Ana.

It was the voice that froze her; a chill of fear and rage threatening to steal her reason.

"Well if it isn't my old toy, Delilah. Good to see you doll. Time has been good to you. How bout we play a round of where's it hurt the most for old time's sake?"

Ari straightened her shoulders and focused. Reality slowed in comparison to her processing speed as she took in Ana, the two men she was trying to fend off with the heavy backpack, and Lance.

I am with you. Be not afraid.

Warmth and heat radiated from her innermost self as Ari's gaze flashed at the man who'd once hurt her for kicks and giggles.

"Okay. Lets." She said, right before attacking with a swirl of kicks, punches, and knife slashes.

Somehow sending a signal to Rob and Dan (though she had no idea how), Ari felt their presence in her head as she mentally shouted.

"Reinforcements needed on the roof. They're after Ana!"

Ducking Lance's round house and meeting him in his inner thigh with an uppercut, Ari grinned. Finally. A fair fight. It was time for a little payback.

***

Ana

The emergency shut down had been her last resort. Ana, moving as quickly as she could to pack everything up, knew two things:

First, she couldn't let them get their hands on her laptop. She and Max knew way more than these people thought they did. If they got their hands on her computer, everyone they knew lives would be forfeit.

And second, Ari was a pimp! Even while she was distracted by the two enforcers rushing her, Ana's attention was divided on evading capture and watching Ari work.

The woman was poetry in motion. Ana wondered (as the goon tried to grab for her again and she slammed him with her backpack) if Ari had been a dancer in her former life.

Her moves were smooth like butter and her speed was undeniable. There was no question in Ana's mind that Ari was accessing her enhancement protocols. But then, Ana's eyes narrowed while she took everything in, so was the guy she was fighting.

The speed of their hands and feet became a blur. Several minutes had passed before Ana saw the guy fly backward and land on his back while holding his gut.

The force of the blow that Ari dealt him had been so powerful that the guy, Ana and the enforcers gawked.

Putting her leg down in slow motion like Neo from the Matrix, Ari asked the guy sarcastically, a mean lip tilt of a smile on her face, "So, tell me Lance. Where'd *that* hurt the most?"

Ana's mouth dropped open further. She would have broken into a round of applause at Ari's quip if someone hadn't snatched her from behind and shouted, "Time to go fellas!"

Throwing her backpack over the left side of the building onto the platform over the bikes, Ana snatched at the arm at her throat.

"Sorry I can't stay and catch up," the guy said, just as Rob and Dan landed on the roof (having jumped straight up from the second landing from what Ana could see).

"Be seeing you doll," He shouted, running toward Ana and whoever held her with what felt like robotic strength.

Feeling a small prick in her throat, Ana's gaze flew to Dan. He was yelling something she couldn't hear for the roaring sound that engulfed her.

And as the world around her went dark, Ana knew that the fear and rage that consumed Dan's visage would be something she'd never forget in life.

I knew he couldn't stay mad at me, she sighed to herself, right before blackness swallowed her whole.

***

Max

Struggling not to throw his laptop, Max reached for his cell.

Feeling it buzz before he could even unlock it and place a call, he tried to focus on anything else in the room besides his heavily breathing wife.

"Status." He grunted, not bothering to look at the caller ID.

"They took her," Dan growled into Max's ear through obviously gritted teeth.

"Her being?" Max asked, his eyes closing as pain chewed through his chest.

"They got Ana."

Max disconnected.

"Baby?" Balboa wheezed. Max's jaw tensed. He refused to repeat to her what he'd just heard.

He had to do something. What could he do? There was no tracker on Ana. There was no way to trace her via her Sat phone since it hadn't moved from what he could see. The computer had been shut down, but the battery responsible for keeping the ROM up to date generated enough power for him to see that it hadn't left the scene either. Without a device, finding her would be almost impossible.

"Max!" Balboa shouted, leaning over her chair to take big gulps of breath, pulling him out of his daze.

"Dios Mio," he growled, moving faster than he'd ever moved in his life.

"I'm so sorry, baby." She mumbled as he grabbed his keys, caught her in his arms and moved quickly toward the door.

"Be quiet." He hushed her. "We're good. You're fine. Say that back to me."

"We're good. I'm fine." Balboa wheezed.

"Right. Say it again."

Max grunted as he got her to his truck, positioned her into the passenger seat and sped the three miles it would take them to get to St. Mary's hospital in Clayton.

He made her repeat it every five seconds as he prayed and begged God in his heart.

Because while he'd made her say the words, they were good and she was fine, the spreading stain of blood on her house dress told a different story.

A story Max couldn't possibly accept to be true. He would not lose his wife or their daughter. He'd save them himself, he resolved, shifting gear to speed through the Delmar Avenue traffic. Or die trying.

***

Amanda

I reached the roof just as the helicopter angled off into the southern sky. Breathing hard, I took everything and everyone in, my vision struggling to account for an obviously missing Ana.

Feeling Cruz come up behind me, not knowing how I knew it was him, just knowing it was; I leaned back. Mentally calculating the odds as quickly as I could, the part of me that knew there was no way I could catch that bird scoffed at my attempts.

Swiping the wet from my eyes angrily, I struggled out of Cruz's hold.

"What happened?" I yelled at Dan, who'd just been talking on his cell a second ago.

Looking up from it, his gaze collided with mine. The lost look of anguish shattered me. My knees buckled right before Cruz caught me and held me up.

"Where is she?" I choked. Horror spread through me in waves, threatening to bury me and take me under. Each face, Dan's, Rob's and Ari's confirmed what I knew my heart couldn't take.

My sister was gone. And no one knew where.

"We'll get her back baby, I promise." Cruz crooned to me, having dropped to the roof with me on my knees, he rocked me while I silently cried.

"I promise you Mandy, if I don't do anything else in this life, I will find her." Cruz vowed solemnly. He kissed my temple gently and kept holding me, all while silent tears wrenched the sound from my soul.

"We'll find her together, Man." Rob grumbled, on his knees now on my left, he took hold of my hand.

Dan was silent as he stared off into the direction the bird had flown.

On an exhale, I glanced to my right where Nina stood, her cell phone to her ear.

It wasn't until she turned that I realized, for the first time ever, she looked both lost and afraid.

"What?" I croaked. Not able to take another shot of grief, not able to let it go either.

Nina shook her head, her eyes wide and, suddenly tired.

"What do you know?" I asked, my voice hollow.

It was when her head dropped back, and she looked up to say a prayer to the sky under her breath that I felt suddenly I didn't want to know.

"Balboa. She's in ICU."

A strange wailing scream rent the air. So loud and grating, I wondered briefly what in the world could possibly be making that horrible noise.

Feeling my throat grow raw while I gulped fresh air into my strained lungs, I realized with exasperated horror, that the answer was me. I was making that disturbing sound. Maybe I was coping the best I could; or trying to get God's attention. Because if we never needed Him before, one thing was for certain, we truly needed Him now.

Part THREE:
WAIVERING TIMES

238

Chapter 27

It was hard to believe that a whole year had passed since Ana was taken from us. A painful fact of life that I could hardly bear to even think about.

Bending to put flowers on the grave site before me, I wanted to weep bitter tears, but I couldn't afford to do so.

Because again, it seemed the clock winding slowly toward a powerful divide that would rend the world in two, had reached a pinnacle.

Blinking the tears away as I walked out of the small cemetery, I glanced to my left, uttering a quick cry of surprise that turned into a joyful streak.

Cruz was home.

Rushing him I felt life enter my body again. The bone crushing hug that greeted me didn't bother me at all.

And the kiss that followed, I would have given both my eyes and limbs just to taste it.

Coming up for air, I closed my eyes and grinned, ecstatic to have him so near me.

Reality intruded however, at the sound of several bikes approaching up the hill.

"Any progress?" I finally asked, having breathed in his scent enough to sustain me for the rest of the day.

His hold tightened on me. An answer all by itself. And yet, it was His voice, God inside of me, that kept me calm.

That voice had been the only reason I'd made it through the last year with my sanity.

"How was your visit?" Cruz asked instead, rocking me a bit before pulling back to peer directly into my eyes.

Only God knows how I ever thought I could live without this man. I'd been wrong about him on so many counts. I'd also been prideful and stupid. My gratitude to God despite my heaviness of heart increased. He'd done so much in the last twelve months that my brain stuttered just thinking about it.

We'd arrived home to St. Louis as a group, numb, worn-out, and rightfully discouraged.

Shae had gotten away, taking Ana right along with her.

Having cried myself into a dry husk of human at that point, my bed called my name like a spellbinding siren. It drew me into its depths, welcoming me to the oblivion that would provide some semblance of

240

forgetfulness, despite not knowing Balboa's condition or Ana's whereabouts.

I just wanted to escape. I wanted to be free from it all. I wanted... to not be tired of everything, including life.

A depression I no longer fought took control of me and sleep seemed to be my only peace from it.

I hadn't felt it when Dee forced me into the shower, into my pajama's then tucked me in. I heard but didn't hear her conferring with my girls (who were concerned and frightened by my condition) outside my door in the hallway.

Nor did I feel it when a body lay down in my bed beside me and curled into me, spooning me, and wrapping me in heavy strong arms.

All I knew was the sweet darkness of oblivion as I was swept under.

Time passed with me finding myself in a dark room, sitting in a chair. I could hear a foreign language spoken somewhere in the distance. As freaky as that sounds, it wasn't near as freaky as barely seeing my hand in front of my face. The place was dark with air that was thick like murky soup.

"Amanda," a quiet voice spoke, echoing as if coming from all around me.

"Why are you here?"

I blinked, trying to get my bearings. I didn't know how to begin to answer that question. Point of fact, I didn't know where "here" was, let alone how I'd gotten there.

"Amanda." The quiet voice sounded more insistent this time, but it asked the same question.

"Why are you HERE?"

I was fidgeting in the chair, twining my fingers and twisting them, trying to figure out how to best answer the question. Because I had to answer it. Somehow I knew that the answer was extremely important. I just didn't know what it was.

I croaked as I opened my mouth to speak. The foreign languages spilling around outside of me stopped abruptly, as if it too, was waiting to hear my answer.

"My sister." I said finally, not sure how to finish that sentence. Was Ana dead? Were they torturing her? I didn't know. I didn't want to know. I just wanted to stay in the dark where everything wasn't so overwhelming. To stay in this remote place where there were no expectations, no responsibilities... where it didn't matter that I was JUST Amanda Same; average nobody that couldn't even keep her family safe. I'd failed Ana again when she'd needed me the most. I'd done it the day I turned thirteen and at the time I'd just turned twenty-four.

Shaking my head, I finished my answer on a breath, "I failed her. I failed my sister."

At that moment, a bright light exploded into the room, nearly blinding me.

By the time my eyes were able to adjust and focus, there was another chair sitting before me in the empty room. On it sat a brown skinned man, his dark hair in locks down his back with tiny curls surrounding his face. Silver

242

flecked, brown and gold eyes shown at me from a face that was both stern and beautiful. Masculine and graceful. Hard and soft. There were so many conflicting traits that warred with each other and, somehow existed in harmony, that it was hard to look upon the man without getting a headache.

However, what I did notice without fail, was his shirt.

Green and white with a swirly pattern, it read in Monster dripping font, "My way IS the highway."

The rest of the man was encased in a regular pair of jeans and his feet were clad in steel toed work boots.

It was when my glance noticed his wrists that I almost stopped breathing.

There were scars there. Jagged, raggedy black scabbed scars. On both of them.

My gaze flew up to collide with the silver flecked brown and gold one, denial ringing heavy in my mind.

My brain yelled at me how this was not possible.

But his side smile and brief nod told me that it not only was possible, but it just WAS. Period.

I knew my mouth was hanging open. It couldn't help it; my brain was at war with itself over what it was trying to process. I couldn't decide whether I should shut it or let a ton of bugs fly in and build a home there.

Luckily, it wasn't up to me to decide.

With a slight chuckle and a shake of his head, the scarred one reached over between us and softly pushed my chin up to close it for me.

"Do you like my shirt?" he asked, leaning back to pull it out for me to make the words clearer to see (though, instinct told me that, without a doubt, he knew I'd seen and read it already."

"I do." I croaked. OMG my mind screamed like a crazy fan. ITS JESUS! ITS JESUS! My brain was on repeat, yet, there He sat; calmly assessing his tee with a nod and a smile.

It was when he dropped the front of it and focused on me, his hands now folded into his lap that my brain finally ceased its fanatical rant.

"Me too. So," he clapped, the half-smile that had hovered on his lips completely disappearing, "Amanda, what are you doing here?"

"I... I don't know," I hedged.

His expression became sterner somehow, if possible. I quickly reconsidered my answer. It wasn't that I was afraid, technically. More that, I was afraid of disappointing Him. Of making Him feel less than proud of me.

"I don't know what to do, I mean. My sister is gone; they took her. We have no way of tracking that. And Balboa is in ICU," I felt my head shaking back and forth. I tried to stop it, but it seemed to have a mind of its own.

"I can't fix this. I don't know how to fix this. I'm just me. Same old Amanda. I don't... I can't..."

I stopped speaking, unsure of what to add. I did notice that the stern expression he'd born moments before had softened. His hard as diamond eyes became soft and melty; and that small smile on his face before had reappeared.

"Okay." He said, slapping his thighs then standing to stretch.

"Lord?" I asked before realizing that my mouth was even open.

He shrugged and held his hand out to me. I took it and stood, feeling the zing of power and electricity surge through me.

"It's only when you are at your weakest that I can do my best work. You not only can't do it, kiddo, you never could. I am the only one that fought and won this fight. I'm the only one that can do it again. So, since you've finally reached the end of yourself, it's time to let me do what I do. Capiche?" He asked, one eyebrow up that was so much like Balboa it brought tears to my eyes.

"Capiche," I croaked, wanting desperately to wrap myself in the peace I felt coming from Him.

Stepping forward, Christ pulled me to Himself in a hug that I never wanted to leave.

"Good. And, don't call yourself the same old anything anymore. Regardless of your name. I don't do shoddy work. And I made you exactly how I needed you to be. It's an insult to me when, having created you in my image, you make YOU sound anything less than spectacular. Understand?"

"Understood," I nodded, my heart flooding with joy and a feeling of such fullness I didn't know what to do with myself.

"Very good." He said in my ear before stating on a whisper, "Now wake up. We've got work to do."

At that second, like with a snap of a whip, my eyes flew open. My gaze heavy on Dee who'd been sitting by my bed reading, I hopped out of the bed and hurried to my closet to get dressed.

"Balboa?" I asked, as Dee looked at me, her head tilted to the side like I'd suddenly lost my mind.

"Still in ICU, not good. They're discussing pulling the plug. The baby has been delivered though, a baby girl. She's alive and okay from what your CeeCee reports."

I nodded, grabbed my bag and motorcycle helmet, shouting behind me, "Let's go!"

And Dee moved, rallying the chicks without question, which is why I loved her to pieces.

Chapter 28

The chicks waited outside of the intensive care unit entrance while I pressed forward. With Dee right behind me, I rushed to room 8 just passed the nursing station, wasting no time to answer the inquiring nurse.

Dee had confirmed that Max was currently at the nursery checking on the baby. That was a good thing. He'd lose his mind if he saw what I was about to do.

Seeing Balboa in that bed, weak and frail almost gave me pause. But a mandate rose inside of me that wouldn't allow me to be distracted.

Rushing to her side, I immediately pulled the life support plugs out of the walls. In quick succession, I pulled the patches of IV's from her skin, the ventilator from her nose and mouth, then rolled the equipment behind me.

Ignoring the beeping noise and the shouting nurse. I waited.

Balboa gurgled, her breath rattled, and her chest heaved. Once, twice, then a third time.

"Who the hell are you!" An Asian male nurse came running into the room, shouting.

My gaze flew to his and my mouth opened. A language I didn't know how to speak rushed fluidly out of me, in a voice that was foreign to my ears.

The man stuttered to a halt, his expression dazed and surprised.

To my right on the bed, Balboa took her last, rattling breath.

"Oh God! She killed her!" The nurse that had inquired of us earlier cried from the room entrance behind the male nurse.

I put my hand to Balboa's sunken chest and with the other, I pinched her nose.

Positioning my mouth inches over hers that had fallen open upon removal of the vent and tape, I breathed a sharp breath into her before rising, and clapping over her face as if to wake her.

"*Attha Cum!*" I spoke, but not in my voice. It was a layered voice, like the sound of rushing waters or falling rain.

Dee was beside me, fighting off the lady nurse and two others that had just entered the room trying to reach me.

Max appeared in the door, fear, and rage in his gaze.

"*Stai Calmo,*" I said to him. And watched his eyes widen and his mouth drop.

"What's going on?" A croaking voice asked from the direction of the bed. As quiet as the voice had been, it was like we entered the eye of a storm.

The noise of battle and aggression surrounding us simply stilled.

And all our heads turned at once to watch an emaciated, but very alive Balboa struggle into a sitting position.

"And bring me my baby." She yawned, her eyes on Max, like they had just been in the middle of a conversation.

Only Max hadn't left to get the baby as ordered. He'd dropped to his knees, his hands on the back of his head and silently wept. Watching his body rock with silent waves of emotion, I knew it was not the time to ask if everyone was okay.

Nodding my head toward the door, Dee and I moved. Passing the Asian nurse on the way out, I stopped to address his question asked of me in a language I didn't speak.

"I'm sorry, I don't understand?" I asked and answered at the same time.

"How did you know?" He asked in halting english.

"Know what?" I asked again, holding up one finger at Dee to ward her off as he grabbed hold of my hand.

"That I'd lost my wife in childbirth? You just... you said... this will not be the loss you suffered, trust in me." I took hold of the hand that had hold of mine and stated softly, "I'm sorry, friend, I don't remember saying that to

249

you; but then, I wasn't really focusing on anyone but Balboa."

He nodded his head and shook my hand before letting it go.

I turned to follow Dee out when he asked hesitantly, "Still... you didn't understand what I asked you the first time?"

"No," I shook my head, "I'm sorry." I stated with a shrug.

"Because, what you said to me, about this not being the loss I suffered? You said that in perfect Mandarin."

I'd left the hospital that day in a daze. Dee, normally one to help me work through my confusion by asking pointed questions, had been eerily silent.

To this day, we hadn't discussed what happened in that hospital room. I'd taken my miracle, the first of many and gladly went home, this time to a peaceful and restful slumber.

When I woke up again a few hours later, it was Cruz in the chair by my bed instead of Dee.

Opening my mouth to ask what he was doing there; I was cut off at the shake of his head. His throat worked for several seconds, like he was trying to swallow a stone.

Until finally he managed to choke out words I'd never heard him say before.

"Don't know why I fought it so long. Loved you the minute I saw you."

Leaning forward, his elbows rested on his knees. I had an unabashed view of the top of his head as he talked while peering intensely at his own feet.

"You were too young. Nineteen. And, according to Balboa, a former victim of sexual abuse. How could I, a grown man, take advantage of the open trust and desire lighting up your face every time I entered the house?"

"I had a talk with Max. Told him how I couldn't trust myself around you anymore." He shrugged and sighed. Then cleared his voice to continue.

"I wanted to give you time. Time to grow up and experience life. But, I knew if I tried to explain it before I left town, you wouldn't understand." He laughed a hoarse, angry laugh, "Hell, I didn't even understand. All I knew was that I needed to protect you at all costs. Even from myself."

"You love me?" I asked him, obviously still stuck at the very beginning of his admission.

Glancing up at me, taking in my head tilt in question, he snorted and looked away.

"Kind of feel like the word is an understatement, myself."

"Okay," I yawned before rubbing my stomach as I felt it growl.

His gaze now burning through mine, he asked pointedly, "You hungry?"

I shrugged, "What will you do if I was?" I asked before crossing my arms.

"Feed you." He answered, moving from the chair to sit next to me on the bed.

251

"How long would you do that before you decided to leave again?" I asked, having dropped my arms to pick at the lint on my covers.

"I was thinking never. Or, at least, when I did; this time I'd be taking you with me." He responded gruffly, pulling my lint-picking hand into his.

I sighed, forcing myself to look at him again, despite the crushing emotion in my chest.

"How do I know that? How do I know you won't leave again? How can I depend on you to keep your word this time?"

Feeling his hand tighten on mine I glanced down only to feel his breath so near me, just touching the corner of my mouth before I heard.

"Because I'll make you, *Cara*. And I'll make you mine in every way you let me. Once you're mine, I'll never let you go. My promise to you and God."

My breath hitched. He was so close that, by merely turning my head to face him, my lips were a hairs breath from his.

"Prove it." I whispered, my gaze on his mouth. I took in his burning gaze at his groan that sounded at lot like "Challenge accepted," before his fiery kiss stole the rest of my oxygen.

It was a long time before I was able to get anything to eat since Cruz had determined to spend the next hour doing exactly that.

***

Cruz

He knew he'd find her at the cemetery. She'd promised Nina she would come here today on her behalf, to put flowers on her Uncle John and parent's graves. And Amanda always kept her promises.

Especially since he, Nina and Robert had been hitting the road intermittently throughout the last year, looking for some trace of Ana. And finding nothing.

To say it had been the strangest, most beautiful, yet, most frightening year he'd experienced in his life would be an understatement.

From his humbled and now, even more so, introspective brother that seemed to develop a fascination with the bible only surpassed by his devotion to his wife and daughter, to the technical advances that kept him awake at night in constant fear; Cruz felt like time was running out for all of them.

After they'd gotten back home from Florida, everyone had been in recovery mode and on automatic. Except for he and Amanda. They'd experienced what most would call, "a honeymoon" phase.

Only they didn't get to experience the soft lighting and dinner date kind of romance that most people did. Because her sister was still missing. And she'd still had enemies.

Like her uncle. An uncle that, the guys, not two days after they got back from Florida, paid a visit.

253

Sam had led the charge, bursting into the hotel room with Max, Cruz, Rob and Dan following quickly behind.

Cruz remembered with disgust the pornography the man had been watching as they forced him, naked, out of his bed and into the living room.

Amanda was Cruz's woman. Had always been. So, the responsibility fell to him to make his point known irrevocably.

By the time they left, Devin knew what the barrel of a gun tasted like. He knew what the knuckles of an enraged man protecting what was his felt like. And he knew that, if he ever thought about approaching Amanda or Ana with his sick propositions again, he'd know what death felt like. That included all the pain dealt along the way to get him there.

Devin, having an epiphany and possessing a newfound appreciation for life, had checked out of his hotel room and left town, never to be heard from again.

Or at least, that's what Cruz thought. Four months later, he and Amanda were making their requisite fawn all over his niece visit (a niece named Maxena Amanda Arpaio or Maxi for short) when Max called him over to the command center.

Handing Cruz his iPad, Max continued to work as if he hadn't just handed his brother an article written in New Jersey about the murder and execution of Devin Same.

Someone had eviscerated the man with obvious fury and rage. The body, found by the local authorities in a sleezy hotel, spoke on how the man had lost everything upon his mother's death due to some family tradition he couldn't fulfill. And while this act had been far from suicidal, surprisingly the authorities weren't spending much time investigating.

Cruz had quietly walked the iPad over to Amanda. Exchanging it with his niece to allow himself to get lost in her cuteness, he'd listened carefully just in case she needed him.

But she hadn't. With a deep sigh, she passed the iPad over to Balboa, pulling the diaper bag and bottle out of her hand.

Balboa read the article, glanced up at Cruz and Mandy, who were at that time fighting over which one should be holding Maxi right now, then snorted.

"This your friend's work?" She asked Amanda who was grumbling because Cruz, obviously having won the battle, snatched the bottle from her.

"My best guess." Amanda humphed as she sat back down and pouted.

"You're not sure?" Balboa had asked.

Amanda shrugged before asking what Cruz wanted to, "Why?"

"See here? Balboa had pointed to a small picture under the paper, "laying neatly on the dresser by the paper?"

"Crap," Amanda said under her breath. "My locket."

Right before the police had banged on Max's door.

Chapter 29

Amanda

Having everyone in my office again, sans Ana was strange. No stranger than how the world was changing at a rapid pace, though.

It had taken them months of investigating to determine that I couldn't have possibly been two places at once thus she wasn't a murderess.

Two days after being cleared, I'd been contacted by the Same family lawyer. Quickly and efficiently he'd broken it down. The Same family was a matriarchal line, thus the fortune, assets and property all transferred to the eldest female heir upon the current matriarch's death.

I had refused to leave for New York to take possession only to be assured that I didn't have to.

Everything was mine to do with as I pleased. And that had been the end of that.

Now, as I leaned back to look at my closest friends and allies for the first time again in almost a year, I deep sighed.

It was clear that we had a lot of work to do, and not a lot of time. But as a group, we would need help.

Dan sat in his chair, closed off to the world, his expression dark and dangerous. There was no smile hovering just at the corner of his eyes like he was entertaining some amusing thought. No lip tilt. Nothing. Cold, flat, and expressionless, his eyes left me with a feeling of despair.

Robert and Nina stood at two different sides of the room, steadfastly avoiding one another. It was clear that something had happened there, though I couldn't imagine what had.

Brody stood at the back of the room with Dee, his arms crossed, seemingly relaxed. Wearing his brand-new eyepatch, he'd gone from evil to just plain sinister. From Satan to a pirate. All in all, it was better, nonetheless.

Because his story had been the most interesting of them all.

While everyone else had been on the roof trying to save Ana, Dee had stayed below, grappling with Brody in a free for all.

According to Dee, one of Nina's knives had found its way into Brody's eye by accident. The twitching, out of control one that happened to "bug" her.

258

Luckily Brody hadn't bled out. Instead, Dee had knocked him unconscious with a chair.

The Gangsta Nuns had taken him into custody and, with a few friends of theirs and one of ours (Cheryl), Brody underwent some massive deprogramming.

Within six months, he was shipped to St. Louis to remain under Dee's watchful eye. And despite his being deprogrammed, Max was adamant that the man not even think about coming near Balboa.

And I didn't blame Max, seeing the strange light in Brody's eye every time Balboa's name was mentioned. Or at least, it used to. Now that light seemed to flair when Dee entered the room. I shook my head quickly to force that thought away. I didn't even want to consider what that might mean.

Instead, I forced myself to focus on what we know from the intel that Brody had provided to our current state of affairs; all of which was NOT good.

My gaze landed on Cruz to somehow siphon the strength I needed. He chin-upped me and grinned. Fighting an answering grin of my own, I forged ahead...

"Based on what we've learned from Brody, there are two possible locations that Ana could be currently held. There is the New York location, and the Granite City one. I'm banking on New York City. That's where Lance's base of operations is and apparently he and Shae are working together."

"I'll take New York," Nina stated, studying her nails.

"Or," Robert gritted, "We can all go together. Travelling in a group would be safest. Some people could even avoid getting shot that way."

"Oh, for the love of!" Nina shouted, crossing the room to jab her finger into Rob's chest, "it was a minor flesh wound! I had a Kevlar shield under my jacket! Why is that so hard for you to understand? You know what pisses me off the most? That you think I would be stupid enough to rush into a room with no gun in hand, without wearing freaking protection!"

Dan rolled his eyes and sighed before stretching out his legs. I looked to Cruz who shrugged, grinning. Apparently this wasn't the first time Dan heard this particular fight acted out; and looking at how furious Rob and Nina were, it probably wouldn't be the last.

"Hey!" Dee shouted, as the two argued back and forth like toddlers.

"Shut it! We aint got all day for you two to decide if you want to kiss or kill each other. Make a decision! Get it together! But most of all, be quiet and quit wasting our time!"

Nina flipped Dee off with a growl and stomped off, back to her corner.

I coughed to hide my snicker, Cruz doing the same.

"Our bad Mandy. Continue." Dee grumbled, with Brody looking at her strangely again.

I cleared my throat and tried a different tact.

"They most likely have sentinels on the ground watching all modes of travel in New York. We hit the ground there, be it flight, train, bus or ship, they'll

260

probably know within an hour. That said, I propose we depend on those that are unknown and focus on a more pressing issue here."

"Who's unknown?" Dan asked, for the first time something other than flatness in his gaze.

"Remember Lace's cousin, Maria? Turns out, while she'd been trafficked extensively and was considered the "bottom" girl, the one that kept everyone else in line, Maria was never chipped. She'd visited Lace several times, trying to get help out of the life, but Zeke was someone Lace didn't want to take on by herself."

"Why didn't she tell Coco?" Nina asked, her brow furrowed.

"Good question. We don't know. All we know is Lace wanted Maria free but wasn't willing to involve the Gangsta Nuns in the process. That was why she didn't give Balboa the intel on Shadow. The intel would be traced back to Maria earning her all kinds of dead."

The group nodded so I continued, "Maria is with Ari in Baltimore now. She's healing, she's traumatized, and she's willing to help. According to her and Brody, there's been a split in the factions. Zeke is currently at war with Shadow. Lance fell in on Shadow's side. The remaining Old Geezer and Zeke are the other. Apparently, the war extends from just being between the two factions, but their technologies. The tattoo method has been spreading at an alarming rate. It's gone from Florida, throughout Georgia and is working its way up the East coast. Thus far it has reached North Carolina. The kids are loving it, turning it into an internet challenge and..."

"Crap," Nina gritted, "It's gone viral."

I nodded with a sigh and repeated, "It's gone viral."

"There's no stopping this." Nina stated the obvious. And she was right. There wasn't

"We are in damage control mode now. Dee, you'll take the Slick Chicks and head Northwest, Cruz and I will take the South. I need someone here to man command central."

"What's the plan?" Rob asked, rubbing his face tiredly.

"We follow the bouncing ball. God has made it clear that we need safe havens all around the country for the unmarked."

"Why?" Dan scoffed, "What good would that do us if world leaders get the tattoo, putting them under Shae's control?"

I shrugged, "That's not my problem. That's Gods. My job is to follow directions. We spread west, we set up Sanctuaries strategically stationed in specific locations He gives us, and we wait for further instructions."

"What about that Dart thing that they shot Brody with," Dee asked, "can't they just make more of those?"

I cleared my throat again, fighting the tightness of it.

"Ana was responsible for the creation of the EMP dart. Beyond a small supply that Max has kept safe for us, there won't be any others made. She had everything we'd need to create them on her laptop."

"What happened to that thing, by the way? Ari said Ana had thrown it over the side of the building?"

Glancing at Cruz who shrugged, I responded based on what Coco had said, "she did, but someone must have retrieved it. We just don't know who."

"So, we don't know which side has it? Us or them?" Nina asked.

"That's exactly right," I nodded.

"Oy Vey." Nina sighed.

"Welcome to my world." I chuckled at a smiling Cruz and winked.

264

Epilogue

"Hey baby," He greeted me, pulling my jacket from me then snuggling me close.

"How'd it go?" I wanted to answer him right off, I really did, but soaking up the warmth from his body and inhaling the tang of soap and mint distracted me.

"Babe..." Cruz chuckled. I ignored him and nuzzled his chest some more.
After soaking in as much as I could I finally answered him, "Do you know how much I love my ring?"

Feeling his chest bounce, I rested my chin on it and moved my arms to wrap them around his neck.

"I kind of got the feeling that you did the minute I slid it on your finger."

Checking my right hand over his shoulder, I grinned as the princess cut diamond caught the reflection of the lights in our cabin, "Because I really really do," I sighed.

"I see," Cruz grunted, swinging my legs up into his arms to carry me to our fur laden couch where he dropped with me in his lap.

"What else do you love Mrs. Arpaio?"

"Oh, I love these Colorado mountains and being so close to my Mom."

Spreading kisses all over my face, Cruz growled. I laughed when he nuzzled my neck.

"And I guess I might just love you. Kinda like a lot actually," I responded, feeling those nuzzles turn into the kind of kisses that would really distract me if I didn't hurry up and say what needed saying.

"Ditto," he grunted, his kisses moving up my chin and to my mouth.

"Wait, wait a..." I didn't get it out before his lips claimed mine, robbing me of air I no longer felt I needed.

It was a long time after when we were snuggled under the blankets in our new bed that I was able to remember.

My chin resting on his chest, this time from a prone position, I spontaneously asked the question, surprising him and myself, "Do you want boys or girls? And how many should we have?"

Cruz sighed, one arm behind his head, the other holding me close.

"I want healthy. I want strong. I want boys that will protect their sisters. And girls that rival their mother's beauty."

I allowed my hand to trace his face, still awed about how everything had somehow worked out for us.

"What about you?" He asked me, taking hold of my hand to bring it to his lips, where he kissed my palm.

"I want boys. Boys that are strong like their father and smart just like he is. And girls with his gorgeous dark eyes and excellent hair."

I bounced with his chest as he chuckled into my palm. And sighed before letting go of this moment, one of which I'd mark as beyond precious.

"Our third Sanctuary just went up in Denver. We've got an underground supply chain already set up and Dee is sending Marla, the Slick Chick with family here, to run it."

"Good." Cruz grunted.

It wasn't, not really. This should have been our seventh Sanctuary house. Or at least, it could have been. But people just didn't see a need for Sanctuaries in small towns. Large cities were a prime domain for what we had to offer, a home for those who are troubled, misfits and rejected. Those without a clan. And soon, those without a tattoo.

It was already spreading, the hype about the tattoo. Having hit the Midwest full on, it was such an in thing that, those opposed to the tat were considered strange and old fashioned. I watched a familiar process known as cancel culture quickly gain ground and become rooted in the tattoo movement.

Tat's now could be QR codes and strips used for financial transactions. They were beginning to design code biometrics into the tattoo that would allow people to access devices, accounts, and data, just with their tattoo.

The tat had opened doors in the tech industry that the world just wasn't ready for.

Wearable data. Trackable data. Controllable data.

Trying hard to trust the One who promised that he would never leave or forsake me, I snuggled into my husband to enjoy the time we had on this earth.

Because tomorrow wasn't promised to anyone. And tomorrow was closing in fast. I refused to allow myself to give in to wavering faith despite these wavering times. Because my God never wavered. So, neither would I.

***

Max

He thought he was dreaming at first, at least, the normal kind of dreaming. But something inside of him told him different.

The place was all white, creepy looking in its sanitary appearance, but starkly empty. It was the strangest room that Max had ever been in. Even stranger as the brown door, inconsistent with the blandness of it all, appeared suddenly on his left.

Brown and hewn from wood based on its splintered appearance, Max was captivated by the door.

Drawn to it, he didn't realize he'd been moving, he reached for the metal knob. It looked hot to the touch, like it would burn his hand, blazing as if from the smelter of a furnace.

Still, Max was compelled to reach out for it.

Touching it and finding it cool despite its appearance, he pulled the door open and walked through it.

Into a colorful room with a huge command center similar to his (only much more up to date with its equipment) smack in the middle.

And at the workstation drinking Mountain Dew red and eating chocolate licorice twists was none other than Anabella Same.

Bouncing her head to a beat he couldn't hear through the humungous headphones on the side of her head, Ana glanced up and caught sight of him, a huge smile splitting her face.

"Bout time you made it here!" She smiled; eyes delighted to see him as if she hadn't been lost to them for a year and a half.

"Where are you? What is this place?" Max growled. He was trying not to be furious with her because it wasn't her fault she'd been taken. And, while he couldn't understand exactly how he was communicating with her right now; he knew beyond a shadow of a doubt that this was his Ana he was talking to.

Shrugging, she removed the headphones and rose from the workstation with a stretch, "It used to be what we called "the white room". At first, we thought it a haven for BW's to meet up, fellowship and be close to God. Until we learned that they were using it to track and study us."

Max remembered the white room. He'd had plenty of discussions with CeeCee, trying to understand it. And had always gone away confused.

269

Many things confused him that he couldn't readily explain with science. Except for what had happened to his wife. He knew science had absolutely nothing to do with that. He had witnessed a bonafide miracle. One that had left him shaken so badly, he'd embraced her faith completely without question moving forward. Her God became his God. Her people became his people.

Forcing out the memory of Balboa's death and return to him, Max focused on a very concerned Ana. Her brow was furrowed, and she watched him as if he was the one who had been missing.

Max snorted. And reminded her of that fact in no uncertain terms.

"I'm fine Max," Ana sighed, after listening to him rant.

"I promise I am. See, not a scratch on me?"

"But where ARE you?" Max asked, frustrated and still a little freaked out at how they were meeting.

"I'm in a safe place. Shadow couldn't hold me for long. Fact is, there's no facility with any kind of security that can hold me for long. Sooner or later, I learn the tech and use it against them."

Max grunted. She was not wrong. Ana had an affinity with technology that far surpassed his own. It had been her genius that thought up the EMP darts, her genius that allowed them to develop the Kevlar shield that saved Nina's life, and her genius that allowed them to track all of their people without them being aware.

That said, Max was growing angrier, not less.

270

"If you got away, why didn't you come home! We've all been worried sick about you!"

She nodded, listening to his every word like she was a counselor and he was on her couch.

"You're right," she added, "and I'm sorry for that. It was the only way I could gain access to their data, more schematics on the tattoos and how they plan to use it in the future. I couldn't do that from home. Plus, they'd come after me if I did return. I'd be leading them right to everyone we deem important. You know I couldn't let that happen. So, I escaped, met up with a friend who retrieved my laptop for me and have been in hiding ever since."

Max grunted. Because he did know.

"So, what now?" He asked, allowing his fascination to resurface for the entire set up and workstation.

"Now we meet here on the regular, I share intel with you, and you take it back to the crew."

Max grunted again, moving to inspect the computer Ana had been working on.

"What's this code here?" He asked, a little awed at the flawless, elegant design of it. The code was stored just above the fiber with nanobots attached to it.

Ana giggled; a sound Max had come to learn was her "showing off" sound.

"That, my man, is the tiny piece of code that sends our little soldiers there to the head where they lodge just behind the eyes, using them as a window; one might say."

Max grunted.

271

"Interesting fact about these. You ready? Know how the Brainwaiver chip's later versions created a tell — the twitching eye, in controlled recipients?"

"Yeah," Max stated.

"Well, these little dudes that work themselves up to the nasal cavity and behind the eyeballs, have a similar effect; they provide a tell; a clue to who is enhanced and who isn't."

"What is it," Max asked distractedly, pulling up more codes and schematics from her screen.

"They cause a shimmer, a bright one, to flash at intervals the longer it invades their eyesight."

"A shimmer?" Max asked for clarity.

Ana grinned before responding, "A waver, one might say."

"Waivering Eyes?" Max clarified before rolling his eyes at the pun of merging the Brainwaiver name with waver and eyes.

***

Ana

"Indeed," Ana grinned, leaning close to look at the code that was fascinating him. Because eyes were starting to waiver all over the place. And she'd been preparing for this moment for months with excitement. All she'd needed to be ready, was time. And the time had finally arrived.

ABOUT THE AUTHOR

Chantay Hadley, is an acclaimed faith-based novelist writing under the pseudonyms *Chantay James* (Christian Sci-Fi and suspense), *C. Marie Evans* (African American FaithBased Romance) and *C. M. James* (nonfiction, Christian Living).

Currently #1 on Romance I.O's uUltimate list for FaithBased Fiction (Curvy Herione, Alpha Male) and #5 (Christian African American Romance, Alpha Male), Chantay published her very first novel in 2005 and has been writing ever since. The owner and founder of Midwest Creations Publishing & Media LLC since 2018, Chantay considers herself a jack of many trades centered around ministry, educating, publishing and mental toughness training.

Combining her passions of serving Christ, writing and publishing, she strives to help others fulfill their potential. A devoted mother of one, she lives in St. Louis, Missouri where she loves God, a good romance, comedy and cartoons.

BOOKS BY CHANTAY JAMES

The Brainwaiver Series:

Waivering Minds
Waivering Lies
Waivering Winds: Novella 1.5 (Waiverings)
Waiverings featuring: Novella 1.5: Waivering Winds
Novella 2.5: Waivering Times
Waivering Eyes (Book 3)

The Valley Series:

Valley of Decisions
In the works: Valley of Shadows (prequel)
Valley of Dry Bones Other works:

Published as Chantay Hadley in Anthology form:

A Hawk's Tale

Attending a book signing soon?

Sign up for the Midwest Creations Publishing
Quarterly newsletter and enter to win Brainwaiver
swag, so, like Balboa, you too can MAN UP and
FIGHT LIKE A GIRL!"

Don't forget to sign up for the Midwest Creations
Publishing Quarterly Newsletter on our website!
https://midwest-creations-publishing.square.site/

MWCP UPCOMING RELEASES AND AUTHOR LIST:

Adair Rowan
(Sci-Fi, Suspense, Science and Tech)

- Concentric Relations: Unknown Ties – March, 2019

Projects for **Adair**:

- Project Ariel

Chantay M. James
(Romance, Sci-Fi and Suspense)

Available to pick up your copy today:

- Valley of Decisions
- Waivering Minds, Book 1: Brainwaiver Series
- Waivering Lies, Book II: Brainwaiver Series
- Waiverings: A Brainwaiver Anthology
- Waivering Winds, A Brainwaiver Novella
- Waivering Times, A Brainwaiver Novella
- Brainwaiver Beginnings shorts: Wattpad (Chantay M. James)

Projects for **Chantay**:

- Gangsta Nuns Series: Book 1, Order of Protection
- Brainwaiver Generations: The Kids (YA Series)

M. Renae
(Christian Living, Marriage, Divorce and Family)

- Allowed 2 Cheat: When Marriage Takes A Wrong Turn.
- Allowed 2 Cheat: Study Guide
- Allowed 2 Cheat: Workbook

Projects for **M. Rena**

- By Faith

C. Marie Evans (Black Romance and Action)

- A Hater's Prayer (July 2019)

Projects for **C. Marie Evans**:

C. M. James (Nonfiction/Christian Living)

- Who Broke My Daughter's Alabaster Box?

Projects for **C. Marie Evans**:

- A Prophet Has No Honor (The Legacy of Sylk Smoov). May, 2021
- Hater's Prayer 2: Annie B.'s Legacy
- Hater's Prayer 3: Legally Bound
- C.J. Series – Action (2021)
  - CJ Run
  - CJ Hide

- CJ Fall
- CJ Rise

Projects for **C. M. James**:

- He Still Breaks Chains: Quick-Hit Hard Truth Series, Book 2
- Cracked Pot Communication for Fractured Folks: Quick-Hit Hard Truth Series, Book 3
- The Power of No: Quick-Hit Hard Truth Series, Book 4

And many more authors are coming soon! Don't forget to check out the website for author swag, events and giveaways!
Stay tuned for bits and pieces of some of our publications!

Midwest Creations Presents...
<u>Author Chantay M. James:</u>
<u>Brainwaiver Universe!</u>

What if you could have anything you desire? Is what you desire worth everything you possess – including your soul?

Waivering Minds, Book I:

Brainwaiver Series

Celine:

A Licensed Clinical Social Worker in Alton, Illinois, Celine Baltimore lives a content, peaceful life. Until one of her patients reveals that her sister has become a guinea pig for behavior modification technology known as "Brainwaiver," then disappears.

Left with a child's journal that paints her once comfortable life in horror and intrigue, Celine finds herself nose deep in corporate secrets, shifty attorneys and rugged, intense men (specifically Enoch Sampson or Sam for short).

Shocked that she's named a winner in the Brainwaiver contest (a contest she'd never entered) Celine learns of more missing children in Alton and their link to the hip new software trying to take over her life; including Sam's teenaged son.

An all-around goof that can't stop tripping over her Aubusson rug (or keep said rug straight) can Celine let go of playing it safe, fight the good fight of faith and get the guy in the end?

Sam:

A widower and ex-CIA agent turned owner of a family owned construction company, Sam picked up a few skills from his former life. Some he wishes he'd never learned. Espionage and secrets had been his business.

Missions and sacrifice had become his life. Growing cold again seemed inevitable... until he met goofy (and determined) Celine Baltimore.

Could he avoid that place of unfeeling and do the unthinkable? Retrieve his son and love again? Because protecting his family was the only thing that mattered to Sam.

It was something that he would do at any cost. It was more than a goal – it was a promise. And Sampson men ALWAYS kept their promises.

Waivering Lies, Book II:
Brainwaiver Series

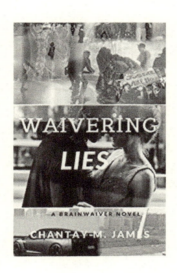

Max:

Max Arpaio is a Freelance Information Systems Security Analyst and part time Bounty Hunter on occasion. When Max responded to Enoch Sampson's call for help to find his missing son he realized something crucial.

The top government secrets and plots he'd stumbled upon long ago are no longer a shadow on the horizon.

And Now that Denise Ferry has taken up the gauntlet to wage a silent war against Brainwaiver, Max has to make a choice: To help the woman he loves but can never have or stand aside and watch as millions are led like sheep to a slaughter. Either way, he's a dead man. It's only a question of when.

Balboa:

Denise Ferry is a Business Consultant, former FBI agent and a severe pain in Max's rear. A woman who has gone from gang member lieutenant to military strategist to agent, she could write a book on espionage and silent war strategies.

So, when Denise engaged in a search and retrieve mission that targeted children for mind control experimentation, she's in for the long haul to wage war. However, she hadn't counted on warring on two fronts: Against the advances of Brainwaiver and to win the heart of Max Arpaio.

A man of mystery with a sense of doom, Max draws Denise despite her efforts to fight the attraction. Can she help him overcome his dark past?
As a strategist she realizes she has no choice.
Without him taking her back against Brainwaiver, she's already lost the war before she starts. And without him in her life she's already lost her heart.

Valley of Decisions:

A Valley Series Novel

by Chantay M. James

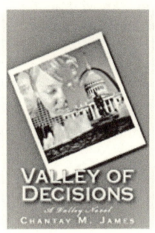

St. Louis, Missouri. Home of the missing.

Sandra Peters, editor for Re-born magazine, has planned her life to the smallest degree - her work, her friend, and her faith.

But when the prominent Christian magazine goes belly up and her friend attempts suicide, Sandra watches all of her plans crumble.

All she has left is her faith and her calling. For some reason, God has chosen her, a woman with an abusive past, to journey to St. Louis to save children. But how? And from what?

These questions plague the jaded young editor as she treks to find her destiny.

Little does she know that her war is not with flesh and blood. Little does she know that only self-sacrifice, unity, and love can defeat the evil that consumes the next generation.

Little does she know that, in the heart of St. Louis, lies her Valley of Decisions.

Author Adair Rowan presents the Concentric Relations Universe!

Concentric Relations: Unknown Ties

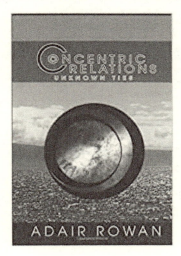

Psychotherapist Dr. Liam Ronaw enjoys a rather plush existence until new client's recite details about night terrors and dreams. Several dream descriptions spark a memory from his childhood. In an effort to help these clients, he follows the various clues as he works to figure out what connection they have to his own past.

Dr. Ronaw follows the breadcrumbs which lead him into a world involving a global coverup, a hidden community and a terrible new threat, the likes of which could spell doom for all life on earth.

Welcome to The Hater's Prayer Saga by author C. Marie Evans!

The Hater's Prayer

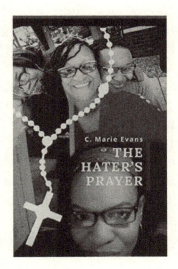

Naomi Carmichael Nee' Brooks was a Hater.

Well, a reformed hater, that is.
Destiny, her sister had been deemed by her church, family and all creation "the golden child," so Naomi knows how it feels intimately and repeatedly to have someone steal her thunder.
And now that she was about to be a divorced mother of three, struggling to make it on a state job, with an ex that was all about rubbing her nose in it,

Naomi wouldn't know what to do if God hadn't given her what her and her bestie called, "the hater's prayer".

With a podcast that's growing by the hundreds, Naomi is sure that life was on the upturn. But she should have known better.

Falsely accused of hurting her kids, her ex-husband coming after everything she's got (which isn't much) and her (not really) hated sister sexually assaulted at a club; all while Victavious "Vic" Carter, the boy next door, has suddenly decided she's the one, can Naomi fully let go of her hater ways, trust God instead of herself, and give her old friend a chance to "shoot his shot?"

As a reformed hater, all by herself she doesn't have a chance. But with her bestie at her back and crazy family at her side, Naomi knows one thing to be true: With God, all things are possible. And seeing Vic through new and enlightened eyes, that may just include falling in love again.

Don't sleep on Allowed 2 Cheat: When Marriage Takes A Wrong Turn by Author M. Renae!

Allowed 2 Cheat: When Marriage Takes a Wrong Turn

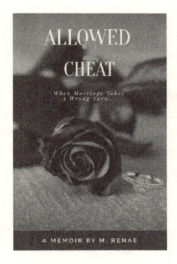

    I loved my husband. Looking back, maybe I loved him a little too much. Definitely more than I loved myself. How do I know? Because six weeks before our wedding I found out that there was another woman.
    Devastated, I called him crying, trying to understand why. He explained that she started off as a friend because I made him give up his best friend

(another woman and as such, a different story entirely, but really the same situation) to comfort me. He goes on to explain that it just turned into more than he expected and how he couldn't stop it since he didn't want to hurt her. He said that he did it to try and get it all (by all I assume "the cheating") out of his system so that he wouldn't cheat once we were married.

I knew then, in my heart, that his cheating would continue for a lifetime. But I was determined to keep the love I thought I found. I was so eager to hold on to that love that I told him, "I forgive you and we will get past this." Sadly, that wasn't the last time I spoke those words.

Throughout the course of our marriage, that refrain was repeated if not openly, silently… over and over again.

So, this is my story.

To protect those I love the most, I've changed names (including mine, just because) and the locations of various events. I also did this because the names are not important, neither are the places.

What holds true, or at least the truth that I'm trying to convey is illustrated in the message of this allegory. A message that so many women need to hear. A message outlined in the following fact that, as you read, you will feel this in your very soul:

BECAUSE I was aware of my husband's cheating during our engagement and set no boundaries or consequences; I gave him permission and consent to continue it during our marriage. I didn't walk away, and I should have. As a result, ten years later I'm still struggling with my sanity and choices.

Don't be me.

Allowed 2 Cheat: When Marriage Takes a Wrong Turn – Study Guide

This is the study guide to be read in accompaniment with the novel adapted memoir Allowed 2 Cheat, When Marriage Takes A Wrong Turn by M. Renae. (Memoir by M. Renae; Novel written and adapted from the memoir by Chantay M. Hadley and Midwest Creations Publishing).

Allowed 2 Cheat: When Marriage Takes a Wrong Turn – Workbook

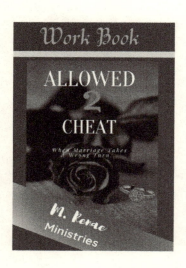

  This is a companion workbook for Allowed 2 Cheat: When Marriage Takes A Wrong Turn (the memoir adapted novel as well as the study guide).
  Learn key skills that will assist you on your journey to healing from damaging relationships.
  With fun exercises and a journaling component built in, your quality time with God will take on a whole new meaning!
  Freedom, joy and emotional stability can be yours! Don't forget to pick up the novel and the study guide for a richer and more fulfilling experience.

Coming Soon:

Waiverings:

A Brainwaiver Anthology

Celine Baltimore and Sam (Enoch) Samson introduced the world to the Brainwaiver Universe in Waivering Minds, a place full of mysteries involving missing children, mysterious technology and race against time to save one from the other, never realizing that the target, in truth was Celine. And as mysteries often do, the saga didn't end with Celine and Sam...

Waivering Winds, Book 1.5:

Waivering Winds sheds light on the in-between-times, connecting Waivering Minds to book two of the Brainwaiver Series, Waivering Lies.

Delilah and KC's story.

As Celine's opposition, Delilah did her thing in Waivering Minds, but it wasn't all good... and surprisingly, it wasn't all bad either.

Learn about her horror story compiled of kidnapping, human trafficking and present day slavery. God and KC have their work cut out for them when it comes to winning Delilah's heart.

But neither one of them is about to give up. Read her story as God and KC show a woman hurting from the pain of her past that she is more than who she thought she was...

Waivering Times, Book 2.5

Novella 2.5 begins midway through Waivering Lies, Book two of the series.

Amanda and Cruz's Story.

Amanda, too young and too focused on saving the world from Brainwaiver (starting with her mom) finds Cruz irritating... and irresistible.

On a mission from God, Amanda is determined to win her war, and the man that makes her wish she never had to fight one.

However, Cruz Arpaio is no fool. Amanda, at nineteen, was too young for a US Marshall in his mid-twenties.

Not to mention that Denise "Balboa" Ferry-Arpaio, his new and military trained sister-in-law would kill him, if his brother Max didn't first.

So, Cruz left as he was told.

Years later, he still can't get the thought of Amanda Same out of his mind.

Determined to return for the woman he knows is his, Cruz never makes it to his destination.

What happens next turns the worlds of Amanda Same and Cruz Arpaio on its head; and kicks off the war that had been a long time coming.

Will Cruz and Amanda find each other again and somehow, reunite and reignite the powerful attraction that both of them can't forget in these Waivering Times?

Only God knows...